LESSONS IN FALLING

diana gallagher

SPENCER
HILL
PRESS

Lessons in Falling
Copyright © 2017 by Diana Gallagher

First Edition: 2017

Lessons in Falling: a novel / by Diana Gallagher–1st ed.
Library of Congress Cataloging-in-Publication Data available upon request

Summary: A girl afraid to take risks since a gymnastics injury must take charge of her future after her best friend's failed suicide attempt stains her view of the world, the people in it, and her future.

Published in the United States by Spencer Hill Press
For more information on our titles visit www.spencerhillpress.com

Distributed by Midpoint Trade Books
www.midpointtrade.com

Cover design by: Michael Short
Interior layout by: Jenny Perinovic
Images courtesy of ArtFamily and Roman Sigaev

ISBN: 978-1-63392-037-8 (paperback)
ISBN: 978-1-63392-038-5 (eBook)

Printed in the United States of America

CHAPTER ONE

THE OCTOBER SUNSHINE glints off of the Department of Motor Vehicles' door as my father holds it open, like he's ushering me into a debutante ball. I breeze past him to join the line of would-be drivers. The girl in front of me whimpers.

Amateur. I've taken this test six times. There's no point in showing fear.

Ping, ping. My best friend's texts roll in. I keep my head down as the line shuffles forward.

Cassie: *You're gonna kill it today!!!*

Cassie: *Come to South Cross ASAP when you're done.*

Cassie: *When you PASS, that is.*

Cassie: *Bring burritos.*

Right. Senior Cut Day. While I'm here, my best friend is busy frolicking by the ocean, never mind the fact that it's cold enough for frost outside. "That's the beauty of it," she'd told me last night. "The teachers don't expect us to ditch on a shit day. You're sure you can't get out of your test?"

"Would you want my father as your life chauffeur?"

She'd laughed. "Fair enough."

I half expect to see a poster of my learner's permit on the wall with the caption *DMV's Most Notorious.* New York State still hasn't passed a law to keep repeat offenders like me from signing up for one test right after the other, so here I stand. The first three tests, I was optimistic. On four and five, the doubt settled in. By now, it's just embarrassing, or in the words of my father, "They're going to start sending you Christmas cards."

"Name?" the DMV attendant says.

"Savannah—"

"*Kaitlyn* Gregory," Dad interrupts.

Nobody has called me Kaitlyn since I was seven. Not even Mom. I'd tugged that name off and taken my more exciting middle name instead. Cassie had seen to it. *Get it together, Dad.*

"'K.S. Gregory,'" the man reads from my permit in an I-don't-have-time-or-patience-for-your-discrepancy tone. "That you?"

"Yes," we say in unison.

The man sighs. "Park across from the playground."

There's no doubt that Cassie's the first senior down to the shoreline. Although it's only eight in the morning, I bet the Atlantic Ocean is warmer than the air. My best friend won't be swimming, although some of the braver seniors might attempt an early-season Polar Bear Plunge. No, she'll be walking over the dunes, stopping at the peak, and digging in her heels to keep from sliding in the sand. Her camera will be slung around her neck. The fact that her attendance has been, shall we say, spotty so far this year won't bother her.

Tomorrow, she'll show our teachers the photographs, dropping her voice so that it falls into her purple-and-green Palestinian scarf. She'll even win over our notoriously hard-ass precalculus teacher. As always, she will be forgiven.

Meanwhile, a permanent layer of dust covers the dashboard, the seatbelt digs into my shoulder, and the gas pedal groans like an old man whenever I press it. The car's a piece of shit. It's as sick of the Town of Ponquogue DMV as I am.

We'll get out of here today, you and me.

I'm sick of failing.

"I didn't feel good about the parallel park you ended on yesterday. Did you?" Dad says in his teacher-chastising-a-young-delinquent tone. Since he's the AP Calculus teacher at my high school, all of my classmates have the privilege of hearing that voice, too. On the rare days he has a sub, like today, it's like Christmas break comes early for Ponquogue.

No license. No gymnastics career. A father infamous for assigning shitty grades. Yeah, I'm pretty much the coolest senior.

"When am I ever going to have to parallel park in my life?" I counter, fully aware that this argument is futile.

"Two cars from now."

"I'm not worried." I am very worried. "I've been practicing." I extend my legs like I'm warming up for a gymnastics meet, eliciting the crack of scar tissue in my right knee. Bad move.

Last night, I tried an exercise that my former gymnastics coach was fond of. "Ten times a night, every night," he'd instruct, "look in the mirror and say to yourself, 'I am a great beam worker.'" We'd all roll our eyes behind his back.

But when you're six road tests in the hole, you're not really one to judge. "You can do this, Savannah," I'd mumbled once I'd shut off the lights, feeling my breath bounce back at me from the mirror, and then threw my face into a pillow. Useless.

Thinking about gymnastics—just as useless. I need to have realistic goals now, like passing this goddamn thing once and for all.

Another text. I know it's from Cass. Nobody else would text me this early (or at all these days—sad, but true). "I'm fairly sure texting during your test results in automatic failure," Dad says sarcastically as I glance at my phone.

Sure enough, it's Cass: *I'm freezing my balls off. Can you bring hot chocolate, too?*

Cass: *Love youuu!*

"So when are you going back to the gym?"

My hands freeze on the steering wheel. Another text arrives, but the words don't register.

Dad steamrolls on, either not noticing or not caring that I've got a death grip on the wheel. "You've been cleared by the orthopedist for a month now."

How many times must we play this game? Too bad Mom couldn't take me today. She wouldn't bring up this nonsense. "I'm done," I tell him for the hundredth time, and for the hundredth time, I ignore the drop in my stomach. It should feel easier by now, shouldn't it? I'd had a career-ending injury on the most important day of my career. What part of *done* doesn't he get? And why does he have to bring it up now?

"You've had plenty of injuries," he replies, undeterred.

"Exactly." A thin man in a black blazer with an equally dark look on his face waits by the curb.

Wait! Not yet! Now I'm the one who wants to whimper. Dammit. Except this is my seventh time here, and if I can't do it now, when am I ever going to be able to?

I slide next to the curb at a cool one mile per hour.

"You should e-mail the Ocean State coach," Dad continues.

The words make my palms sweat and my heartbeat accelerate. I don't want to talk about gymnastics, I don't want to think about it, and right now, that dour-looking DMV employee looks like a hell of a lot better company than Dad.

I press the brakes too abruptly, causing the car to jerk forward.

"Bye, Dad. Good talk."

My father sighs and drops a quick kiss on my forehead before opening the door. "Good luck, Katie." I'd roll my eyes at the old nickname, except now I'm too nervous to do anything.

When the road test administrator slides in next to me, it feels like all of the air is sucked out of the car. His legs must be twice the length of my body, knees crammed against the glove compartment. I imagine him already docking me a point: *insufficient leg room.* "'K.S. Gregory,'" he reads flatly. "What does 'K.S.' stand for?"

"Kaitlyn Savannah." Perhaps he agrees that "Savannah" is the far more interesting name.

"Pull away from the curb," he says instead.

I signal and take an exaggerated look over my shoulder before pulling away from the curb. If I had dared glance to the side, maybe I would have seen Dad by the playground, watching his daughter and the fifteen-year-old Civic move away from the curb.

Ten minutes. That's all the time it will take to pass this thing, get the hell out of coming back here for the eighth time, and achieve something for the first time in months. I cannot, under any circumstances, fail again.

I will my hands to stop shaking. They ignore me. Typical.

The speedometer needle hovers safely at 30 mph, though the pick-up truck riding my bumper looks ready to plow over me. I've lived in Ponquogue my whole life and have passed by these landmarks countless times: the lighthouse statue, the OCEAN BEACHES sign that was bent in the last hurricane and still hasn't been fixed, the WELCOME TO PONQUOGUE sign painted on driftwood and propped against the flag pole.

I've never had those Get-Me-Out-of-Ponquogue urges; rather, it was inevitable that I *would* leave for the Ocean State University Buccaneers. The green-and-white sweatshirt that my parents gave me last Christmas became my unofficial uniform for months. Now it's stuffed with my old leotards in the darkest corner of my dresser.

"Left," the man says as I approach the fork in the road. At the heart of the fork is 7-Eleven, the place of 2 a.m. Slurpee runs when Cassie calls me, unable to sleep. She could text, but since it's Cass and she's impatient, she always insists on calling to make sure I wake up. "I'll buy you one," she'll say in greeting. "Also, I'm outside."

Today, migrant workers linger on the curbside in baseball caps and jeans flecked with paint. Just across the street, a man sets up shop on a beach chair adorned with American flags. Propped up beside him is a sign that reads, "Secure Our Borders—Give Jobs to Americans."

"*Left!*" the man grunts.

Oops.

I hit the signal and pull a wide left-hand turn. Plenty of space before oncoming traffic.

The man mutters under his breath.

Slowly, gently, my death grip eases despite the sweat on the steering wheel. Lots of sweat. Sure, my parallel park is a hair too close to the car behind me. However, our bumpers never collide; I'd learned the hard way from tests four and five.

It's like a balance beam routine during competition with only a few skills left before the dismount: feet pound down the beam, punch off the end, flip, and stick the landing.

For the first time since that fateful April afternoon at Regionals, a wave of confidence courses through me. I've *got* this.

We return to the opposite side of the street from where I began. I'm almost bouncing in my seat. I'm done, out of here, conquered glorious attempt number seven. Through the window, Dad steps away from the playground, makes his way over with that infamous smirk brewing on his face. I give him a thumbs-up and he raises an eyebrow, surprised.

That's right, Dad, you're looking at a licensed driver. Consider yourself relegated to shotgun.

"Work on controlling your steering," the man says, handing me the paper with my score. "As well as paying more attention."

Sure, sure. I nod vigorously. Hell, I'll agree to anything right now. The paper trembles as I scan the litany of deductions. It's a little longer than I'd expected, but so what? You can still get points off and pass—

Two. Freakin'. Points.

Between me and my license. Between the me who always fails and the one who thought she'd broken through today.

"Sorry." The man's already halfway out the door.

The paper crumples in my hand. That brief flash of confidence, of belief in myself? Clearly I'm delusional. When the feeling had reminded me of completing a beam routine, apparently my subconscious forgot to add, *Warning! This experience is eerily similar to others that you've failed at. Do not trust.*

Dad doesn't say anything when he returns to the driver's seat. He might want to, but I'm too damned focused on watching the cars in front of us. Did any of those drivers pass today? Are they driving right now?

"How much?" he finally asks.

"Two."

"We'll go driving this weekend," he says with a little laugh, and I don't say anything.

Besides that too-wide left-hand turn, there are no major violations on the piece of paper. Just the same phrase again and again: "Failed to use proper judgment."

I press my forehead to the cool window and imagine myself in the thicket of trees that we hurtle past, running far and deep into the shadows.

When my phone rings, I debate not looking. Whatever Cassie has to say is sure to make me feel worse, although she won't mean to. *Kicking serious DMV ass?*

More like getting my own kicked, I type and then drop my phone into my backpack before I press Send. What's the point?

Too soon, we're in the Ponquogue High School teachers' lot. Three-quarters of the senior lot spaces are empty, with seagulls waddling on the concrete before flying off. Right. While I was embarrassing myself, the rest of my grade drove to the beach.

When Dad opens the door, wind slaps my face. He looks away. He's about to say something uncomfortable.

"You don't have to be miserable, you know. Just have to...try again."

Tears jump into my eyes, and not of the *I'm so inspired* variety. "Sure."

"Cassie managed to pass, after all. If New York State's willing to put that girl behind the wheel—"

The bell rings inside the red brick building. Already, I imagine sneakers screeching over linoleum and lockers rattling open. Underclassmen scuttling along in the daily grind. "See you later," he says.

Is this my future? My father driving me back and forth from whatever college I end up going to?

Cassie managed to pass, after all. Dad's idea of an inspirational speech.

I wait until he's disappeared through the D-Wing entrance. He'll find out about this by the end of the day, for certain; teachers in passing will say, "Guess Savannah's taking advantage of Senior Cut Day, huh?" and the sniveling nerds hoping for an A will tell him I missed Spanish. It will serve as breaking news. Unlike my best friend, I actually show up on a daily basis and do my homework.

But he's the one who left the keys on the driver's seat.

I make it down the driveway and over the bright yellow speed bumps without security noticing a vehicle heading off-campus. Soon, I'm at the light as mid-morning traffic passes in front of me, rocking the car.

The sign says I can signal right for Ponquogue Village or left for the ocean. Cars become more sporadic, making a last-ditch effort to beat the light as soon as it turns yellow. Red. On green, I exercise my right of improper judgment. I turn left.

CHAPTER TWO

A S I BUMP down Main Street, I fight the urge to duck in my seat. The paint curling off the Anthony's Pizza (Great to Meet Ya!) sign, the flashing neon "Open" sign of Empanadas Sudamericanas—they feel like scowling witnesses. *You shouldn't be out here.*

Technically Dad has returned to AP Calculus by now, interrogating my classmates as to the whereabouts of their homework. Cassie would have the windows rolled down already, ignoring the cool burn of the air, drowning out the wind with music. "God, Savs, relax," she'd say.

I scan radio stations, catch the middle of AC/DC's "Back in Black," and take a deep breath. *You got this.* That image again—me on a balance beam—and I turn up the music louder to forget it.

I follow the hill past the mansions that overlook the ocean. Back down the hill is the rest of us. We're the gateway to the Hamptons, neighbors on the same stretch of ocean, yet as my older brother, Richard, likes to joke, "We're Poor Hampton." Most of us have two parents (if we're lucky) who work and stomachs that sink when we start tallying up how much college tuition will cost—especially now that I won't have an athletic scholarship to cover mine.

The road smooths out, the trees flatten, and the dirt turns to sand. In front of me arches South Cross Bridge, iron and concrete. No matter how many times I've been here or how much I hated getting up for work at the beach on summer mornings, it always fills me with a flutter of excitement. It spans the bay, connecting the main land to the strip of barrier island and South Cross Beach. Coasting in at four miles per hour, I pass the booth where I'd spent my summer saying, "Excuse me, ma'am, you need to pay for a day pass." It's boarded up for the winter with a sign that says, "See you next season!" I park next to the one car that's crooked between the lines and adorned with "COEXIST" and "My child is an honor student at Ponquogue Elementary School" bumper stickers. Cass finds the latter hilarious.

My feet sink in the sand, the wind whacks strands of my short hair against my cheeks, and I take a deep gulp of the salt air. The waves curl and crash in high tide—loud, indignant, toppling one after the other—and while it's stupid, I can't help feeling that they're angry on my behalf.

I breathe better down here.

I could have the worst practice at the gym, an argument with Dad, radio silence from Richard. Then I get in the passenger's seat of Cassie's car, walk through the pavilion teeming with little kids and ice cream cones, and run across the sand. Something about the incessant beating of the waves against the shore can make anything feel lighter.

I watch the waves until a tiny bit of the embarrassment ebbs away. Who needs gymnastics? Who needs a license, dammit?

A gaggle of my fellow seniors tosses a Frisbee back and forth. Several girls lay out in bikini tops, either impermeable to the wind or not caring. In solidarity, Andreas Alvarez scampers around with no shirt on. "Put down the damn metal detector and have some fun already!" he shouts at Marcos Castillo, whose metal detector skims the ground near the Frisbee game. When Marcos shakes his head, Andreas fires the disc at him anyway. Classy.

Next to the rocks that jetty into the foaming water, a girl is barefoot and crouched low on the sand, pink skirt flowing around her legs as the ocean sweeps against the shore. The cold is nothing to her. Long blonde ringlets flap against her face as she raises the camera and points the tremendous lens at me. In that exact instant, I stumble over a piece of driftwood. Graceful. She should turn the camera toward herself. I'm the one who's a mess.

"You did it!" she shouts, lowering the camera. "My baby girl is all grown up."

"Yeah, about that." I wipe bits of dried seaweed from my jeans.

"No burritos? It's okay, I'll forgive you this once." Cassie trails behind me as I climb onto the rocks. They're slick with spray, but I've spent so much of my childhood leaping across them that I barely notice.

"More like *nada*," I say to the ocean. I should have just texted her. Despite the thundering of the waves and that familiar clamminess from the salt air, there's no drowning out the way it feels like shit to voice the words.

She scampers next to me and extends to her full height, nearly six feet and slender as the single birch tree in her yard. "No."

"Yes." *Failure to use proper judgment.* I glower at the blue-green waves. They're just as riled as I am, crashing against the rocks and spraying with a hiss.

Her arm loops around me. We look ridiculous side by side, something people at every party this summer made sure to point out to us. Without fail, someone would toss Cassie a beer and then spot me. "Cass, is this your little sister?"

I reached five feet when I was twelve—with a victorious shout in the nurse's office when she read off the number to me—and haven't grown since.

Cassie squeezes me close. She's not laughing at me, although she probably wants to. Heck, I would if it were anyone besides me. "The DMV sucks," she says. "They know nothing."

"Yep."

"You don't need your license. I'll drive you."

"Forever?" I raise a doubtful eyebrow.

"Who needs art school when I can be a professional chauffeur?" she says, and although I roll my eyes, I can't help but laugh.

"I'm going to move where I can use mass transit for the rest of my life."

Cassie's smile slips as her eyes widen, like I've said something truly profound. "That. Is. Brilliant."

"It's for the common good, I think."

Her words sprint now, almost as fast as she waves her hands. "Think about it, Savs. You, me, New York City. Roommates."

"I wasn't planning on applying to any schools in the city." In fact, I still don't have a clear plan on where I'm applying besides where I'm *not* going: Ocean State.

"NYU. Columbia." She ticks them off on her fingers. "You know you'll get in."

"How about the gazillion dollars in tuition?"

She doesn't bat an eye. "We'll get jobs, obviously."

That's the thing with Cassie. She says something totally unreasonable—that she'll drive me around for the rest of my life. That she and I can just move to the city and get jobs—and she says it with such confidence that it actually sounds possible. For the first time all day—in months—hope blooms in my chest. I might have a future that isn't a failure.

A tiny part of me still asks, *What about gymnastics?* After all, there are no NYC colleges with teams.

Well, what about gymnastics? I haven't stepped foot in the gym since I blew out my knee right in front of the Ocean State coach. There's no point. My body has given up on me one too many times.

When I don't counter with another question, she squeezes me closer. Despite the salt air, she smells like lavender and cinnamon as always. "It'll be so awesome that they'll send a reality TV crew to record our shenanigans."

I focus on that blossoming hope. Living together in an apartment the size of a closet, surviving off Ramen noodles—with Cassie, it'll be an adventure, shimmering with possibility. I'll walk briskly over cement sidewalks instead of on four-inch-wide balance beams.

"Gymnastics is the boyfriend you need to get over," Cassie says firmly, as though she knows exactly where my mind has wandered. "You would have had to quit eventually."

I'd wanted to finish at the final meet of my senior year of college, teammates surrounding me. Not like this.

I need to channel the same spirit that took Dad's car and turned left out of the school parking lot. To make a bold plunge that doesn't involve hurtling over the vault or swinging from bar to bar. If I have a definitive future plan, then my father will have to accept it when I tell him I'm moving on to bigger and better things outside of the gym.

I take a deep breath. "I'm in. Let's do it."

Cassie lifts me in the air and stumbles on the rock. We both scream and then burst out laughing.

"We almost died!" I yell.

"Sorry!" she yells back. "I'm just so glad you're not ditching me next year."

The guys stop playing Frisbee and watch us curiously. On the outskirts of their circle, Marcos passes the disc from hand to hand like he's contemplating his next move.

"I was never going to ditch you." The spray catches my ankles, and I step back.

She shrugs, popping off the camera lens cap. "Rhode Island, same thing. Strike a pose. We need to capture this moment."

"Rhode Island, same thing" prickles at me. So does the cool water seeping through the bottom of my jeans.

"Something cool," she says. "Do a handstand."

I can't count how many handstand photos I have, taken by Cassie, now stowed away in a folder on my computer. It's as natural a position as walking on my feet.

She already has the camera raised to her eye. I press my palms to the cool rock and kick up. As soon as I'm up, I know it's going to be a good one. I split my legs, my fingers twitching as they shift their weight to keep me steady.

Click. "Point those toes, Savannah Banana."

"What are we, seven?" I mutter to my hands, which slowly turn red from the cold and the strain.

When we were seven years old and glued next to each other on the bus, Cassie had said, "I wish I had a normal name like Kaitlyn. Cascade is so weird."

I hadn't known what Cascade meant. "My middle name's Savannah."

"Savannah." Her eyes had lit up. "I love that. I'm calling you Savannah from now on."

Ten years later, everyone's adopted Savannah as my name. Besides the DMV. And my dad.

The shutter snaps again. "Here marks the day that Savannah and Cassie decided to get out of this shit town forever, amen."

"It's not that bad." The familiar head rush hits me, blood steadily flowing to my forehead.

"That's like saying the guy with that 'Jobs for Americans' sign outside of 7-Eleven should run for president. Doesn't compute."

A thud against the sand. "You think I can jump that high?" Andreas squawks. The shuffle of feet, the shouts of a few guys, and then one voice calls above them, "Savannah, watch out!"

Thwack. The Frisbee hits me straight in my surgically repaired right knee. I cry out, more from shock than pain, and then I'm tipping, my hands scrambling to find purchase.

On land, this would be no problem; I'd bail out and flip over.

Up here, there are two choices: land on a rock or fall into the ocean.

Stay up, stay up! Gravity makes the decision for me. My legs flail, my left hand walks forward and slips, and I plunge straight into the water.

The cold consumes me so quickly that I can't breathe. My arms and legs swing into action, moving automatically to the surface, fighting the tug of the receding tide. I throw my hand to touch the rock and instead find more water.

Get out!

The blurry distant sun is eclipsed by the crash of a wave. I battle the burn in my lungs and try to coast on the momentum of the next incoming wave that roils at my back. My arms are strained from exertion and my legs kick furiously. *Up.* That's my only goal. The sun's still too far away, my lungs are heavy and my arms are heavier—

A strong hand grabs my arm and yanks me to the surface.

I gasp in gulps of air and turn to Cassie. "Thanks—"

Except my rescuer isn't Cass. She's still on the rocks, staring down at us with her mouth open and her camera hanging around her neck.

It's one very damp, very flustered Marcos Castillo.

"Are you okay?" He treads water and breathes just as deeply as I do. His dark hair is plastered to his forehead and his eyes don't move from mine despite the wave that ripples against his neck.

Those words move Cass to action. "Get out of there, Savs! You'll get hypothermia."

A small crowd gathers around the rocks. Great. "Damn, Savannah, that was awesome," Andreas crows. "Do it again."

"It was *your* fault." Cassie extends her hand to me. Although I can climb out on my own, I take it anyway. Her blue eyes are worried and her voice is strained. "Stupid Frisbee."

Marcos climbs up after me. His red shirt and jeans might as well be painted on. Meanwhile, I feel like I've just gained a thousand pounds in water weight. "I am so sorry," he says. "It was my fault. I thought Andreas was gonna catch it—"

"Nobody could have caught it!" Andreas calls back. "It was like ninety miles over my head."

"When you didn't come out, I was like, holy shit." Marcos runs a hand through his hair, trying to squeeze out some of the water. Instead, it sticks straight up.

I hug myself, shivering as the wind blows. I'm colder now than I was in the ocean. "It's okay." I don't like all of these eyes on me. I shouldn't have done the stupid handstand to begin with. Once again, as this morning showed, mixing gymnastics with any other life endeavor leads to disaster.

"Savannah's like a champion swimmer," Cass adds. "She would have been fine."

I snort. "I'm not a champion swimmer unless you count that time you made me race those Australian guys."

"That's why I said *like* a champion swimmer."

Marcos's head swivels back and forth between us, the water spraying off of his hair.

"Anyway," I say loudly, hoping Andreas and company get the hint, "I'm fine. Thanks, though."

Cass slings an arm around me despite the fact that I'm soaking wet. "Show's over."

My teeth chatter as I nod in agreement. I really hope Dad's got a towel lying around in the trunk. Right now I don't care if it reeks of sweat from his bike rides.

"Hot chocolate," she says. "On me."

As we cross the dunes, I glance over my shoulder. The boys have resumed their game. Andreas takes off running, yelling, "Can't get me, suckas!" Marcos hangs back on the fringes, watching us.

Outside of her car, Cassie dries me off like I'm a puppy.

"I can do it myself." My voice is muffled under the towel.

"You look so tiny and pathetic." She gives my hair an extra yank. Her phone rings and she fumbles for it in her beaded purple bag. As soon as she checks the caller ID, her forehead creases.

"Who is it?"

"No one."

Definitely her father. He's a physicist at Brookhaven National Laboratory who developed a microscopic chip that shoots nanoparticles. Or something. Any time the laboratory has a scientific breakthrough in the news, the odds are good that he's part of it. Cass actually understands his research—she used to read out loud from his old physics textbooks when we were kids while I'd groan.

The phone rings again. "You should answer," I say.

"You should go back to school before you get in trouble."

Yeah, that's not happening. "What happened with your dad?"

She exhales long and loud. "Same bullshit, different day. I'm the one scientific aberration he can't figure out."

"What will your parents think about the city?"

She tugs away the towel and folds it with quick, sharp thrusts. She doesn't like me digging like this—whenever I'm at her house, she whisks me up to her room before I can do more than say hi to her parents—but I want to know.

"I'm sure they won't care so long as you're with me," she says.

Her text tone rings. As she reads the message, her face relaxes.

"Who's that?" I know it, but I could be wrong—

"Jules wants to take photos in Southampton." Dammit. I was right. She tugs her keys from her bag. "It'll probably be a couple of hours."

My stomach sinks. I'm being ditched for The Other Best Friend. "What about hot chocolate?" The towel helped, but I'm still soaked and freezing. I want her to stay with me, with the heat and the music cranked up in the car, finally dry and focusing on that glittery city. Not to frolic off to Juliana de los Santos, who I'm pretty sure hates me.

Cassie's already unlocked her door. "Text you later! Love you!" The door shuts, the brake lights glow red, and she backs out in a sweeping arc. I jump out of the way.

"Love you," I say to the exhaust puffing out of her tailpipe. Any lingering therapeutic effects from the ocean have dissipated as I stand here on the concrete, sopping wet and without a license. Terrific Senior Cut Day.

I turn to Dad's car, and my eyes hone in on the front driver's-side tire. The one that's now completely flat.

Wonderful.

Because this day couldn't get any better.

CHAPTER THREE

"THAT DOESN'T LOOK good."

"Nope." My hand pokes at the tire uselessly, like it'll stop playing dead and wake up.

Marcos squats beside me. Unlike me, he's in a dry sweatshirt that smells like fresh cotton. "Got a donut?"

Today is the most I've ever talked to Marcos. When I became serious about competitive gymnastics in third grade, I only saw my peers—besides Cassie—at school. I didn't care about the day-to-day Ponquogue drama. School was where I rested between practices and did what I had to do to wow a prospective college coach with both gymnastics and grades. Outside of practice, I hung out with Cassie or my teammates. Now, school's pretty much the only place I go.

Marcos nods at my phone. "Do you have an app that's going to fix it?"

I crack a smile. "I'm looking for a tutorial."

His eyes widen like he's impressed. Or he's just realized how freakin' cold that last gust of wind was. "I can help if you want."

I don't have any other options besides calling Mom, which means she'll call Dad, which means I'll be scolded while still soaking wet and getting colder by the second. I extend a hand. "Work your magic."

Marcos takes the donut from the trunk and effortlessly carries it to the front of the car. His shoulders are broad, the kind that would make a male gymnast envious, and he places it lightly on the ground. "I can teach you."

I probably won't be allowed out of the house again until I'm forty. I nod anyway.

"First we've gotta get this guy off of the ground." He places the jack under the car. I've seen this before—Richard loved tinkering with Dad's car when he came home for college breaks—but a refresher won't hurt.

"That handstand on the rocks was really cool." His voice sounds distant beneath the car. "What happened to your knee?"

I kneel beside him. "A Frisbee."

His shoulders shake as he laughs. "I mean in the spring. I saw you on crutches."

What *hadn't* happened to my knee would be a better question. "Tore my ACL, MCL, and meniscus."

"Shit." He scoots back and looks at me sympathetically.

I look away. "I'm fine now." The days I didn't work at the beach parking booth were spent doing physical therapy. My knee's as good as it's going to be, besides the crackle and pop of scar tissue when I bend or straighten it quickly.

He takes a wrench to the first hubcap and passes it to me so I can unscrew the others. "You're strong," he says. "You really didn't need my help getting out of the water."

It feels a hell of a lot better down here than it did standing. Warmer. Safer, like we're crouched by a kindling fire.

The guys laugh up on the dunes. Someone calls, "Castillo, where you at?" and Marcos shows no reaction. Instead, he helps me slip on the donut and runs his hands over the flat tire.

His palms are callused, like mine. "You cut this up pretty good. See what I mean?" He tilts it toward me, revealing a long slit. "You're probably going to need a new one."

Lovely. More things my father will scold me for.

Once the donut is secured, all lug nuts and hub caps are tightened, and the deflated tire is plopped into the trunk, we stand facing each other. What do you say to a guy who hit you with a Frisbee, jumped in the ocean after you, and saved you from calling your dad to say, "Hey, I stole your car and tore up your tire. Come get me"?

I settle on: "Thank you so much. This would have been a disaster without you."

He slips his hands into his jeans pockets and grins. "I owed you for the Frisbee fiasco."

My eyes dart directly to his front tooth, crooked like a little kid's. "Well, um, I'll see you around?"

The grin expands. Two dimples deepen in his cheeks. "We're in the same lunch."

"Oh, cool."

"And gym class."

"I totally knew that," I lie. I spend the period passing the football with Cassie (when she's there, that is; otherwise, I pair up with a random person). I'm surprised Marcos noticed we were in one period together, let alone two.

He laughs like he knows I'm full of it. "See you tomorrow, Savannah."

I start up the car, the radio blasting, and pretend that I don't notice him watching as I inch out of my spot.

....

AFTER I PULL into my dad's usual spot, I contemplate my choices:

Go inside and move through a normal day, with a stern, public talking-to inevitably waiting from Dad.

Spend the rest of Senior Cut Day hiding in my bedroom.

I started off today with *Failure to use proper judgment.* Might as well see it through to the finish. So I tuck the keys behind the donut, cut through the woods, and walk the three miles home.

I turn the doorknob slowly in hopes that the wind will mask my entrance. Wait. Listen. Repeat.

"Look what I found," my mother calls.

Just like that. Busted.

She emerges from the family room and eyes me sternly. She's tiny, not a whisper over five feet, and in her US Army sweatshirt and sweatpants, she looks like a kid. It's probably why the children at Dayshine Preschool love climbing on her; they think she's one of them. "Dad was one step away from calling the police, but I suspected you were with Cassie."

"How much trouble am I in?"

Her face relaxes ever so slightly. "If you help me clean up in here, I might be able to talk him down to twenty-five years."

It's the sound from the family room, rather than the promise of a lighter sentence, that lures me further. Recorded cheering. The reverberation of feet slamming against springboards and launching into the air.

On the carpet is a sea of my old gymnastics footage. Everything is color-coded by level: the Level 5 chronicles are in red, Level 6 and 7 are pink (I moved up a level mid-season and felt like a prodigy), Level 8 and 9 are blue, and Level 10 is green. I'd picked green because it meant go, except apparently for me, it meant *get out of this sport*.

She gestures at the TV. "I love this one. Level–"

"–Five State Championships. Yeah, that was classic."

"Look how cute you girls were." The camera pans to a shot of my teammates and me standing in front of the judges before we competed on bars. I'm the shortest, my knees bouncing because I was that pain in the ass who needed to be moving all of the time. Next to me in height order are Ally, Monica, Jess, and finally Emery, always the best in our group. Even at age ten, she stood with confidence.

Ten-year-old Savannah sprays water onto her hand grips. Then she's jumping up and down on the springboard until Coach Vanessa, ever the disciplinarian, yanks her down. Next she's warming up, moving from the low bar to the high bar with feet flexed and legs splayed. Coach Matt rolls his eyes because everyone knows that she'll only show off her proper form when the judges are watching. She releases the bar, flips once, and lands flat on her back. On camera, Mom gasps.

Now my mother smiles. "You won bars after that."

"Why are you looking through all of this stuff?"

"Making the most of my vacation day." She busies herself with filling up the glass cabinet under the TV.

In the grand scheme, it's better to see Mom enjoying these relics rather than stressing out over yet another news story. I'll walk into the kitchen some mornings to find her zeroed in on the headlines: *Roadside Bomb Kills 3; Reported PTSD Cases Rise; Troops Deployed to Trouble Spot.* When my brother graduated from Notre Dame and headed to Fort Benning for Officer Candidate School, normal motherly concern surged into an anxiety that no amount of reassurances can calm.

She'll come home from work and say, "How was your day, sweetie? Good, good," before I respond, and drift between the phone and the Internet, searching for any sign of my brother. Even with the phone pressed to her ear, I'll hear the ringing on Richard's end.

Straight to voicemail is the worst. It could mean nothing. Richard could be off in a field in North Carolina, teaching the recruits to crawl on their elbows. When he's deployed, it could mean that he's the subtext behind those black-ink headlines, crouched low in the sand where no one can see him. On those days, we all retreat to our own spaces like an unspoken shelter-in-place. Mom treads lightly up and down the stairs as she says, "Maybe I'll have better service here?" Dad escapes to the garage, spinning the wheels of his bicycle as he prepares for a trail ride. I used to flee to the gym, but now to my bedroom, laptop open and door closed.

If Baby Gymnast Savannah wiping out puts Mom in a good mood, I'll allow it.

I join her on the carpet, handing over my color-coded Greatest Hits and Misses: Level 7 Long Island Classic (three falls on beam), Level 8 New England Invitational tweaked my shoulder on bars), Level 9 State Championships (third-place floor—major hit).

Onscreen Savannah stands in front of the balance beam. For once, she's not wiggling. She's terrified.

Good call, Baby Savannah. You were on to something. When she mounts the beam, she leaves behind sweaty footprints on the blue mat.

"What do you think about NYU?" I say.

Mom rocks back on her heels. "I'm sure you'll get in." Yet there's no excitement in the way she says it, just caution. "It's expensive, though."

"I might be able to get a scholarship." Hopefully. Maybe.

Mom's lips twist in the way that means she needs to let me down gently. "You know, I wish you would"– I steel myself–"find something else that you enjoy. What if you try out for a school play?"

"Have you heard me sing?"

She fights back a smile. We both know it's not for the faint of heart. "What about dance? Your floor routines were so beautiful."

Too close to gymnastics, and not close enough. "No, thanks."

There's one last green label and Mom reaches it before I can. Her eyes widen ever so slightly.

I know it before she says it.

"Level Ten Regionals–"

I turn away, ignoring the little voice that tells me I'm the one in trouble today, not her. "Throw it out. Burn it. I don't care."

. . . .

BEFORE MY KNEE, it was my shoulder. I taped bags of ice to it and gritted my teeth against the cold.

Before my shoulder, it was my wrists. I wore matching braces, called Tiger Paws, on them every time I tumbled and vaulted. They prevented my wrists from stretching too far.

Before my wrists, it was my back. "You're too flexible," the doctor told me. "You need to strengthen your core." I did, to the point where Cassie announced in the locker room, "Your abs are bigger than your boobs."

I followed all of the rules. Every repetition of every exercise with the best form I could muster, shaking and sweating—I did all of it. Where did that land me? In a crumpled heap on the floor. The sad fact is that after one surgery and six months of rehabilitation, what's to stop my knee from snapping again?

There's only one guarantee: stopping completely.

CHAPTER FOUR

"**W**ILL THE FOLLOWING students please report to the assistant principal's office? Savannah Gregory, Cascade Hopeswell..."

In the godforsaken math wing, I know that my dad's ears have perked up.

On the way to the office, I halt. A janitor works to scrub off black ink on a row of orange lockers. Surrounding him are the safety signs that caution *Wet floor! Piso mojado!*

He's gotten the "F." The rest reads, UCK YOU SPICS. Students press against the far side of the hallway as if they're afraid the ink will touch them.

The Y falls directly on Andreas's locker, I know that—I've seen him bouncing back and forth from it numerous times. Roberto, rumored to sell weed in the boys' bathroom, is usually on the other side right under the O, and Preston, ranked third in our class and courted by Ivy League schools for both his soccer skills and his brain, occupies the K.

Ponquogue has changed since I was a kid and Richard was in high school. The influx of immigrant families moving here means there are now several Colombian and Mexican eateries (like Pav's Place, for which we are all the better) on Main Street. When Richard was on the varsity soccer team, it was primarily a bunch of preppy white kids who grew up taking sailing lessons and then turned to a less expensive sport.

Cassie's beaten me to the office waiting area. "Did you see the lockers? Who the hell did that?"

When I shake my head, she tugs her camera out of her bag. "Check it out." Armed and ready to show Mr. Riley the fruits of her artistic labor.

Cassie came to all of my meets and took photos. Her early ones were just-misses—me landing a dismount, coming out of a leap, grimacing as I ran toward the vault. Once she learned the timing, she caught me in the air. Feet kicking over my head, flipping over the balance beam, high-fiving my coach. Strong, flexible, confident. Too confident.

When I scroll through the photos of my handstand, they move like stop-motion animation. Like all of Cassie's photos, the balance is perfect and every detail is crisp. A wiggle, a waver—there comes the Frisbee.

"It's like a UFO." Cass presses the forward button so that the Frisbee moves in, out, back again, and we're cracking up when the office door opens and a freshman exits with his head down, clearly chastised.

Crap.

"Miss Gregory. Miss Hopeswell," Mr. Riley greets us in his low, dark voice. He has the broad shoulders, cropped hair, and unwavering gaze of a Navy SEAL.

I bite back the urge to speak before Mr. Riley can open his mouth. *I'm sorry, Mr. Riley. Failing one's road test seven times brings out the delinquent in a person.*

"Miss Hopeswell, I'd like to speak with you first."

Cassie grabs my arm. "Savannah goes with me."

"Miss Hopeswell, I'm afraid these discussions are confidential." To Mr. Riley's credit, his tone never changes.

"I'm just going to tell her everything you tell me anyway."

Surprisingly, Mr. Riley chuckles. "If you're sure."

Once we face him in identical metal chairs, he says, "Miss Hopeswell, there is the matter of your scholarly performance. Your chemistry, English, and precalculus teachers have expressed concerns about your academic output." Mr. Riley makes each subject sound like doom. "You're one absence away from failing physical education. It's only October, Miss Hopeswell. You still have nine months of school."

Wait, what?

Cass always digs in at the last minute; it's her greatest source of inspiration. The essays that she types on her crumb-smeared laptop three minutes before the bell are excellent. Detailed and smart, posing probing questions. She achieves the "where did that come from?" score on final exams in math and science, showing hints of her father's brilliant brain. She doesn't hit rock bottom.

Mr. Riley is mistaken.

Isn't he?

I turn to Cassie for confirmation. Her mouth sets in a firm line as she stares straight at Mr. Riley. "Art schools don't care about flag football."

Mr. Riley slaps the desk. We both jump. "Do you know how many students think they can slack because they're talented in one area? There are thousands of applicants working for the same ten spots in art school, Miss Hopeswell. What if it doesn't pan out? What will you do?"

Bad, meet worse.

She's staring at her hands. Index finger bent. *Crack.* Repeat on right hand. *Crack.* Her bottom lip trembles, but she won't give in. She won't break the silence.

My stomach feels as heavy as his words. I want to whisk Cassie out of here, say, "Thanks for your time and concern, but we'll take care of this." Whatever glitch has happened with Cassie, I'll help her out of it. School's the one thing I'm confident I can still do well. She'll help me plan for our shenanigans-filled future in the city, and I'll help get her through this.

"Cassie and I were just talking about precalc."

Both of their heads turn toward me. My ears are already flaming—they might as well be throwing up smoke signals that say, "She's lying!"

I soldier forth. "She asked if I could tutor her because she's been so busy working on her art school portfolio. We're starting this weekend."

Mr. Riley offers a curt nod. "I'm pleased to hear that, Ms. Gregory."

Cass ceases cracking her knuckles. I can see the relief on her face. The lie worked.

"Well, this has been great." She stands.

"Hold on." Mr. Riley should voice movie trailers with that booming tone. Cassie freezes. "As for you, Ms. Gregory."

Oh, God. I steel myself for, I don't know, my father turning me in himself.

"The Board of Education wants to honor your PSAT scores from the spring."

Cassie snaps her head toward me.

"Um, wow. That's really, uh..." Last year, I'd had two goals: place at Level 10 Nationals and blow the SATs out of the water. So I'd studied like hell for the PSAT because although it wasn't the real test, it'd bring me one step closer.

Any sense of pride is obliterated by the way Cassie stares at me like I've betrayed her with my penciled-in answers.

"You had the highest score in the grade," Mr. Riley says, either obliviously or deliberately rubbing those words into my best friend's heart with the sole of his stern black shoe. "Your commitment to your studies is impressive. Certainly Ms. Hopeswell will benefit from your assistance."

If I had the highest score, Cassie couldn't have been far behind. Then again, with what Mr. Riley said about her classes... "Thank you," I say. Hopefully that's enough to conclude this conversation. "It'll be mutually beneficial, I'm sure."

Cass says nothing. Doesn't offer Mr. Riley a fake smile, an angry stare, even a long sigh. She doesn't look at me either. There's no lift of her eyebrows to show she's ready to mock him when we're alone again. Her entire face is expressionless.

As soon as his door opens, she bolts out of the room.

CHAPTER FIVE

"**S**AVANNAH, WAIT!"

I whirl around without recognizing the voice—male and deep, though nothing like Mr. Riley's.

Marcos jogs up to me, backpack bouncing against his shoulders. "Do you have a second?"

I need to find Cassie. With that chill in her eyes, I wouldn't be surprised if she's stormed out the entrance like a hurricane, not bothering to stop at the front desk to sign out. There's a chance I can still catch her.

Marcos runs a hand through his unruly, dark curls. "I'm sorry again about yesterday. From here on out, I will make sure that no Frisbees come your way without your permission."

Before I can stop myself, my lips lift in a half-smile. That's enough for his shoulders to relax. Broad shoulders that nicely fill out his red T-shirt without the "I'm so jacked" swagger of other guys in my grade.

"Glad to see that chivalry's not dead after all," I say.

He laughs, dimples deepening. Any last vestiges of annoyance from yesterday are swept away by that laugh.

"I'm looking for Cassie." I glance over my shoulder in case I catch gold hair and a bright yellow dress fluttering past the windows.

"Oh, yeah, I just saw her. Looked like she was heading toward the courtyard."

Safely surrounded by four walls. I exhale. It's not that I don't trust Cassie behind the wheel; it's just that, even in the best of times, she's the definition of "distracted driver."

He grips his backpack straps like he's gearing up for something. "Um, I dropped something off at the office and overheard part of your conversation with Mr. Riley. The part about tutoring."

In twenty-four hours, I've gone from never talking to this guy to him taking an active role in my life. A disruptive one, I might add. "Oh, yeah, Cassie doesn't actually need tutoring." She needs me right now, though. I know that much.

"How much do you charge?"

I need to shake him off. I have a best friend to find. "You're better off asking my dad."

He smiles and that crooked tooth somehow emphasizes the warmth of his grin even more, like an exclamation point. "That's why Mr. Riley congratulated you on your PSAT score, right?"

Which then sent Cassie sprinting out of the room.

"Sorry," he says, sensing my impatience. "I need to get my GPA up for this free tuition scholarship at Suffolk." He hikes up his backpack onto his shoulders. "I don't have much cash, but I work at Pav's. I can hook you up with free fajitas."

What does it say about me that I'm not swayed by his dimples, his callused hands, but by the prospect of sizzling hot chicken wrapped in a warm corn tortilla? "Okay, deal. Let's talk in gym."

"Thank you, Savannah!" he calls from behind me as I take off, causing several freshmen to look at us and giggle.

. . . .

BY THE TIME I throw open the door to the courtyard, the bell has rung for fifth period and I'm certain the door to my Spanish class has already been slammed shut. *Tarde*, Señora Gutierrez will cluck.

Cassie leans back against the white stone ring around the fountain, face tilted to the sun. Her yellow dress and pale skin glow in the light.

"I was wondering when you'd show up." Her voice is staccato.

I join her on the stone and wince. It's chilly, even in my jeans. How the hell she's sat out here in a dress for this long is beyond me. "I was intercepted by Marcos Castillo."

Normally any mention of a guy is enough to get Cassie grinning and elbowing me. Today, nothing.

"I'm sorry about Mr. Riley," I say. Was it my fault? No. I didn't ask him to embarrass both of us. But I am sorry that she had to sit there while the assistant principal played us off one another.

Her voice is as empty as the fountain. "At least you got him to shut up."

"You're gonna blow everyone away with your portfolio." It's true that I've not yet seen the results of said portfolio, although I've stood on numerous beach rocks over the summer and gazed deeply at the waves while her shutter snapped. *Come on, Cass. Look at me.*

With a sigh, she draws herself up and meets my eyes for the first time. The look is steel blue, committed.

Have we reached a turning point out here in the courtyard? Will Cassie stand up, dust off her dress, and tell Mr. Riley to screw off via a perfect rest-of-the-year GPA?

"It's just like my dad." She's off the stone and pacing now. The skirt trails after her, a yellow wave. "He thinks I'm going to become some freakin' greeting card photographer. He keeps talking about 'viable career paths.'"

I'm not going to lie—up to this point, I'd kind of assumed the same. I can't count the amount of Slurpee-fueled sunrises she's roused me into seeing with her. "Tell him what you want to do," I say instead. "He's a logical guy. Throw some facts his way."

She throws her hands up. "What if I want to make *art* and see where that takes me? What if I don't ever want to be in school again?"

Yeah, that won't fly with Mr. Hopeswell.

There's a shot that her mother, who sculpts in the basement and leaves half-finished projects around the house, will understand. Then again, Mrs. Hopeswell also started a small pharmaceutical company that was bought out by a major corporation before Cassie was born—so maybe not.

"Exactly," she says to the expression on my face. "Every night, I get the same thing. You'd think someone who experiments for a living would get it. I swear to God that if it were fourteen ninety-one, he'd be insisting that the world was flat."

I have to bite the inside of my mouth to keep from smiling.

Cass isn't kidding. "Face it, Savs. I suck. I've failed Mr. Riley's precious system. My *academic output* is unsatisfactory."

"You're the smartest person I know." I stand up to stop her pacing. She sidesteps me. Anyone watching our dance from the window would be amused.

Since ninth grade, I've seen her face constrict with boredom and her shoulders slouch during class. I've always thought that the tethered look on her face, like Sisyphus's as he pushed his rock, was a sign that school was too easy for her. That boredom was the reason she started writing her essays an hour before they were due, gulping down iced coffee and clacking away in the parking lot. She would use her driver's seat as a workspace and stick Post-It notes to the dashboard carrying such wisdom as "diction on p. 18." "Quick, Savs, give me a three-sentence overview of your feelings on Jake from *The Sun Also Rises*," she'd say, voice and hands jittery from the caffeine, while I'd already finished my essay days ago. She thrives on the challenge.

"You always pull it together," I say now.

"I don't want to pull it together." Did I say her face was cold earlier? Now it's ice, a snowstorm in October. "I don't believe in their rules and test scores and writing bullshit essays so our teachers can keep their jobs. Just because I *can* do chemistry doesn't mean I want to because New York State says I should."

She could go on all day like this, using me as the shoreline that her words beat against. It's too cold today to stand out here for long and in the corner of my mind, I see Señora Gutierrez's sharp gaze sweeping the room and saying, "¿*Dónde está* Savannah Gregory?" Second missed day of Spanish in a row. I have to convince her to get back inside. "Hear me out, okay?"

When she looks at me this time, there's a hint of thaw. I take a breath. "For right now," I say, "we have to play the game on their terms. Then it's all over in June and you're done with this forever."

"Remember that time Mr. Riley told me I wouldn't get into art school?" So much for the thaw. "This place makes me ill." She drops her eyes to the cracked cement, where patches of weeds struggle to break through. "You didn't tell me your PSAT scores."

You didn't tell me you were failing classes. "They don't matter."

"So how'd you do on the actual test?" she persists. Now her eyes are on me full blast, daring me to tell her.

It's my turn to stare down at the cracks, watching the ants make their final dash for food before winter. "Okay."

"How okay?"

Leave it alone, Cass. None of this will make her feel better. These are the games that Mr. Riley wants to play.

Surprisingly, she softens before I reply. I've outlasted her. Not easy. "You know what, I don't need to know. I *do* know that you bailed me out back there and that I owe you."

I exhale. "I really can help if you want. I take pretty good notes."

She rolls her eyes and slings her arm around me. "Just don't bring up any notion that I should go along with Mr. Riley ever again, and we're good."

Yesterday, she comforted me. Today, I'm her anchor. At the end of the day, we're thicker than humidity in July.

As kids we played together, schemed together, nursed bruised knees and silly crushes on boy bands. She was quiet unless she was with me. Together, chances were that we were screaming as we sprinted into the ocean and laughing as we splashed each other. We whispered together under the trees as the neighborhood kids ran around searching for us in Manhunt, never giving up our spot. I rode my bike to her house when Richard was first deployed, blinking tears out of my eyes. She met me at the curb and grabbed my hand. Although her hand was bony, cool, without calluses, it was just as strong as mine. Sometimes I think she hasn't let go.

She keeps her arm around me now, reminding me that I'm her anchor, that she will run to me if she needs to be safe.

....

DAD EMERGES FROM the garage as I'm scrolling through apartment listings. I'd managed to avoid him last night by telling my mom I had a test to study for and locking myself in my room. No such luck today.

I type in a new search. *Did you mean "Brooklyn" or "Burger King"?* Whatever, Google, just get me out of this.

He sits across from me in the armchair. He's dressed head-to-toe in cyclist Spandex—bright orange and blue—and I thank my lucky stars that he prefers riding the trails instead of the roads, keeping my classmates from having more fodder. "What's this about you swimming around?"

That's what I mean. He doesn't miss anything. I fold my hands over the keyboard and look him in the eye. "I needed to absolve myself of my sins."

His lips twitch. Classic Richard Gregory, Sr.—he wants to laugh; therefore, he won't. "All of this free time is no good for you."

"I'm plenty busy. I do homework." He doesn't look impressed. "And stuff."

"Hanging out with Cassie does not constitute extracurricular activities. Have you thought about when you want to retake your road test?"

If I never go to the DMV again, it'll be too soon. "I'm applying to NYU," I tell him, "so no license necessary."

Dad is momentarily speechless, which is no small feat. The wrestling is clear within him: I've misbehaved, yet for the first time since Regionals, I've offered up a goal for my future.

Then his brows furrow, he clips and unclips the bike helmet, and I know exactly what he's going to say before he says it. "NYU doesn't have a gymnastics team."

I fight the urge to retort. After all, I did drive off in his car and blow out a tire. Humoring him is the way to go here. I choose to be neutral. "True."

He holds up one finger. "Option one."

So much for distracting him with my shiny new life plan. I will not roll my eyes. I will not give anything away.

"You're grounded for the next week."

I can already picture Cassie's reaction: "You're *what?*" She'll have to venture for Slurpees on her own. *Or she'll call Juliana instead.*

"What's option two?" I ask.

"You go back to gymnastics Monday afternoon."

"Seriously? What kind of deal is this?"

My dad smirks, satisfied that he's finally gotten a rise out of me. If his mug is ever to be immortalized, it'll be with this look. "The kind that's good for you."

I think he misses gymnastics more than I do. He wasn't a stage dad, the kind that reality TV cameras would love, but he enjoyed the behind-the-scenes work of tracking my competitors' results.

"Kim Mansfield from Rochester got a nine point eight on floor!" I'd moan to my parents.

"Sample size of one." Dad would immediately pull the laptop from me to see for himself. "Not reliable."

"I'm sure she's a very nice girl," Mom would say mildly.

Using it as a threat, though—that's crossing the line. Yes, technically I've been cleared by the orthopedist. Theoretically, I should be healthy and whole. Gymnastics *isn't* good for me, though. My body has shown me that. "Option one."

A flash of disappointment crosses my father's face, waiting for me to change my mind, but I don't.

CHAPTER SIX

ON SATURDAY NIGHT, I stand on tiptoes, looking out the window for Cassie, when my parents begin to argue.

"Richard said he's going off the grid this weekend," Mom says from the kitchen. "Again."

"Guess that's how they make real men," Dad says. "Take away their cell phones."

"That's not—"

"Sounds like what I do with my ninth graders, in fact."

Mom supports Richard's enlistment in the Army. Dad's never been fully okay with it. As I've learned since my gymnastics retirement, which means dinner at regular hours with my parents, he lets his displeasure be known in small, zinging remarks.

Mom approaches in the shadows of the foyer. The dish towel turns over and over in her hands. "Where are you going?"

That's enough to make Dad join her in an instant. Now they're inconveniently united against me, the streetlight outside catching Dad's graying brown hair and stern eyes.

"Cassie wants to go to homecoming," I say.

They trade glances instead of outright telling me no. I've spent a contrite week coming home promptly after school, fielding Cassie's texts of *Should I bake you a file into a cake?* They're considering, especially Mom. Sure, I cut school with Dad's car. However, my social life hasn't been exactly what one would call thriving. "Why don't you invite your teammates over?" Mom used to ask. I didn't have the heart to tell her that it hurt too much to text them and hear about how great their skills were progressing while my greatest achievement that day had been bending my leg to a ninety-degree angle.

Mercifully, Cassie's headlights shimmer in front of the house. Before she can honk, my hand is on the doorknob. "Thank you," I say before anyone can stop me.

There's a hitch in her voice as my mother says, "You...you have fun tonight. Be safe."

She'd cringe whenever I came home with a new injury, like it hurt her more than it hurt me. "You'll get through it," Dad would tell me, but I knew he meant it for both of us. It was manageable—almost a running joke—when Richard was around, but as soon as he enlisted, there was tension like a breath held in our house. Savannah needs a back brace (yeah, I was the coolest girl in ninth grade with that one). Richard's phone goes silent without explanation. What's next?

Mom's greatest wish is *be safe*, because the alternative is too painful to consider.

....

CASSIE'S NOT ALONE. Juliana rides shotgun. Her wide brown eyes glance at me and then return to the windshield.

Cassie blows me an air kiss when I slip into the backseat. Juliana says in greeting, "Andreas won't shut up about your flips."

"Oh," I say. "Sorry about that."

That's it. For the entire ride. I drown in the bass behind Cassie while Juliana, in my usual seat, monopolizes my best friend's attention. I listen for an opening, for an opportunity to make a joke or ask a question, but I can't catch a word over the music. From time to time Cassie glances at me in the rearview mirror, smiles, and returns to whatever Juliana's talking about. So much for *let's celebrate Savannah's freedom,* as Cass had texted me an hour ago.

I cross my arms and stare out the window.

Ponquogue homecoming patronizes the football team by letting them play in the afternoon. Boys' soccer, three-time state champions, plays under the lights on Saturday night and the town squeezes in. Add in the fact that our opponents tonight are the Galway Beach Purple Tigers, and it's safe to say that at least half of my school is here for the pissing war.

"This better not go into overtime," Juliana says as the brake lights ahead of us flash red, like she has power over how long the game will last. "I gotta work brunch in the morning."

When we finally maneuver into a spot on the grass that's an inch wider than the car, I crawl out of the door. Cass, meanwhile, nearly whacks the car next to us. "Oops," she says, looking at Juliana, and they both start laughing. They make it down the embankment and into the actual parking lot faster than I do; I've got my eyes on the ground, making sure I don't slip on an errant ice cream cone or stumble over that soda can or—

Slam into Marcos Castillo.

He reels back, staring at me in astonishment. Dark eyes framed by darker lashes, chiseled jaw that looks none the worse for the wear. I blink to clear the stars from my eyes. Yeah, that jaw is no joke.

"That was a hell of a hit," he says.

"I think we just made out," I blurt out.

His eyes widen, and then he laughs. "Then you and I have very different definitions of making out."

Behind me, Cassie absolutely loses it. Hands on her knees, curls bouncing up and down on her shoulders, laughing so hard that it turns silent. For the first time in recorded history, Juliana grins in my general direction. Of course, it's at my expense.

Could my ears burn any hotter? Forget *failure to use proper judgment*; *failure to interact with peers like a normal human* is more like it. Staying at home and arguing with my dad about gymnastics would be better than this.

I turn toward my original target, the soccer field, ignoring Cassie's silent laugh that turns to cackling. "You're hazardous to my health," I tell Marcos sternly. "I'm forwarding you my next hospital bill."

"Me?" He jogs to keep up with me. I focus on the lights illuminating the field, blazing white against the dark sky. "I think you broke my nose."

I feign an examination. His dark hair curls over his forehead, still mussed from our collision. I fight the urge to reach out and smooth them, the way Cassie would do to me. His nose, I might add, is as strong as his jaw. It would make for a fine profile on a coin. "Your septum might be a little deviated, but you should recover."

Behind us, Cassie and Juliana whisper heatedly. Just like in the car, I've missed something between them.

Marcos holds my gaze, a small smile toying at his lips. Smartass and teasing.

I stare right back. One beat. Two. His smile widens. It makes me jittery, like I'm waiting for the judges to signal me.

Focus, Savannah. I turn away, find the lights again, and walk as fast as I can on legs that suddenly feel like liquid. "We've got a goddamn game to watch."

....

THE BLEACHERS THUNDER with hundreds of feet stomping the metal. "Ponquogue! Ponquogue! What what what!" rises from the far side of the stands as I slide into the first available sliver of metal bleacher. I'm not sure what this battle cry is intended to inspire, but everyone around us whoops and cheers.

Marcos's shoulder presses against mine, rocks again when Cassie and then Juliana slide in. *Sit next to me!* I want to call out to Cassie. I wait to catch her eye, but instead I'm met with curls as she faces Juliana.

It's fine. I'm not a child. I can handle myself solo.

Hot dogs and high-fives pass from hand to hand. Maroon-and-white sweatshirts are everywhere, between them a few ambitious boys with faces painted half white and half red. Across the turf in the visitors' stands, the purple and black Galway Beach fans boo all of Ponquogue's cheers.

During my brother's freshman year, the team earned the moniker "Tiny but Mighty" from an intrepid sports writer. ("Tiny but mighty!" Josh Wolfson crowed at every pasta party hosted at our house, in case there was the chance that someone in the neighborhood hadn't heard him the first time. This was usually met by an inappropriate response that had my mother whisking me out of the kitchen.) They defeated a perennial powerhouse from Syracuse to clinch the state title, the first in school history, and thus tradition was solidified under the Gatorade shower. Small school, tremendous upsets.

"Monday's cool?"

I blink. "Huh?"

"Tutoring." Marcos turns to me, his breath brushing against my ear.

I'm saved from responding when the bleachers buckle as everyone around us rises in a roar of noise. Ponquogue's finest take the field, their maroon-and-white uniforms not yet grass-stained.

My heart thumps with the same excitement I'd had when I'd stood for the national anthem before a meet. Same for when I'd stand up before the start of Richard's games. Soon after, Cass and I would play under the bleachers when we grew bored of watching the boys endlessly run up and down the field.

Andreas bounds out to the center of the field for the coin toss. Marcos sticks his fingers in his mouth and lets out a sharp whistle, his elbow knocking into me.

"Yeah, Andreas!" I shout. Never mind that I've rarely talked to him outside of FrisbeeGate.

"You got this, Dre!" Marcos adds. "Let's go!"

Andreas waves to the crowd with a cheeky grin, pausing momentarily to hike absurd orange socks over his shin guards.

Ponquogue wins the toss. "Yeah!" I shout again. Cassie leans all the way past Marcos to stare at me. "You okay, Savs?" she says. "Take it easy."

Weirdly enough, I do feel okay. The stresses of my failures, the fact that fall is normally the time I'd be gearing up for competing—those facts feel minuscule under these blazing lights, under the possibility of witnessing something exciting.

I lean forward to meet her halfway, except the bleachers rattle with another thunderous pounding and I almost tip over. "Better than ever."

A callused hand on my bicep tugs me back gently. I take a breath and inhale the scent of fresh cotton from Marcos's sweatshirt. It's tinged with something else—coconut shampoo, I think. The combination smells incredible. It makes me want to burrow my head in his sweatshirt for the winter.

Get a grip.

The lights shine off of Dimitri Bondarenko's head before the ball is kicked into play. Five minutes later, Juliana shouts, "You gotta be kidding me, ref! Are you blind?" as Andreas earns a yellow card for tripping a six-foot-tall Galway Beach Purple Tiger.

At the end of the first half, Roberto Aguilar goes deep into enemy territory and shoots. It's in. The crowd goes ballistic. Screams and hip thrusts like some sort of soccer dance. Maroon and white. Black and white and brown. Little kids bounce on their daddy's shoulders as they're lifted above the girls shouting nonsensically.

Whether or not it's the love of Ponquogue soccer or the thrill of vanquishing Galway Beach on a Saturday night, the whole school must be here. The whole town. How many of them will forget the game by Monday? Which hand, raw now from clapping and fist-pumping on a cold night, wrapped its fingers around the marker to write UCK YOU SPICS?

"Nailed it!" Cassie shouts. She's up on her feet, eyes shining in the heavy throb of the lights. Surrounded by every Ponquogue resident, she seems positively buoyant, floating on their excitement. I watch her for a moment until I leap to my feet too, shouting along with everyone else until that energy becomes part of me, until I stop wondering who did what and why.

....

DURING HALFTIME, WHEN the stands thin out with people venturing toward popcorn and porta-potties, I catch Cassie's annoyed voice. "Let's get out of here. They're gonna win. I need sleep."

"You'll be fine," Juliana says. "You can nap on me."

"You don't even like soccer."

"True," Juliana agrees. "But if we leave, I'm never gonna hear the end of it from Andreas."

I'm still riding the warmth of the crowd's energy. If Cass can make other friends, so can I. So what if any time I'd tried to talk to Juliana during work breaks over the summer, she'd looked straight over me and laughed at everything Cassie said? Perhaps we can come to a new understanding. "Why?" I say. "Are you guys dating?"

Both Juliana and Cassie turn to stare at me. That united look is like ice on Mt. Everest. It's something I can't scale.

Or...not.

Juliana seems slightly perplexed, as though she forgot I was here. It's true that I haven't stumbled over anything in the past forty-five minutes. Cassie, on the other hand, frowns at me. *You don't know anything,* that look says.

It's like when she slammed her bedroom door shut in my face when we were nine and I'd made fun of her glittery sneakers. That had been warranted. What the hell did I do now?

Marcos laughs uncomfortably, just in case I thought that things couldn't become more awkward. "That'd violate the bro code, right?"

After a beat, my too-slow mind catches up. Oh. He means that *he* and Juliana dated. Adorable. That's probably why Juliana's looking at me with confusion; she's wondering why the hell I asked her if she was dating her ex-boyfriend's best friend.

Well, here are the facts. I don't care about any code. I don't give any shits about Juliana's love life. And I wish Cassie hadn't looked at me like that because I sure as hell would love to not feel like an idiot.

Then Cass slaps Juliana's arm and says, "I could totally see it!" and Juliana shoves back, saying, "Shut up—you say that about *everyone*." She's fighting back a grin, which explodes into a laugh when Cass continues, "You and that guy from Anthony's Pizza had chemistry!"

"Not like you and gas station guy," Juliana retorts, causing Cass to tip her head back and laugh.

"Who's gas station guy?" I can't help asking.

Cassie's eyes stay on Juliana. "Hey, he gave me ten cents off per gallon."

"Got us to Montauk and back," Juliana agrees.

"When?" Apparently I'm a glutton for feeling like an idiot.

Cass shrugs. "Time flies." Those two words inexplicably send Juliana into a fit of laughter. Inside joke, I guess.

Marcos raises an eyebrow at me, expecting me to clue him in. I can't. The longer their exchange goes on, the more moments are checked off the list of *you weren't there*. For a fleeting moment, I wonder if I should have chosen my father's second option instead of opting to be grounded. Cass would have called me instead to go to Montauk, the tip of Long Island. We would have had our own jokes from the day.

I shouldn't care. I should count down the seconds until the players run out under the lights again. At the end of the year, I'm the one she's moving to the city with.

Heck, I used to have other friends. When I'd wake up before dawn for a competition, a group message would be underway between my teammates.

May throw up on the runway today. Emery, our unspoken leader, always kept it real.

Can someone bring bobby pins? This is out of control. Monica sent a photo of her dark brown curls, all of which were perfectly tamed.

Mom's stopping for snacks—who wants what? Ally had her priorities straight.

Their texts after my surgery—*Visit soon plz! Jess got her blind change to Jaegar! OMG Emery got an email from Nebraska!*—hurt too much. They were flipping, swinging, learning new skills while I was figuring out how to roll out of my bed, grab my crutches, and hobble to the bathroom with the least amount of pain.

So I'd stopped answering, and after a while, they'd stopped sending.

I exhale and watch my breath turn to smoke.

"How's your knee?" Marcos says.

I turn to him in surprise. "It's okay. Why?"

His own knee starts bouncing. "Your presence has been sorely missed on the Olympic team, I'm sure."

This guy has the uncanny ability to make me smile against my will. "Pretty sure the Olympians are getting by without me."

"Are you cleared to get back in the gym?" He folds his hands over his knee. A slender scar winds around his middle finger. I have one like that, too, straight down the front of my knee.

"There is no 'back in the gym'. I'm done."

Marcos actually looks concerned by my response. His thick eyebrows shoot up and he places his hand on top of mine, like he hopes to reason with me, only to hastily rescind it. "Why?"

I'm sick of defending my decision. I'm also confused by the residual tingles that shoot through my fingers upon Marcos pulling his hand away. Cassie's right. My relationship with gymnastics is done, and it's time for everyone else to accept that and move on, too. "Too many injuries. The ACL was the icing on the cake."

"ACL tears are common in soccer," he says earnestly, like he's a team doctor or something. "Plenty of players make a full recovery."

Congratulations. My ACL was the grand finale in a career littered with pain. Not doing gymnastics is the only way to ensure I'll fully recover. Thanks, but no thanks, Marcos Castillo.

He mistakes my silence as me considering his words. "You see what I mean?"

"You're friends with all the soccer guys," I counter. "Why aren't you on the team?"

That strikes a nerve. His shoulders stiffen and his gaze turns back to the field. "It's not my thing."

I should feel glad that I shook him off. Instead, guilt washes over me. Whatever's up with not being on the team clearly bothers him.

"Oh," I say. One round syllable.

The whistle blows for the second half.

. . . .

WHEN ANDREAS DEMOLISHES Galway Beach's defense for the decisive goal, the slamming of feet to metal rattles my teeth. "What the crap is going on?" Cassie calls over the ruckus.

"The earthquake," Marcos says. "It's what they do for Andreas."

As soon as the final buzzer goes off, the stands erupt. Juliana grabs Cassie's hand, Cassie pulls the elbow of my sweatshirt, and we roll with the crowd onto the field, a maroon-and-white landslide of noise. The field lights dazzle, and when I blink, I see white explosions.

Damp arms around my shoulders and rock-solid chests against my face. It's one tidal group hug and no one's left out. The mascot, Dashing the Dolphin, leaps across the field. So many high-fives that my hands hurt. The guys don't discriminate against those who didn't play.

"Over here!" Preston Bolivar lifts his phone to his glasses. I reach for Cassie and instead catch jersey, slick in my hands. Andreas, the star. I try to wriggle away, but his arm captures my shoulders—we see eye to eye—and Marcos appears on my other side. Andreas makes a sound like a wolf howling to the moon, and I crack up; everyone does. The vibration makes the whole line buckle. The phone's camera flashes and another cheer rises.

It's almost like something worth being a part of.

CHAPTER SEVEN

"**W**HAT'S UP WITH Marcos?" Cassie says, spinning her sunglasses between her thumb and index finger.

I take a gulp of iced black coffee (blegh) and return to typing. I'm not used to this much caffeine, and my fingers keep misfiring on the keyboard as a result. At some point, my thesis statement referred to Hamlet as "Hamster." Ten minutes before the first bell, I'm still only two pages deep. I'd completely forgotten about the assignment until I woke up this morning. So much for that GPA that's kept what's left of my pride afloat.

I fumble for one of Cassie's ubiquitous Post-It notes. There are no blank ones, so I scrawl "Real madness or fake?" on one that reads, "Do I dare to eat a peach?" It slips out of my fingers and tumbles into the abyss of scarves and flip-flops on the floor.

"The madness thing has been overdone," Cass says, reading over my shoulder. "Although you know that Beth O'Leary is going to act like she's the first person to wonder if Hamlet was faking it."

I stab at the screen. "Here I discuss how Ophelia should have told Hamlet to screw off."

Cassie snorts. "The assignment's a textual analysis. Good luck with that."

"Then what's the point of all of the coffee mugs with Shakespearean insults if Ophelia never got to use them? Fuck the nunnery, man." This is the worst. I *need* days of preparation, not the last-minute dance that Cassie thrives on. "What'd you write about?"

She tugs the coffee from me and takes a noisy slurp. "C'mon, Savs. You know me better than that."

AKA she didn't do the essay. Even after Mr. Riley's meeting. I should ask why not, but with another page to write, I need to stay focused.

"Seems like you and Marcos hit it off swimmingly," she says.

"I guess." *Thanks to you talking to Juliana the entire night.*

Nine minutes until the bell.

I had to bribe Cassie with the promise of buying her coffee in exchange for her picking me up so early. Driving out to Montauk for the sunrise? No problem for Cass. Waking up early for school? Forget it.

"Ugh, I forgot Ophelia in my intro." Amateur mistake. Scroll, scroll, accidentally exit the document— "You have to be kidding me!"

Cassie shuts off the radio. This means trouble. Now my palms are sweating enough that the keyboard glistens. "Can I be honest with you for a second?" she says.

Can I be honest? she'd asked when I'd attempted eye shadow in sixth grade and smeared blue up to my eyebrows. Or when I'd missed a spot of sunscreen and had an odd shaped patch of brilliant red skin on my back.

I'm not going to like this. I know it already.

She adjusts my ponytail, smoothing down the free-flying pieces. "Marcos is nice and all, but can you imagine Papa Gregory dropping you off for a date in El Pueblo?"

Whoa, whoa. She's rolling down a mighty slippery slope here. (I didn't hit my head hard enough to *actually* nap against Marcos's laundry-fresh sweatshirt, right?) In the flat area between Main Street and the bay, down the hill from the mansions, tiny bungalows are crammed together on barely paved roads. It's the place my classmates call El Pueblo, where many of the immigrant families squeeze together.

"Hold up." I raise my hand for further emphasis. "First of all, El Pueblo is not an official place."

Cassie sighs. *Two weeks older, so much wiser.* "Just because it's not on your precious Google Maps doesn't mean that—"

"Secondly, what date?" Let's be honest, at the first notion of *a date*, Dad would log into the school system to check the guy's GPA.

"You're kidding, right? Marcos didn't take his eyes off you the entire night. Even Juliana noticed." A wicked glint in her eyes. "After your super-hot 'make-out session.'"

I roll my eyes. "Oh, God, don't bring that up ever again." Which is basically my way of saying, *I know you'll never let me forget it.*

She cracks herself up, tipping her head back. "It was adorable. You were like a fawn standing on your legs for the first time."

I try not to smile; I really do. Then I recall the stunned look on Marcos's face, combined with the caffeine in my system, and I start laughing with her.

A knock on the window.

Cassie screams in surprise, I yelp, and then we're cracking up afresh. It's like the sleepovers when we've been up far too late and something that isn't funny at all gains hilarity the more we laugh.

"Holy shit, we summoned him." Her eyes bug out comically, and as she rolls down the window, I can barely look Marcos in the eye for fear of laughing again.

He rests his forearms on the window frame and smiles at both of us. I'm distracted by that single crooked front tooth. It's so damn cute, I bet he got out of trouble all the time as a little kid.

"You smell baby fresh," Cassie greets him. "What's your secret?"

I whack her arm. "Cass, you can't just ask people about their personal hygiene."

"Says who?" Her eyebrows lift and her lips purse in mock propriety. The laugh I attempt to hold back comes out as a snort.

Marcos smiles uncertainly. He definitely thinks we're ridiculous. "How's it going?"

"Fine, thanks." Cass elbows me—I *told you so*, that move says.

Marcos turns to me. His jaw flexes just a moment before he speaks. It's almost hypnotizing. "How's sixth period for you, Savannah? Meet in the library?"

"That's when we have lunch," Cassie says before I answer. Her tone has shifted from playful to cool.

"We could work in the cafeteria." Marcos's smile wavers a little.

"Work?" Cass turns to me, confused.

"I found out Savannah was tutoring you, and she offered to help me out."

"Oh, right. *Tutoring*." Never have three syllables held so much sarcasm. "Well, that sounds fun. I wouldn't want to interrupt."

Marcos raises his eyebrows, but I have no explanation. I can't focus on math, or Cassie, or the fact that his dimples have disappeared. I *still* have to finish that damn essay. "Sixth period sounds great."

"Bye, Marcos." Cassie nearly shuts the window in his face. I'd give him an apologetic look, except he's already turned away. "What the hell is going on, Savannah? Library trysts?"

"He overheard our meeting."

"Make sure you tell Mr. Riley. He'll nominate you for sainthood." Just mentioning the assistant principal's name makes her eyes darken.

"What's the real problem, Cass?"

The directness of my question makes Cassie drop her eyes to her shimmering silver scarf. It's unseasonably warm today after the cold weekend, humid enough to bring back hints of early September, and all of that makes me sweat more.

"Juliana invited me to a party in El Pueblo over the summer. It was at this guy Nelson's house—he graduated a couple of years ago." She tucks in her right index finger and cracks it. Middle finger. Ring finger. "They have, like, twenty people in one house there. Lots of poverty. Lots of crime. Juliana lives there, and she says it's a shithole. Not a place for a girl like you, Savs. You wouldn't be able to handle it."

What's that supposed to mean?

"Marcos, well, let's just say that that night, he wasn't exactly—" The rest of her words are buried by the first bell.

Shit. My essay isn't close to done, my battery's about to die...

Cassie shuts the laptop before I can start typing again. In contrast to the panic that consumes me, she seems perfectly calm. Maybe she's relieved to have gotten her feelings toward El Pueblo off of her chest. "Tell Mr. Raia your computer crashed. I'm sure he thinks you're a little shining star, just like Mr. Riley."

"But—"

"It's fine, Savs. I do it all the time." She tucks the laptop into my backpack before I can protest.

And look how well that's going for you. I swallow back the thought.

As I approach the entrance, trying not to run while Cassie saunters, her words about El Pueblo echo in my mind. *Not a place for a girl like you.* She said it so certainly. To her, Juliana is one kind of girl and I'm the other—the can-handle and the can't.

Well, not anymore.

....

THROUGH THE REMNANTS of caffeine and "working on my lab report" in AP Chem, I manage to finish a semi-coherent essay where I may or may not have referred to Hamlet as a fishmongering rapscallion for his treatment of Ophelia. It's complete, I'll give it that.

Going to the art room. Try not to make out in the stacks, Cass texts me when the bell rings for sixth period. That's her version of giving me her blessing.

I arrive at the library first and open my laptop. When I click on my math folder, my fingers slip on the track pad and open a photo file instead.

Emery and I stand with our arms around each other at the end of practice. Four inches taller than me, her biceps ripple even while at rest around my shoulders. Her green eyes are half-closed as she laughs at something I've said. Both of our cheeks are smeared with chalk and our hair falls loose from our ponytails. We've just finished the final practice before Regionals, and my smile in the photo says it all. Confident. Focused. Determined.

My heart swells with both fondness and pain.

All of it for nothing.

Get over it already.

If Cassie saw me like this, my lips pressed together so hard they may turn permanently white, she'd delete the photo before I could protest. "There," she'd say. "You're free."

Hovering the arrow over the trash bin icon feels—

"What are you looking at?" says a deep voice from behind me.

I jump. "Good afternoon to you, too."

My heart slows from a gallop to a steady thump as Marcos's gaze drops to the laptop. He inclines his head ever so slightly as I shut it.

"Who's that girl?"

"My friend, Emery." Is "friend" the right word when you haven't texted since a cursory *Happy birthday! Miss you!* text in July?

He blinks as though he's running through a mental index of names. "She go here?"

I roll my eyes. Tall, athletic, elegant—covered in chalk and dressed in polka-dot Spandex shorts, Emery was still all of those things. "Galway Beach, and she has a boyfriend." Last time we texted, at least.

"Hey, hey." He raises his hands in surrender. "Not going there. Just curious. I've never seen you with anyone besides Cassie."

Right. The way he's *always* curious.

"What's Cassie's deal?" he adds. "She looked like she was going to eat me alive."

"Not up her alley. She's vegetarian." It's a stupid answer (albeit true), but it makes Marcos chuckle. I can't exactly say, "She was in the middle of warning me to stay away from your part of town," now, can I?

"Emery was one of your teammates?"

For crying out loud, can the guy take a hint? I don't want to talk about Emery because that twists right back to "when are you going back to gymnastics?" and the fact that Marcos, despite his handsome face and one crooked tooth and excellent shoulders, just doesn't get it.

"I'm sorry." His tone is no longer teasing. It's soft now as he leans on the table, trying to make me look at him. The smell of coconuts and fresh laundry come closer. I'm eyeing the wall above him sternly—I am—except my heart's galloping again. "Sometimes I don't think. If I see it, I'm gonna say something."

"Yeah, I've noticed."

He crosses the finger with the scar. "No more snooping. Promise."

My lips lift in spite of themselves. I decide to play a game called *How long can Marcos Castillo go without asking a question?*

He flips through his planner, revealing line after line of tiny block letters. "So I could use your help with triangles."

This I can do. My father might actually be less pissed at me if he catches wind of this. "Okay, what aspect?"

"Cosine, tangent, cotangent." His face flushes ever so slightly. "The works, really. Know what I mean?"

"Do you have any specific problems you want to work on, or are you looking for more of a smorgasbord?" How long does it take him to write with such meticulous penmanship? I see "5 to close" written down for today and something's scribbled in for Saturday—

The planner whisks away. "Ah-ha! Now you're the one spying."

At least I'm working on those extracurricular activities Dad was harassing me about.

Marcos flips through his textbook. "Just when I think that I have sines down, they have to go and throw a wrench into things with cosines." He looks up at me with a self-deprecating grin. "Do I sound like I know what I'm doing?"

"On a scale of one to ten, I'd put you at a solid six right now."

He shakes his head. "Uh-oh. Wait until we get to cotangents."

For the first time since I landed on the ground screaming in April, I'm excited about what's next.

....

IN BETWEEN TEACHING Marcos about cofunctions, I learn that he works at Pav's Place twenty-five hours a week, that he swears up and down their fried avocado tacos are heaven, and that he has an older brother named Victor with whom he shares a car.

When I tell him that Richard was on Ponquogue's first state championship team, he leans back in his chair. "You were exposed to soccer greatness and never played?"

"Too boring."

His jaw drops. "Boring!" The freshmen at the computers giggle at his outburst.

I ignore the heat burning my ears. "It's glorified running." The only kind of running I used to enjoy was toward the vault, but that was sprinting for something higher, faster, better.

I wonder again why he's not on the team. Perhaps he tried out and didn't make the cut. It's possible that working so much would interfere with practice and games. Wouldn't he have said that outright, then?

He places both palms firmly on the table. "I'm going to change your mind, Savannah Gregory."

Go for it. When he says it like that, maybe I need to keep an open mind after all.

The wooden doors swing open and Cassie flies through. She's a hurricane in a blue dress, her beaded bag bouncing against her hip and her hair half-tugged up into a ponytail while the other half streams free. "There you are, Savs."

"What's the matter?" I say automatically, because by virtue of her presence, something important is happening. Cassie's not one for the library. "Too many dead texts," she calls it.

"We need to go," she says.

"We do?"

She loops her arm through mine, stronger than usual. "I have to show you something. See you later, Marcos."

I almost pull back. Can't she wait?

Marcos's brows furrow, but all he says is, "Thank you so much, Savannah. I'll bring you tacos tomorrow."

Tacos. That gets Cassie's attention, but her blue eyes focus on me instead. "Let's go."

I wave to Marcos as Cassie moves us along with surprising speed. She steers me straight to the courtyard. As we step outside, the first droplets of rain fall. Shielding her camera with one hand, she presses a button to illuminate the tiny screen.

This is what she had to rush me out of the library for?

Her bitten-down thumbnail presses briskly through a series of photos. Waffles, her cat, glaring at the camera; Juliana in the cafeteria, hands raised in the middle of talking; the sunset, burning and brilliant. The photos are perfectly focused and balanced. She really could work with greeting cards if she wanted to.

"There." UCK YOU SPICS. The black-and-white photo makes the locker text ominous.

"I can't believe they still have no idea who did it."

"I have a theory." The screen goes dark. "But that's not why I wanted to show you."

The rain picks up force, and I hastily tuck my hair into the hood of my sweatshirt. Since all of my gymnastics sweatshirts are on the Do Not Wear list, this one's a hand-me-down from Cass that says, "Ponquogue Rocks!" with dancing starfish. By hand-me-down, I mean that it last fit her in sixth grade.

"I know it's exciting that Marcos is into you," she begins. "As he should be. You're awesome. But he's no saint."

I'm not so convinced that he's into me. Into my knowledge of trigonometry, I'll give her that.

"At that guy Nelson's in El Pueblo, a bunch of guys from the Galway Beach soccer team showed up and things got out of hand. Fast."

How come this is the first time I'm hearing about it? Cassie's all about the breaking news, the here and the now. Ruminating on previous events and contemplating the best time to discuss them, not so much her style.

"He punched a guy, Savs." She looks at me without any kind of *wink wink*. The worry is palpable. "I heard Andreas and Juliana yelling, and the next thing you know, Marcos put this kid on the floor. It was unreal."

Marcos—who smells cotton-fresh, who helped me change my tire and frets over cotangents—punched a guy? I try to imagine the hand with the scar connecting with someone's face. "Was he provoked?"

She shrugs, impatient that I'm not immediately saying, *Oh, no, Cass, you're right!* I'm trying to explore all angles here. "I have no idea. There was a *lot* of cheap beer flowing."

"What happened after? Did the police show up? Was the kid okay?"

She turns back to the camera. "I don't remember. Just be careful, okay? Things like that aren't going to win Marcos any friends, and I don't want to see you get caught up in it."

The first roll of thunder. I cringe. "Noted."

CHAPTER EIGHT

ON FRIDAY NIGHT, keys press into my hand as Cassie opens the passenger door. "I already had a few shots," she says, sinking into the torn plush passenger seat. She flicks aside a Post-It note that reads, "I have heard the mermaids singing, each to each."

I hesitate. The keys are warm from her palms. They signal power. Independence. Something I tasted when I drove Dad's car to South Cross. Something that the DMV is adamant about withholding from me.

Cass scrolls through her text messages. I read the sender of the most recent: *Jules*. "Oh, sorry," she says, looking up. "I brought you some fun, too. Figure we'll break it out when we get to the bridge." A Friday night that won't be spent holed up in my room or driving aimlessly with Cassie—my social life has escalated.

Still, I'm wavering. "I can't drive with someone under twenty-one."

"That sure stopped you last time." She presses her head back against the seat and looks up at me sideways. Her curls frame her porcelain face. Never a tan for Cass in the summer; only sunburn that fades to white. "We both know you're a better driver than me."

When I turn over the engine, the car rumbles to life, rattling my hands on the steering wheel. It's a powerful surge, a little more than I expected, and I just hope I can control it. Despite bumping the seat forward, my leg strains to reach the gas pedal. The side-view mirror hangs on thanks to duct tape and miracles.

Before I can talk myself out of it, I push the gear into Drive.

As I glide down the road at approximately ten miles per hour below the speed limit, scanning from side to side for deer, Cass says, "Ready for this gem?" She holds her phone in front of my face.

I dare to let my eyes dart away from the road. "What's that weird crop circle on the floor?"

"That," she says, "is two thousand dollars a month." She scrolls to the next ad. "'Awesome bedroom in sweet building with roof deck,'" she reads. "We might be able to afford this one if we share a bed."

"I am not sharing a bed with you," I say. "You steal the blankets."

"That was once!" The screen's glow illuminates her grin. "This one is 'the coolest brownstone.' Wow, twenty-three hundred—what a steal."

"We could commute," I offer. We can sit side by side on the train, watching the scrubby pines of Long Island's East End whisk away into growing buildings.

"We are *not* commuting." Her smile vanishes. "The point is getting out of here."

"How are we going to pay for uncool brownstones in gross buildings with no roof decks, let alone those?" See also: tuition, books, miscellaneous fees, Ramen noodles...

A text message arrives and she types back furiously. "We'll work at the beach again next summer."

"Are they raising minimum wage by twenty dollars an hour?"

She drops the phone into her lap. "This was your idea. I thought you were committed."

Moving somewhere I wouldn't need to drive had been a joke. While the idea's appealing, for once I'm countering *failure to use proper judgment*. I've already had one future plan, Ocean State, blow up in my face.

"It'd suck if we moved to different places next year," Cass continues. "We'd never see each other."

I swallow. It was the one consideration that gave me pause in my recruiting journey. If I went to Rhode Island, we would still text and call, send each other silly photos and songs, but it wouldn't be the same. We wouldn't be able to walk the two streets to each other's houses, go on late-night 7-Eleven runs, drive around in circles in the South Cross parking lot until we're dizzy and laughing.

She picks up her phone when a new text message arrives. *Jules.* Again.

I wonder if she's telling Juliana, *Savannah's bailing on moving to the city with me,* and if Juliana is writing back in kind, *Savannah is the worst.*

As I ease across the intersection, the opening guitar chords of a familiar song begin playing over the radio.

"Is this what I think it is?" Cassie straightens up.

"Seventh grade summer anthem? Hell, yes."

"Remember when we met those kids from Australia down at South Cross?" She's already grinning. The city has been dropped in favor of silly lyrics and doofy-looking boy band members that we'd swooned over. "They were all, 'We're pro surfers,' so you challenged them to a swim race?"

"You mean when you volunteered me?" *I bet my friend Savannah could take all of you,* she'd said, fists on the hips of her mint-green bikini bottom.

They'd eyed me over their sunglasses. *Her?*

The wind had sent Cassie's hair flying, yet she'd never budged. *Count of three. One...two...*

Sprinting into the water, the adrenaline of competition coursing through me, Cassie shouting from the shore, *You got this, Savannah! Show them how we do it in America!*

"Either way, I beat their asses," I say. They'd pretended to chase me out of the water, so I splashed through the foam and back up to Cassie. She'd thrown her arms around me despite the fact that I was soaking wet.

She nods sagely. "I was honored to know you."

Next thing I know, we're belting out song lyrics with the windows rolled down, screaming over the frigid air. The infectious beat on the highest volume obliterates any remaining tension. Cassie reaches out her hand and lets the wind bat it back, her curls tangling in her face, too busy singing to push them away.

"Drum solo!" I yell, forgetting my vehicular fear for a moment to bang my hands against the steering wheel.

"Someone get this girl a record deal!" she yells back.

I thrash my hair, completely destroying all of my earlier efforts to straighten it, and she laughs. "Dammit, Savannah," she says as the reverberation begins to fade. "What would I do without you?"

"Swim against Australian surfers on your own."

She whacks my arm and we crack up again.

I wish that we could keep driving. Pass the bridge to South Cross and see where we end up. Montauk for the sunrise. New York City, the opposite direction, for the lights. The two of us, the way it's always been.

Ah, but not tonight.

．．．．．．．．．．．．．．．．．．

I PARK IN the tiny lot next to the bay, where during the day fishermen cast into the water and boats push off from the launch. Tonight, the bonfire throws light and shadows against the cement underbelly of the bridge.

As soon as I shut off the engine, a Thermos is pressed into my hand like a trophy. "Driver of the year," Cassie proclaims. "You should take my car to your next test."

I take a cautionary sip. Hot chocolate mixed with something strong and minty. "I owed you hot chocolate," Cass says, watching my reaction. Her eyelashes are thick with mascara, her blue eyes luminous. "And for Mr. Riley."

"How are we getting home?" I take another sip. I can't deny that after the wine coolers from summer bonfires, this is a significant step up.

"We've got hours," she says with a wave of her hand. "And I'm not going to go wild. We can expect the usual shitty delicacies here, unless someone was really ambitious and stole a handle from their parents."

I stare at the lid of the Thermos, debating whether or not I should have more or dump it once we're out of the car.

"Cascade Hopeswell!" a male voice shouts.

"Call me that again and I will push you into the fire!" Cassie calls back. She's met with laughter.

My feet sink into the sand and its coolness stings my ankles. The autumn night wind is sharp, not dreamy like the humid summer gusts, and I hug Cassie's sweater close.

I follow her footsteps to the base of the bridge, home of the bonfire. Everyone likes to pretend that the cops won't notice the flames and smoke down here, and truth be told, the cops like to pretend they're not happening either. As I approach the cement pillars, I wave at the faces lit orange by fire.

They're preoccupied elsewhere. "Cass!" One, two, three hands rise to slap high-fives with her.

"Don't touch the Ponquogue scum," someone says jokingly.

"Don't be a hater just because our soccer team blew yours out of the water," says Cassie, apparently a sports expert now. "Galway Beach can't do it like we do."

"What took you so long?" Juliana grabs Cass for a side hug.

Me.

"Little Cassie!" Always Late Nick (so named due to his propensity for arriving a half hour after his shift started) greets me. "You haven't gotten any taller."

"Your jokes haven't gotten any better."

"Touché." He tosses me a Coors. "Hope you can handle the hard stuff."

I make the rounds over the pebbled sand. Yeah, I'd been relegated to solo parking lot duty while Cassie peddled French fries with everyone else here. Doesn't matter. I'm sure there's plenty to learn, especially since I barely know any of them. Surely we'll find common ground.

"Hey," I say to Soft Pretzel Stephanie, who Cassie said was really meticulous about putting equal amounts of salt on each warmed-up-in-the-microwave pretzel. I can respect attention to detail. "How's school going?"

"Sucks," she says with a laugh, sipping from her Solo cup. "You?"

"Sounds about right," I say.

We chuckle, and her eyes turn elsewhere.

On to the next.

I try Music Man Mark, who had inspired us all to try karaoke out on the deck one night after work. That was fun. He's already too drunk to look at me with any kind of focus. "Who are you again?" he slurs.

Ouch.

I'm a quarter of the way through the Thermos and have yet to make meaningful headway. In the meantime, Cassie's keeping this fiesta from being a total wash. Sure, there's fire, but the light source everyone revolves around is my best friend. Her silhouette swings long and her flushed cheeks glow from the flames. Her eyes squeeze shut as she laughs, everyone around her smiling wider.

She used to call me exactly twenty minutes after practice, when she knew I'd be home and eating dinner. "Wanna hang tonight?"

"Speaking of hanging, I can't lift my arms," I'd say. "Tomorrow?"

She'd sigh, long and dramatically enough to make me hold the phone away from my ear. "I don't have any friends besides you." Not true, but she always made it out to be that way. Until this summer, when apparently grease and humidity were enough to forge bonds between the snack-bar employees. And Juliana.

"Remember how he tried to take apart the string cheese with his teeth?" Cass says now, and those around her start laughing, one girl spitting out her beer.

No, I don't. I was the one sitting in the ticket booth, shielding my eyes from the sunlight glinting off of cars. At any given moment, I could have slipped out without anyone noticing. Like right now.

....

I HAVE CASSIE, but up until junior year, I'd also had
Beth O'Leary on my side. We'd gone way back to
kindergarten days, sat in honors classes together, and
mutually bemoaned AP essays over brownies. The sort
of things that Cassie couldn't be bothered by, and it
was nice to have someone else who was.

One problem: Beth's sweet sixteen fell on the
same day as Regionals, and the Cha Cha Slide was not
coming between a shot at Nationals and me.

Cassie had been twisting my hair into place for the
competition when Beth called me. "I'll see if we can
get back," I'd said, "but it's in Massachusetts—"

"I had a candle for you," Beth had said. "I was going
to talk about that AP Comp essay we wrote about
Heart of Darkness and how we went through our own
struggle."

"That essay was the worst," I'd agreed.

"What am I supposed to do now? Give the candle
to my uncle or something? Everything is going to be
thrown off."

That was when Cassie had ceased twisting my hair.
"Give me the phone."

"Cass—"

She'd tickled me.

"What the hell?" I'd half-shouted, half-giggled, and
she took her chance to grab the phone and enact her
idea of vigilante justice.

"Beth, Savannah extends her sincerest apologies,
okay? The gymnastics gods didn't schedule this event
to dick you over." She'd listened. "Okay, you are
legitimately full of it. Do you know Savannah's start

value on floor? Do you even know what that is? Well, let me tell you, it means she does flips for bonus points and can get a perfect score if she nails it."

I'd wavered between knocking the phone out of her hand and listening to more of her loose interpretation of gymnastics rules.

"Do you know how hard she's worked? Were you there the time she busted her lip on bars but finished her routine? Blood everywhere. Yeah, didn't think so.

"Look, she's going to the Olympics, okay? She'll send you a card or something."

"I'm not going to the Olympics." It had been my first coherent thought, followed by, *Well, that bridge is burned forever.*

"I never liked her anyway," Cassie had said, resuming her taming of my hair. Her fingers shook ever so slightly. "When I moved here, she told everyone that my mom was in a mental asylum."

"We were seven," I'd ventured. "I'd like to think that we've all evolved since then."

"I don't care who Beth thinks she is or how great her grades are. Nobody should guilt you like that."

Sorry about that, I had texted Beth later, when we were on the road to Regionals and Cassie ran into the McDonald's bathroom. *I hope you have a great party! I'll be there in spirit.*

She never wrote back.

....

CANS POP OPEN and beer fizzes like the ocean receding. So many people here, but they don't make the air any warmer. I take up post against the pillar, sitting on the sand and watching the fire play off the waves. They're calm, low tide—nothing like what I plunged into on Senior Cut Day.

The moonlight glistens on the crests. Despite growing up here, reading the waves still challenges me. One could build and build and fizzle into a small swell. Another might look like it'll fade out but there it is, towering above you until your only choice is to dive under as it crashes over your head.

"Savannah freakin' Gregory? Is this a mirage or is this real life?"

Before I can react, a body collides with mine. The arms wrap me so tightly that I cough and drop my half-finished Thermos to the sand.

"Where have you been? Why haven't you come to the gym? How the hell is your knee? How the hell is your life?"

"You did really well at Level Five States." That's the first response that comes to mind.

Emery Johnson, Level 10 Regional all-around champion, continues to squeeze me without letting up. Her dark hair is cut close to her chin and swoops across her forehead, her denim jacket smells of bonfire smoke, and her arms have lost none of their strength.

Outside of the gym, my teammates and I traveled in a herd. You could find us eating fro-yo together with leotards rolled down to our hips underneath our tank tops. We'd flip into Ally's pool or gather around Jessica's TV for an obligatory viewing of *Stick It*. Running into Emery here, on Ponquogue turf and out of context, throws me off.

"What are you doing here?" I choke out against her shoulder.

"My friend Amber's dating that kid Mark." She looks at me inquisitively. "Are you drunk?"

"Partially." I reconsider. "Partially past partially might be more accurate."

She examines me with narrowed green eyes. "You look great, but you haven't answered my questions."

Yeah. I look away, hoping she'll think I was too drunk to hear that second part. "Things are things," I say with a profundity that would make NYU admissions proud. "Trying to figure out the college...thing."

She nods. "Ugh, I know."

No, she doesn't know. I'm looking up scholarships and overpriced apartments; she's fielding e-mails and visits from college coaches. She'd never brag about it—if there's one guarantee along with Emery being an outstanding athlete, it's that she's humble—but even so, I dust off the Thermos and take a quick sip, hoping it'll quell the jealousy.

Cassie has backed away from the bonfire to stare at us.

"Hey, girl," Emery says, stepping toward Cassie to hug her. All of my teammates at South Ocean Gymnastics knew Cass; she and her camera were a staple at my meets. "Let's chuck her a leotard, see what she can do," my coach, Matt, would joke.

"Hey." Cassie offers a thin smile and keeps her arms pinned to her sides. The most touchy-feely person I know avoiding physical contact? Strange.

"When are you coming back?" Emery presses, turning to me. "Don't give me this retirement bullshit. The team is in shambles without you."

Right. Monica will still be using an entire can of hairspray before every meet, Ally will dangle from her knees on the high bar like a kid on the monkey bars, and Jess will be making pouty faces at herself in the mirror as she fixes her ponytail. "I highly doubt that," I say.

Juliana appears next to Cassie and says something to her that I can't catch. Is this going to be like the soccer game all over again, being stranded in favor of Juliana?

Emery sticks out her hand. "Hey, I'm Emery. Savannah's friend from gymnastics."

Juliana shakes her hand slowly, probably wondering why this acquaintance of mine is being so friendly. "Juliana."

"You work at Pav's, right?" Emery says. "That place is my kryptonite. I could eat my weight in burritos three times a day."

To my surprise, Juliana smiles. "If you saw what went down in the kitchen, you might not feel that way."

"Give me guacamole or give me death," Emery says firmly. She's never met Juliana, she hasn't seen me in months, yet she fits in without any stumbles or hesitation—the way, to be honest, I wish I could.

Cassie's eyes flick back and forth. Whenever her lips part to jump in, the banter rushes on, leaving no room for her. It's strange to be part of a conversation that gallops along without her participation, without her dictating the ebb and flow of it.

The wind carries over the conversation taking place behind us. "Those refs at the Ponquogue game were on crack," someone says.

"I don't think it's fair when you're playing against all Mexicans," Always Late Nick says. "I bet their whole team is illegals."

"Seriously," his friend says. "My cousin Tommy, he's like the only white guy on the team. He says that Ponquogue's gonna have to build an extension on the high school because there are so fucking many of them."

"They should take some of ours," Always Late Nick says.

Cassie's eyes go wide.

Emery chokes on her drink.

Juliana's ponytail whips against me.

I'm the one whose mouth opens. "What does that have to do with anything? Maybe your team just sucks."

"Excuse me?" Always Late Nick's dopey, drunk grin is gone.

Now that I have the floor, and apparently the soapbox, I can't stop. Half a Thermos of Cassie's magic will do that to a girl. "By the way, 'all Mexicans' is a gross generalization. How about Salvadorans, Guatemalans, Hondurans—"

Every other conversation has ceased. Drinks hang suspended in people's hands. The only sounds are the wood crackling beneath fire and the waves, quiet yet relentless.

Then a hand yanks my forearm. As always.

Cassie pulls me to a thin patch of rocks. The salt air masks the smell of alcohol from the party but not from her breath. "You can't say that kind of stuff here, Savannah."

"He's being an idiot."

"I know." Her eyes dart back to the crowd at the fire. Heads are bent together and eyes glance toward us. Nobody makes a move to follow.

"Is Cascade Hopeswell actually abiding by someone else's set of rules?" I say a little too loudly.

Her eyes turn cold. Pissed. "Remember what I told you about Marcos and the party? Sometimes it's better to keep your opinions to yourself."

"I thought we were among friends," I say, reflecting back on my one-line exchanges with the rest of the South Cross Beach summer employees. Deep and meaningful, they weren't. "Emery's my friend," I add belatedly, if winding up at the same party together and calling me out on my unresponsiveness counts as friendship.

"How real of a friend is she when she didn't even visit after your surgery?" Cassie wedges her beer into the sand. "None of those girls did. Who was there? Me."

She's right.

Up by the fire, Emery and Juliana are joined by Music Man Mark and his girlfriend. Even Soft Pretzel Stephanie has roamed into the mix. Emery says something that makes their shoulders shake with laughter. Making friends, as I've tried and failed to do. My former teammate's laugh travels, loud and clear and free of stress.

Cassie's gaze follows mine. "Remember what I said before. I'm the only one who's got your back."

. . . .

I SETTLE BACK into my spot next to the pillar, leaning my head back and letting the alcohol turn my memory to mush so I don't have to consider why Cassie thinks I should hold back from correcting assholes.

"Hey, Savannah."

I don't turn. I don't look. I do my damnedest to ignore the smell of coconuts and cotton. I'm about zero and twenty with human interaction tonight.

He settles in next to me and just like when we changed my tire, the air is immediately warmer, the wind softer.

"What are you doing here?" I say to the rippling waves. "You didn't work at the beach."

"Juliana invited me." He runs a hand through his curls. "Said you and Cassie would be here."

"Cassie told me you punched a guy." There is absolutely no thought before I say this. It slips straight out, plunks into the conversation like a stone dropped in water.

Our shoulders brush together. "Yeah, I did. It wasn't the greatest decision, but someone had to take a stand."

I keep my eyes on the water and try to keep my focus off the tingles I feel from his close proximity and the headiness of the smoke and the alcohol. "What happened?"

A long sigh. He drops his voice so that I have to tilt my head to hear. "A bunch of assholes from the Galway Beach soccer team showed up. They talked shit to Andreas, he of course decided to give it right back to them because he can't shut up, and people started pushing each other." He pauses, turns to face me all the way. He's backlit by the fire. "I went to yank Andreas out of there and one of them clocked me in the face, so I went after him."

"Did you really need to take a stand?" I think of Cassie's face as she pulled me away from the fire.

He nudges my chin so that I have to look at him. "He's my best friend. I'm not gonna let him get shredded by guys who weigh a hundred pounds more than him just because he runs his mouth."

When he says it like this, I can imagine it. Defending Andreas's honor. Defending Ponquogue soccer. I almost smile.

"You're one to talk about taking a stand," he says. "I got here when you were yelling at that guy."

I wave my hand to preemptively shoo away the rest of the sentence. Already been chastised by Cass, thanks. I don't need round two. "Let's forget about—"

"Thank you."

Up this close, I see the dark stubble lining his jaw. When I reach out to touch it, he inhales sharply. It's rough as sandpaper beneath my fingers. Neither of us pulls away. He's close enough that I could just tip forward and then...then what? Would he catch me? Would he lean forward too and meet me halfway?

Marcos clears his throat. I feel the vibration all the way up to his jaw. "Speaking of best friends," he says, "why did Cassie take you away like that?"

My fingers freeze.

"What about Senior Cut Day," he continues, "when you fell in and she just stood there watching? You could have hit your head on a rock."

I roll my eyes. "Cass isn't much of an athlete." *What do you mean, doggie paddling isn't a stroke?* she'd asked our swim instructor when we were eight.

"She knew I'd be fine."

"She's no good for you."

"Excuse me?"

He looks taken aback by the strength of my voice. That's right, Marcos—you can't go around acting like the authority on my friendship with Cassie.

"You were so good at gymnastics," he says. "Then, poof, you're done with it."

"You don't know anything about my gymnastics," I say heatedly. "You saw me do one skill, one time. Guess what? Five-year-olds can do the same thing. Nothing special."

"Andreas found your YouTube channel."

Goddammit, is anything sacred? Yes, my YouTube channel, made for college coaches to see my routines and skill upgrades, is publicly available. It's fair game for anyone to view, although I never imagined people from school would watch it recreationally. I need to take it down ASAP.

"You were amazing," he insists. "You were wearing all sorts of braces, so you've obviously been injured before."

"That was the problem."

"Yeah?" he says. "I don't think you're really afraid of getting injured. I think you're terrified of failing."

I jump to my feet, the alcohol and the anger pounding through me. "You don't know anything about me."

I'm not terrified of failing. You can't be afraid of something you live and breathe every day.

Up by the smoke, Cassie sips from her drink and listens to whatever Juliana's saying. Her eyes find me, and her eyebrows quirk. *Everything okay?*

Marcos rises, blocking my view. "I think you're smart." I can hardly hear him through the rushing in my ears. "I think that you're a hard worker and really disciplined to get as far as you have in gymnastics. And I don't think Cassie has your best interests in mind."

I've heard enough of this bullshit. I step around him, one foot slipping into the water. He reaches out to help me. I wave him off. "If you'll excuse me, I'm going back to my best friend."

Marcos doesn't know anything. He wasn't there in the days after my surgery, when everything I ate made me nauseous and walking to the bathroom felt like a marathon. Cassie brought magazines, crackers, ginger ale. She stuck around despite the painkillers making me nod off mid-conversation. I woke up and she was on the bed next to me, knees holding her magazine in place. "Just in time, Savs. I've learned who my celebrity boyfriend is thanks to this super-scientific quiz. Ready? Question one."

Over the laughter from the fire, I hear him say, "Okay." Fleetingly, I think of turning around.

Instead, I let the moment wash away.

CHAPTER NINE

CASSIE HAS THE distinction of being the first announcement on Monday morning. "Cascade Hopeswell, please report to the main office."

Everything cool? I text her.

No answer.

Are you here? I try again.

Nothing.

I slip into the bathroom before gym and call her. When she picks up the phone, she doesn't say anything. She just waits.

"They're calling you to the office. Where are you?" Ah, a new message on the door today: FUQ CALC. Right to the heart of the matter.

"Failing gym." The words lack her usual certainty. They wobble.

"Do you want me to come get you?" I say, which is so stupid because what am I going to do, hotwire Dad's car and make a run for it?

"I gotta go." There's so much silence from her end that it's hard to believe she's in any hurry. "I'll text you later."

I squint as though I can see across the miles and into Cassie's home. "Are you sitting there alone?"

"Dad's at a conference in Georgia, Mom's at yoga, and sitting isn't the right verb. I'm lying down." Blankets rustle in the background.

I lean against FUQ CALC. "So come here."

"I just can't, Savs." A long pause. "It's like…you know how a squirrel ran in front of your car during one of your road tests and you couldn't move?"

Don't remind me.

"That's how I feel about everything right now."

I'm going to be late to gym. My fingers trace the penmanship of DIEGO <3. Cass always fights back, whether it's to catch up or to say *screw off*. When she misses class, it's for something that she finds more important—taking pictures, holing up in the art room, driving off-campus for burritos. This—the lying down, the lack of conviction in her voice—is unfamiliar. It worries me.

I'm reminded again of how I'd wake up in the mornings after surgery and already know it'd be a shit day ahead. I know that feeling of heavy limbs and a resigned heart before the day is even underway. "Maybe you're getting sick? I'll get the homework for you."

She snorts. "Right, that's exactly what I want." The faintest bite in her voice.

"Well, what do you want?"

"Can you stop with the questions? God."

My fingers halt on the O in DIEGO.

It's like the look she gave me when I asked Juliana if she was dating Andreas. It's the shutting of a door that says *you don't get it.* How am I supposed to get whatever's going on if she won't tell me?

Another silence, long enough that I wonder if she fell asleep or has put me on hold and walked away. I don't hang up, although now my irritation matches my worry and the bell for first period has long since rung. *Tell me, Cass.*

"Sorry," she says so softly that I nearly miss it. "Come over later, okay?"

....

WHEN I RUN onto the field twenty minutes late, Marcos hands me a handwritten note, the old-fashioned way. His words are as deliberate as his penmanship. *I'm sorry for getting in your business. You're right; I don't know you guys as well as you know each other.* After that, I meet him for sixth-period math tutoring. He stays safely on his side of the table, no longer close enough to touch. His eyes, though, are just as warm when we look up from the textbook and I pause in the space between finishing what I've just explained and asking if he has any questions.

Of course he has questions. He's Marcos. He leans back in his chair and says, "What's your favorite play?"

"I'm going with *Hamlet.*"

He wrinkles his nose. "Eh, couldn't get into that one. I'm more of a *Julius Caesar* guy. Favorite movie?"

"*Lord of the Rings,*" I say immediately. "All of them. My brother made me marathon them with him, so I never had a chance."

His eyes widen. "Seriously? Same here." He raises his hand for a high-five and I slap it, our calluses lining up against each other. "Except Victor had to do the extended versions. Who do you think would win in a throw down, Elrond or Galadriel?"

It's the best part of my day.

....

ONCE I'M HOME, I work my way between the pine trees, cut behind the Vogels' chicken coop, and arrive in Cassie's backyard. The blanket of pine needles and twigs cracks beneath my sneakers.

Cassie's house is a nondescript ranch, save the lawn trinkets on the way up the walk. Shimmering glass shapes dangle from the birch tree, glowing turquoise and amethyst in the sunlight. Hand-painted flower pots and half-finished mosaic tiles form a disjointed path up to the steps. While Mr. Hopeswell works inexplicable scientific magic in the laboratory, Mrs. Hopeswell tries to make her own magic.

"Tea?" Cass greets me. She's in a dress and full makeup, like she's on her way out or has just dashed back in.

Entering Cassie's home is like stepping into a universe that runs parallel to Ponquogue, one filled with statues of exotic animals, prickly carpets depicting images of men riding elephants, and wooden floors that shine a brilliant orange-amber. Despite the gleam, it's always a little too cold and drafty in here.

I accept the cup of steaming tea. We settle in across from each other at the kitchen table, Cassie squirts an indiscriminate amount of honey into her cup, and I decide that I will let her ask the questions.

I last for ten seconds. I'm as bad as Marcos. "How are you?" I venture.

Cassie doesn't blink. With a sweep of her hand, she sets the honey back down. "Better than this morning. What'd I miss?"

"Do you really care?"

She grins as she lifts the mug to her lips. "No, but you'll feel better if you tell me, so go for it."

The teasing look in her eyes. Her normal voice, laughing as I scowl at her because we both know she's right. I choose to believe her.

....

TUESDAY. WEDNESDAY. THE rest of the week passes without Cassie missing school (though she rolled her eyes about it), without that defeat creeping into her voice, without me asking questions that she doesn't want to answer.

Until 3:03 a.m.

Who's playing "Stairway to Heaven" directly next to my ear? It can't be time for school, can it? My hand gropes around the nightstand and finds my phone. I fumble for it and it knocks me in the temple. "Deliver us from evil," I mutter.

Cass, reads the bold letters.

Too late for gallivanting to 7-Eleven. Too early for her to tell me why she's skipping school again.

Led Zeppelin's singing about the two paths you can go by and it's too loud, too much, just let me sleep, Cassie.

The phone falls to the floor.

CHAPTER TEN

Y OU CAN TELL what kind of day it will be by the noise that hits you when you enter Ponquogue High School, your shoes squeaking on the red-and-white tiles that saw their better days in 1980.

The normal pitch is high tide. Shouting and chatting and last-minute text tones chime. Impassioned lovers press together after a night apart. The soccer team whoops and high-fives, euphoric after last night's victory against Center Moriches. High tide means that PHS maintains equilibrium. *Oh-my-gawd-I-can't-believe-it* and *what's good for this weekend?* blends with squawks from the band room and other signs of students trying to do something with their lives.

It's slack tide you have to watch out for. Everyone's afraid of being heard. Conversations take place in huddles next to lockers. Lovers hold each other closer than usual. Something has happened. Like UCK YOU SPICS.

Low tide is the worst. The student body moves so quietly that the squeaking shoes echo. Teachers avoid eye contact. The announcement: *Please report to the auditorium instead of your first period class.* That happened on my second day of high school, when William Peacock and Molly Shroud were killed in a car accident on their way to school. Low tide means something has gone terribly wrong.

When Cass didn't answer my texts, I rode with Dad to school. As soon as we pulled into the parking lot, he received a terse phone call for an emergency teacher's meeting.

"What's going on?" I said.

"I don't know," he said. He left the car before I did, making sure to take the keys with him. I figured the meeting was for something like when Ella Mancuso hacked into the system and changed grades.

I must have been wrong. PHS is silent this morning.

No sound ekes out from the band room. Catalina Dover, saxophone virtuoso, sits against a row of lockers, staring up at the lights. Jacki Guzman, my locker neighbor for the past three years, turns to me with glassy eyes. "I'm so sorry," she whispers. Then she bolts around the corner.

Uh?

A cluster of freshman girls disperses as soon as I look over. Andreas and Dimitri, the forward on the soccer team, offer me high-fives, but Andreas's wide smile doesn't hold. Before I can ask what's wrong, they vanish.

Cassie will know. She has a better pulse on this place than I do. She'll loop her arm around me, whisper the story, and start scheming afresh about how we'll share a Brooklyn closet together.

No sign of her at her locker. I pop it open—we know each other's combinations—and examine the contents. A photo of me and her from the beach this summer, our eyes covered with sunglasses and our hair darkened with water. We almost look like sisters. A pack of gum, a textbook that looks like it's never been cracked open, a notebook. Nothing freshly dropped off.

She could be ditching *because* it's a low-tide day, one of the few occasions when teachers will let kids off the hook. Hell, even Mr. Riley can't argue with that. *Where are you?* I text her.

By the time we gather in the auditorium, she hasn't responded. Beth slips into the seat two away from me, her birdlike features narrowed with concern. Around us, there's the hush of taut conversations, and no matter how hard I focus on catching a syllable, a hint of *anything*, nobody dares to speak loudly enough.

Juliana leans against a seat in the back row with her arms crossed, lips pursed. She has the air of someone who has been interrupted. I look beside her, around me, and there's no sign of Marcos.

For the first time, I feel a drum of fear. What if Cassie was in a car accident this morning? What if Marcos was? I search through my phone until I realize I don't have his number.

No, Cassie has lightning-fast reflexes behind the wheel despite her tendency to focus on everything besides driving. She'd whip right around someone blazing her way. Marcos—I can't imagine him being nearly as distracted as Cassie. It has to be someone else. I wipe my palms on my jeans and try to calm my breathing.

Behind all of us, in the Standing Room Only zone, are the teachers. Mr. Raia and Mr. Kessler in conversation, Mr. Raia's tie frumpier than usual. Next to Mr. Kessler, my father. He's eyeing me like he wants to say something. At that exact moment, a text arrives and I nearly drop my phone. Except it's not from Cassie. It's from Dad, sent ten minutes ago and arriving now thanks to PHS's superb cell service: *Find me so we can talk.* Then the stage microphone squeaks to life, and I turn back with a whisper of relief. At least Dad's here.

When Mr. Riley walks onto the stage, all noise leaves the room. I don't want him to speak. Marcos isn't here. Cassie isn't here. I want to climb over all these legs to the aisle, run to the door. *I don't want to know.*

Where the hell are you? I text Cassie, because if I send her enough messages, I'll finally receive an answer.

"I've gathered everyone to address the rumors that are flying around." Mr. Riley's voice is commanding as usual, but there's a slouch to his perfect posture. "A student attempted to take her own life early this morning."

Her own life.

Suddenly I'm as cold as if I've cannonballed into the Atlantic on a January morning.

Around me, everyone gasps.

I'm reduced to looking around wildly, a last-ditch search. *It's not her. It can't be her.*

Mr. Riley holds up a hand, swallows before he speaks. The lights catch the sheen of sweat on his forehead. "The student is presently in critical condition at Stony Brook Hospital."

She doesn't do rock bottom. She finds her way out.

No, she's asleep in her bed, cocooned by her quilts. She's slipping between the rocks at the beach, camera in hand, and she'll laugh at me when I spill my fears about this morning. *God, Savs,* she'll say with an arm over my shoulder, *I would never do that.*

Jacki's apology. Andreas's shaky smile. If it were Cassie, I'd *know.* I'd pull her back before she went too far. I'd have all the right words.

"I encourage you to visit the guidance counselors if you need support or someone to talk to," says Mr. Riley. "I know that high school isn't an easy time."

I have to find her. I have to bring her back.

Juliana stands at the door, immovable as the crowd files out, silent as a church. Her face is cool, unyielding, and she doesn't flinch when the girl in front of me wipes at her eyes. Only when I get closer does she shift. She's waiting for me.

"Did you know?" Her voice gives nothing away.

I want to tell her that Cassie's out sick. Show her I'm the closer friend, the one who knows Cassie best.

Instead I say, "No."

She shakes her head. Messy dark curls swing over her shoulders. "Me neither."

In the hallway, her voice drops so low that I have to lean close. How strange it is that the two of us are walking together. Cassie would laugh if she saw us. Sling an arm around both of our necks, bringing us closer still.

"Marcos found her," Juliana says.

Marcos. My stomach drops. How did he wind up in the same place as Cassie?

Plenty of girls look like my best friend. Rope thin and blonde. Maybe Marcos thought the girl looked like Cass and it was enough to spark all of this. A freshman with the face of Cassie and the mind of Ophelia.

"He has this metal detector," Juliana says before my mind can sprint too far, trying to find both of them. The distant memory of Senior Cut Day returns—the boy with a metal detector, Andreas yelling for him to have some fun—and I nod.

"Sometimes he walks around before school to see what he can get. He took it to South Cross Beach at sunrise and it started beeping. Pieces of a metal bracelet." She draws in a shaky breath, the first crack in her cool veneer. "He followed the beeping under the bridge."

Oh, my God.

I have to focus, I have to hear what she says next, but the throbbing in my ears and my head feels like waves crashing over me without receding.

Juliana's lower lip trembles. She pauses, steels herself, spits out the last part. "She was floating in the water. She wasn't breathing when he pulled her out."

Blonde hair spread like a sunburst in the water. Catching the first light of dawn.

I'm the one who's supposed to be able to bring her back, not Marcos, a guy she barely knows. A guy who happened to be there instead of me, the one who has always been there.

"It's so cold," I blurt out. Like that logic changes anything.

She draws in a long breath. "Her car was running. Like maybe she was going to change her mind, you know?"

When the bell interrupts, we awkwardly pivot away from each other. I stand rooted to the linoleum, an island in the sea of whispers.

An arm around my shoulder, except it's too tall and thick to belong to Cass. My father. "How're you doing, kiddo?"

That's when I know. Dad knows better than to acknowledge that we're related in the hallway. He knows that I would only allow this under the most extenuating circumstances. And here are the circumstances: the near-death of my best friend.

"Fine." I move away before he can feel me shaking. "I gotta get to class."

....

JULIANA DIDN'T KNOW, either. That's what I keep telling myself.

Her car was still running. She didn't mean it, I decide in AP Lit. Mr. Raia talks about the multiple choice section of the AP test with more gesticulating than usual. He keeps looking to me like he expects me to flee the room in hysterics. No, not I.

Maybe she was photographing something, slipped, hit her head. By precalc, I'm so certain that my hypothesis is correct that I don't understand why Cassie hasn't waltzed back in and given me a wink, prepared to tell me all of her stories.

I call Cassie's house during lunch. The phone rings and rings. I imagine the sound echoing against the twisted animals with their frightening faces and the orange-red pottery. Surely Mrs. Hopeswell, freshly relaxed from yoga, will answer with, "Cassie? She's right here."

No answer.

In Spanish, the lyrics to "Stairway to Heaven" won't stop replaying. 3:03 a.m. and no voicemail. *Why did you call, Cassie? Why didn't I answer?*

After the last bell, everyone flees. I walk toward Dad's car in the too-sunny afternoon, and a beaten-down boy with hair swept to one side like a wave steps in front of me.

"Marcos?" The blood rushes through my veins at hyper speed. *Where's Cassie, how'd you find her, how is she now?*

"I'm sorry." His brown eyes are nearly squinted shut with exhaustion. "It wasn't good." Instead of coconuts and laundry, he smells like sweat and saltwater. The bottom of his jeans bleed a deeper blue than the top, hours after—

I fight down the rising panic. I have to hear it from Marcos. I have to know the official narrative. "Do you know what her status is now?" Calm as a journalist.

He shakes his head. "They took her in a helicopter."

I imagine the chopper landing on the small outcropping of rocks beside the bay, sand flying everywhere, Cassie's curls flowing like she's facing the ocean instead of lying there—

"It was an accident." I ignore my shaking legs, the waver in my voice.

Marcos looks at me sadly. Sympathetically. "I found a note on the passenger's seat."

The panic rises higher. *I can handle it.* I repeat the mantra as I would before competing on beam. "She has Post-Its everywhere. Stuff for her essays. Hell, I've left notes in there." I'm rambling. I don't recognize this high-pitched stranger speaking in a rush.

"There was only one." Marcos sounds too tired to fight me on this. "It said, 'Till human voices wake us and we drown.'"

CHAPTER ELEVEN

CARS, SCHOOL BUSES, trucks seem determined to push us back as Dad and I inch up Nicolls Road. At every red light, my hand clamps down on the door handle. *Go, go, go.* I can see the hospital's towers above the trees, the dying sunlight catching the windows, and I'm staring at them as hard as I can, as though I'll be able to see Cassie from here.

When he finally pulls up to the curb of Stony Brook Hospital, I'm out of the car before it comes to a complete stop. I run through the sliding doors and almost barrel into an elderly lady in a wheelchair. "Cascade Hopeswell," I say to the nurse at the desk, voice trembling.

The nurse eyes me critically. "Relation to the patient?"

"Sister. Savannah, Savannah Hopeswell." *Shut up,* I can't stop, am I too late?

She scans the paper in front of her. "She already has two visitors. I'm sorry."

Has. Present tense. Still breathing.

"But—"

"I'm sorry," she says firmly. "Come back tomorrow."

....

I SLEEP WITH my phone clenched in my palm. Every hour between midnight and six a.m., I wake up, certain that it's the vibration of a text message. It never is. It's just my mind.

"My mom works on the neonatal floor at Stony Brook, and she says that Cassie's out of critical condition," Jacki Guzman tells me at our lockers, wiping away a tear in relief. "She's stable now. It was, like, a miracle recovery. Aren't you so glad? I am so, so glad."

Out of critical condition. While I don't know how accurate secondhand information from a neonatal nurse is and I'm pretty sure that all sorts of laws are being violated by these details being shared, it's enough to fill me with hope.

Word catches that Cassie is out of danger, and high tide returns. When she comes back to school, there will be whispers. Right now, though, everyone is as jovial or annoyed as they'd be on any other day.

How are you? I text her.

An instant later, the response: *Got a hot doctor.*

Finally.

I'm shaking and laughing a little because of course that would be Cassie's response—flippant and irreverent—and when Jacki shuts her locker and watches me with concern, I ignore it. Who cares?

My fingers rush to reply, hitting all the wrong letters and forcing me to retype. The same panic from yesterday rushes through me, as though if I don't reply fast enough, she'll vanish. *They wouldn't let me in yesterday.*

Yeah, I don't remember much of yesterday. So casual, as if she's telling me about a night of drinking.

The next message arrives just as briskly. *Please visit? I miss you. All I do here is sleep.*

Whatever led her to the water, she's back again, away from rock bottom and swimming back to the surface. She'll be back, she'll get through this, and I won't let her fall again.

Clutching the phone so that those precious words don't slip away (*she's alive, she's okay*), I find Juliana in the cafeteria next to Andreas, who's in the midst of illustrating on his napkin with a ketchup-dipped French fry. When she looks up and sees me, she seems almost grateful for the interruption. "Cassie texted me," I tell her. "She's okay."

Several nods bob around the table. "Cool, cool," says Dimitri, taking a tremendous gulp of milk.

Juliana's eyebrows spike up enough so that I know Cassie didn't text her.

I win. In some feeble way.

....

"MISS!" A NURSE calls. I'm already past. I'm the girl racing her best friend down to the shoreline.

When I round the corner, Mrs. Hopeswell has her back to me as she leans against the wall. "Alan?" she calls.

I slow to a stop. My breathing is too loud for this corridor.

She turns around and gives me a ghost of a smile. "Oh, Savannah." Based on the wrinkles in her green blouse and the disarray of her hair, she probably slept on a hospital chair. "How are you, honey?" She's Cassie with dark hair, a little shorter and a little plumper, with the same luminous eyes that pin you in place.

What's the appropriate response?

Luckily, she doesn't wait for my reply. "She's awake." Her fingers circle each other without taking hold. "She's looking forward to seeing you."

Did Cassie tell her about our meeting with Mr. Riley? Did he leave a message on their voicemail, wanting to meet with her parents? Were those conversations about focusing on "viable career paths" so bad that she believed her parents would rather not see her again?

"Savs?" Cass calls from the room.

I expected wires and machines. Vestiges of salt water and purple-blue skin from hypothermia. Instead, Cass sits cross-legged on top of the blanket with a Chinese checkers board, hair in a simple ponytail. Her cheeks are egg white.

When she smiles, I extend my arms for a hug, for once being the initiator of such affection. I probably won't let go. The nurses will have to wrench me away. She's okay. She's *okay*.

She's cool under my arms, hugging me back without the usual vigor. "I'm sorry," she says. Her eyes are glassy. I've never seen Cassie cry. Not when the kids used to tease her for being so tall, not when she dated Toby Mickelson in eighth grade and he dumped her before the Moving Up Dance. "It's just...it's been a bad time."

I settle in next to her. "It'll get better from here."

Unbidden, my mind flips back to *You wouldn't be able to handle it*. Cassie meant that about El Pueblo, sure, but was it also a code for her? What about Juliana—what does she know?

She musters up a shaky smile. "So what's everyone saying about me? Did anyone cry? I will bet the three dollars in my wallet that Jacki cried."

I wonder if her mother listens at the door. What have their conversations been like? What about with the doctors—is Cassie steering around them, too?

Whatever she's been hiding, I want her to feel like she can tell me. "So how are you..." Doing? Feeling? What are you supposed to say when your best friend—laughing, scheming, singing to silly songs on the radio—tries to kill herself?

She nods like I've filled in the blanks. "They put me in the psychiatric emergency room and let me tell you, it's some wild shit in there. Like *One Flew Over the Cuckoo's Nest*. Don't give me that look, Savs, I did read it."

The last thing on my mind is her schoolwork. Instead, I'm seeing her walk into the water, shivering but not turning back. Her engine rumbling, puffs of smoke coughing out of the tailpipe. The final line to "The Love Song of J. Alfred Prufrock," a poem we'd studied last year, scribbled in her loopy cursive and left on the passenger seat.

"Police officers are stationed down the hall, just in case. There was a lady who was yelling the entire time I was there. Makes you reconsider the whole living thing." She half-smiles. "Kidding. I don't want to end up back there, that's for sure."

We fall quiet, listening to the clink of marbles against the checkers board. Roll in, roll out. No method to the way she's placing them, yet she doesn't seem to mind.

"What happened that morning?" I say finally.

Cassie coughs as though she hasn't heard me. "I'm thinking about going into filmmaking. Art direction, cinematography, special effects. What do you think? You could write the screenplays."

I turn to her, disturbing the precarious balance of the marbles. She swoops over to catch them, fingers shaking. "You know you can talk to me, right?"

"Yep." She rolls the marbles around in her palm. "Lately I've seen so many images, and all of them are moving." That half smile again. "Could be the drugs talking." She returns them to their hollowed spots on the board. *Tap. Tap.* "I think I should consider film school instead of art school. My dad seems to halfway approve, though he probably just feels bad."

Is this the way she talks to her doctors, leading them down detours until they get lost and give up? Even I'm having a hard time keeping up.

Do better.

I failed to follow when it mattered most. If I can piece together the answers now, I won't lose track of her again.

"Why did you leave the car running?"

The slightest flush of pink blooms in her pale cheeks. "In case I changed my mind."

She wasn't set on it. I cling to that. She wanted a way back.

When one of the marbles slips loose, the ping of glass against metal resonates in the near-empty room.

"If I had died," she says, looking at me frankly for the first time, "you would have spoken at the funeral, right? None of those other assholes making up bullshit about how much I meant to them."

"Of course," I say automatically. Always Late Nick, all the summer friends who held Cassie's attention by the bonfire—they're not here. They don't matter; they never have. "Why did you call me that night?"

"I don't remember." She lines up the marbles on the board. "But I knew you wouldn't answer."

That hits me straight in the stomach, swift and strong as a fall onto the balance beam. "I would have if I'd known—"

"Thing is, Savs, your life's like a hallway. Along both sides, the doors are wide open." Her fingers touch each marble. "People are hanging out the doors. *Savannah! Come in! Bring your PSAT scores!* My hallway? The faster I walk, the faster the doors close. It's only me in there." She tilts the board. The marbles stream across the metal grooves and tumble to the floor. She doesn't make a move to pick them up and neither do I; I'm rooted to this clinical white blanket, unable to budge until she finishes. "I know what you're thinking. I could have tried harder, right? Gone to class and shit. But I couldn't have done anything differently. Do you know what I mean? I wouldn't have been able to change a thing. It wasn't in me."

I want to yell. I want to tug on her bony shoulders and shake her until her eyes focus and she realizes what she's saying. Instead, my stomach hurts as though her words physically struck me.

Failing my road test, blowing out Dad's tire, messing up in the gym—none of it compares to the crushing reality that if I'd answered the phone, I could have stopped this. She's all but said it herself.

"I'm sorry," I say instead, and I hate that my voice wavers because I need to be the strong one. I can't fail again.

She inspects the board as if she hasn't heard me.

I try again. "What are you going to do now?"

She runs her fingers over the grooves where the marbles had been. "They're keeping me under observation to make sure I don't make any sudden moves, I guess."

I wish she had said, "Open those doors."

....

CASSIE'S EULOGY. I feel ill even considering it; after all, I would have been the obvious choice to speak. I'd have to stand in front of Ponquogue's senior class, packed into a church that Cassie never attended. "Hi, everyone, I'm Cassie's asshole best friend who didn't answer the phone the night before her suicide." I would have been the one to throw flowers on her grave.

I'd start with the Cassie that I knew first, when poetry and Beth O'Leary (of all people) solidified our friendship. While kids at every other school on Long Island ran outside for Field Day and ate hot dogs to celebrate, we'd crowded into the library for the First Grade Poetry Jamboree. As the crowd had strained to hear Sarah Langhorne's "My Puppies and Me," Beth had leaned over. "Where's your mom, Cascade?" she'd asked innocently.

"On her way," Cassie said just as smoothly.

Christina McGovern peeked around Beth's shoulder. "Beth said your mom's in the loony bin."

Cassie stood completely rigid. The applause thundered around us as Beth and Christina stared at her expectantly.

Then Beth shrugged. "I heard it from Liam? On the bus?"

"Liam is stupid," I said firmly. "Cassie's mom got a flat tire. She'll be here soon."

Despite the fact that there was no way to prove how I had this information, they retreated as I grabbed Cassie's arm and pulled her away from the sweaty flock of first-graders.

By the final day of school, Cassie and I were best friends. It was simply understood. She braided my hair on the bus and gave chilly looks to anyone who teased me for being short. By the first day of second grade, I was officially Savannah. I slipped on the name like a too-big coat that I'd someday grow into. It was a mature name, one without the childish ring of "Katie." It didn't sound like anyone else's name in my family.

The Cassie that everyone knew best was the girl in middle school. She became fingers and a right eye squeezed shut behind a camera. Sure, everyone believed they were a photographer with their cell phones, but Cassie was actually good at it. She came to all of my meets and captured me upside down. The hallway displays for the photo classes became Cassie's displays. I became cooler because I was that mid-air girl in the pictures. Everyone was cooler in her pictures. They were deeper; they had contours and shadings.

Maybe Cassie should have taken self-portraits. Maybe that would have helped.

CHAPTER TWELVE

THEY MIGHT HAVE changed their numbers. That's my first excuse.

The second excuse is the one I fear—that they're pissed and have rendered me irrelevant after those early weeks of well-wishes and *Come to the gym soon!*

Cassie has been in the hospital for three days, which means I've had three nights of sleeping for three hours apiece and plenty more hours spent staring up at the shadows playing across my ceiling. I've reimagined every conversation. The afternoon we spent in her kitchen after I'd called her that morning, the way she'd shifted from defeated to *no big deal, everything's fine* so convincingly. Her arm around me as we stood facing the ocean, her eyes glittering as we talked about New York City. The way Mr. Riley shut her down.

The constantly replaying loop of memories yields one conclusion: I should have known. I shouldn't have accepted her evasive answers. Instead of letting the phone roll out of my hand, I could have talked her out of it, or talked to her for so long that she fell asleep and stayed in bed that morning instead of driving to the bridge.

Not only am I a shit driver and gymnast, but I'm a shit friend, too.

I stop at Emery's number. She was the one I felt closest to, the one who laughed the loudest at my jokes and rolled her eyes when Jess preened in the mirror. I click her name first, and before I can talk myself out of it, I add Ally, Monica, and Jess to the group message.

Hey, strangers, I miss you! I'm sorry I disappeared.

Weak, but honest. It's the best I've got right now. The reality—*I'm sorry I was too jealous and wallowing to feel happy for you, or to even talk to you*—seems a little heavy for an icebreaker message.

"I don't know about those girls," Cassie had said as we hung out in the backseat of my dad's car on the way home from a meet, eating potato chips (the perfect post-competition snack, obviously). "I think you only like them because you're under the influence of chalk."

"We spend almost thirty hours a week together," I'd said.

"You're always trying to beat them. What kind of friendship is that?"

Yes, Monica was as tightly coiled as her dark curls, and Jess would cheat during strength and get us all in trouble. We understood each other, though; the same exhaustion burned in our muscles and we'd struggle to lift our arms as our coach Matt said, "Just one more bar routine." ("Just one more" meant we had at least three more.)

Cass, however, did have a valid point. Relegated to the couch with a glass of water and a vial of painkillers, it hurt me too much to see the videos they posted and read their enthusiastic texts about new skills and future plans when I no longer had either. So when I offered evasive answers to their questions about my knee, they'd stopped asking. I'd let them drift until they were out of sight.

Somehow, with Cassie right beside me every day, she'd nearly slipped away. I can't be that friend anymore. I have to be alert. It might be too late for my old teammates to forgive my absence from their lives. If there's a shot to make amends, though, I'll take it.

In the early morning rush at Ponquogue High School, with a volume level that has mercifully returned to high tide under a full moon, I check for a response. Story of my life lately.

Seeing you at the bonfire was quite possibly the highlight of my eighteen years of existence, Emery replies. She's written back to me individually instead of to everyone.

By the end of first period, no one else has replied, confirming what I suspected to be true. I'm a terrible friend.

Another message from Emery. *Sooooo you're coming to practice today, right?!*

For a moment, I actually consider it.

When I was younger, it was the safest place I had when Richard first deployed to Afghanistan. It was my own world that came with its own set of problems and challenges. It was one that I knew how to maneuver. I was certain if I practiced hard, the outcome would be what I wanted. Then, of course, I learned that the latter wasn't true.

As the hallway thins out, I maintain the same slow pace. Is it just me, or are people avoiding eye contact? Either it's because I'm the near-dead girl's best friend, or my father is handing back a test today.

This is not the normal, safe senior year I've been banking on. To say the least.

Emery's relentless. Gymnasts are focused, that's for sure. *So. Practice. Yes?*

No. No.

I turn the corner for my locker and smash into Marcos's chest. He stumbles into Jacki and her locker slams shut. "Ow, ow, ow! You just broke my hand!" she exclaims. Tears, immediately.

"I'm sorry." Marcos takes her baby-pale hand in his and examines it. "Can you move your fingers?"

Get your hand out of his.

Where did that thought come from? I fling open my locker and it resounds with an unreasonably loud bang. Subtle. "Don't you guys have class?"

"Study hall." He flips her hand over, looking at the knuckles.

Jacki hiccups her way to calmness. "I'm gonna have to go to the nurse," she says, voice cracking, but the tears have subsided. I bet her hand wasn't even in her locker. I bet she's scared of loud noises like children who fear thunder. I know the difference between just sound and real pain.

"Hey, Savannah." Perhaps satisfied that Jacki's injury will not require surgery or, I don't know, a hand replacement, he approaches me. His fingers rest on the edge of the locker door, holding onto it hopefully. The same hands that plunged into freezing waters, pulled Cassie to the shore, kept her alive.

His dimples crease as he smiles at me like it's the most natural greeting in the world. "I like your hair."

That's all it takes. *I like your hair.* The spiky pieces stand up with static cling from my run-in with his shirt.

I close my locker and put my hand on that coconut hair. Pull his cool lips to mine. He tastes like morning.

We both pull back and stare at each other, his dark eyes wide and maybe a little shocked. As I'm catching my breath and his lips begin to curl into a smile, I do the only thing I can think of:

Run.

"Got chemistry!" I call, immediately regretting the choice of words as I hear him laugh behind me.

CHAPTER THIRTEEN

I DILIGENTLY ANSWER the first questions posed in AP Chemistry so that I can spend the rest of class figuring out the turns my life has taken:

My best friend attempting suicide.

My former friends (well, most of them) not responding to my text messages.

Kissing my best friend's other best friend's ex-boyfriend. In public.

Would I have landed here if I'd landed on my feet at Regionals?

Over the summer, I'd sit by myself in the parking booth and watch the blurry asphalt haze straighten out as the day cooled off, the heat advisory expired. I'd watch the sun plunge toward the water, tucking itself behind the reeds on the bluffs, and if the wind blew just right, I'd hear Cassie laughing up in the snack bar. With sticky salt air on my skin and sand under my knee brace, I told myself that I was happy. Sometimes, like the wink of a green flash, I was.

Whether it's a glitch or tenacity, Emery sends me the same text. *So. Practice. Yes?*

The pros of going to practice: Seeing my old friends in person instead of hiding behind a text. Seeing my coaches. Doing something that has nothing to do with how I failed Cassie.

The cons: the three-inch scar that runs down my knee.

Once the period concludes, I fake looking for an imaginary essay in my folder so that if, say, anyone wanted to ask me about the morning's events, I'd look completely unapproachable. I text Cassie: *Well, this morning sure took an interesting turn. How are you? Want me to visit later?*

It's when I've almost reached the exit that I make the grave error that a gymnast who has almost completed her routine does: I relax. I think I've got this without having finished. My mind returns to Emery's texts, how my *no* from this morning has softened into an *I don't know.*

"If I suggest a *Lord of the Rings* viewing party, would that be moving too quickly?"

Marcos is trying not to laugh; I can sense it. I bet he knows that I've found a way not to bump into him since this morning. With Cassie around, noise and light and spur-of-the-moment is the norm; without her, it feels like sensory overload.

"I think 'quickly' is the wrong word." My eyes move directly to his lips, cool and soft and far too kissable. So much for avoidance. "We're talking twelve-to-sixteen hours of footage here."

"Definitely too much too soon," he agrees. "We might need to ease into it with just *Fellowship*. What are you doing this afternoon?"

Despite spending 90 percent of the day on the lam from him, sitting together watching Aragorn and company kick ass sounds like an excellent retreat from my own mind. The idea of sitting with him for hours, alone, makes my heart speed up and my palms sweat. If I should be spending time with anyone, though, it's Cassie.

I sneak a glance at my phone to see that she's responded. *Talking about your feelings all day is exhausting—who knew? I'm going to watch some bad TV and nap.*

I reread each word, searching for subtext. Is she okay? Is she hiding anything?

"Or not?" Marcos's smile has slipped. He shifts his weight from foot to foot.

I don't know what Cassie would do if the situation was reversed. I don't know if I should go with Marcos or push Cass harder, not accept her no. I need to go somewhere where I know all the rules, the right things to do.

Up until last spring, I'd never had to weigh these options. There was one place I went each day after school, without fail.

It comes out all at once. "Tomorrow?" I say. "I have practice."

....

COLLECTING EVERYTHING I need still feels automatic. Red leotard. Leather handgrips in blue bag, with chalk floating off the bag in small wisps. Finally, the beast with cross straps and hinges that creak as I pick it up: black knee brace, never worn.

As it dangles from my hand, I consider returning it to the closet and hiding myself in there, too.

My hair has just made it into a ponytail with an excessive amount of bobby pins when my phone rings. "Let's do this, chica!" Emery yells in my ear.

It's time to trade one bold move for another. If only the thought didn't make the brace tremble in my hand. Gymnastics isn't the sort of sport that you can do when the mood strikes you. You need the strength, flexibility, and spatial awareness from regular practice. If not, you'll get hurt. Or you can be like me and go to every practice *and* still get hurt.

"I can't believe you're back." Emery gives me a one-armed hug as she blazes away from the curb. "This is better than Christmas. This college shit is giving me an ulcer."

Yeah, I know all about that.

Dear Savannah, I was highly impressed by your performance at the New York State Championships. I look forward to seeing you compete at Regionals! I ran around the house squealing when that email arrived.

"Praise Jesus I finally convinced you, because not having a goddamn team is the worst." Emery merges onto Sunrise Highway.

"Wait, what?"

"You know how everyone went MIA after your surgery?"

I'm the only one who has your back, Cassie told me.

"I think I was the one who went MIA." It's a relief to say it out loud, to admit my own responsibility.

"Hey," Emery says, "you were recovering from ACL reconstruction. I'm sure that sucked, and you were probably loopy half of the time from all of the pain meds, right? Without you, though—it's all turned to shit."

"What happened?"

"They're all gone." Emery expertly switches lanes. "Jess has this boyfriend that she's obsessed with. Matt told her that if she kept showing up late and leaving early, she was off the team. So she *quit*. Idiot. Have you seen the pictures she posts of him? He better have a great personality, that's all I'm saying."

My brain's spinning. *They're all gone.*

"Monica broke her ankle and decided to do diving, and Ally switched to Flip Factory even though it's like an hour away and so overrated. Oh, man, I love this song!"

"G-Man? Seriously?"

"Don't tell." Emery winks at me. Then she starts moving her head in time to the beat and rapping along with G-Man.

So that's why nobody responded to my text message white flag. All of this time, I assumed they were doing great things that I could no longer be a part of. They're done with South Ocean.

It occurs to me fleetingly that they should be able to answer anyway, that we should be able to catch up on each other's lives despite the fact that our leotards are stuffed away in the depths of our dressers, except they're doing exactly what I did: shutting the drawer. Instead of our pack of five, gathering on the podium to hold up our team trophy, it's down to Emery and me. I can't help but wonder if the reason she wants me back is because she wants someone to train with, not because she's missed *me*, Savannah, the collector of various injuries.

"C'mon!" she yells, turning up the volume.

All right, then.

I join, although the only rhymes I can make out are "what," "butt," and "we be swingin' yo-yo's 'round dem mofos." Somehow G-Man calms my nerves, which is about the only positive thing I can say for such lyrical mastery. By the end of the song, I'm relaxed enough to pop the question. "How's recruiting going?"

She shakes her head. "I reached my all-time low last week. Ocean State's head coach came to visit, and the guy didn't smile the entire practice. I landed on my face every vault. Every. Single. One."

Buccaneers Gymnastics. The sweatshirt crammed into the recesses of my closet that I should have been wearing on my official college visit.

I shouldn't have asked.

Her green eyes meet mine. "Not one smile. Who wants to be on a team like that?"

I appreciate the effort to make me feel better, to ignore the fact that Emery won the meet that I was wheeled out of on a stretcher. Besides, what are my expectations for today? It will be a victory lap, without the victory, on my journey to bigger and better things. Closure, perhaps.

We leave the highway and drive down the pine tree-lined road. This was the point where I'd sit up straighter in the passenger seat, willing my parents to drive faster—*come on, we're almost there!* Emery turns right into the industrial park that advertises foreign car repairs, international shipping, and, at the very end, gymnastics.

It's a tan warehouse with slender windows and a steel door. Above the door is the white-and-blue sign: *South Ocean Gymnastics, Training Champions of All Ages.* Small children exit the gym, holding their mothers' hands and hopping up and down like they're still on the trampoline. "Remember how we were like those kids?" Emery kills the engine. The car plunges into silence. "I can't believe my mom never chucked me out the window."

Now that we're at the door, every urge that said *do it* now says *go back.* I fight against telling Emery that I'll just kick around in the lobby while she works out.

Here goes nothing. Literally.

CHAPTER FOURTEEN

I F ONLY NOISE were enough to make me invisible. Children run everywhere in the lobby–pulling on sweatshirts, wrangling with the snack machine, playing tag as their parents chase them. It's pandemonium. It makes me never want to have kids.

I follow Emery's short brown ponytail and bubbly pink scar on her shoulder past the glass viewing windows and into the gym. My feet sink into the blue mats, corresponding nicely with the feeling in my stomach.

When I started gymnastics ten years ago, I couldn't believe how huge and complicated it all looked: rows of balance beams to the left, three sets of uneven bars to the right, foam pits and two trampolines, a fuzzy blue runway leading to the vault, the wide blue floor exercise in the corner, and mats everywhere. Mats of all colors and sizes and shapes, including one that's shaped like a donut, which I think is for the sole purpose of rolling kids around. Pervading every piece of equipment are the smells of chalk, mat vinyl, and a scent that I can only describe as feet.

Banners hang from the walls. In the summer, when our only source of cool air is from giant industrial fans, they flap in the breeze. There's "3rd Place Level 7 Team, Long Island Classic," "2nd Place Level 5 Team,

Finger Lakes Invitational," and the like. Just above the floor exercise is the banner that our coach Vanessa is most proud of: "1st Place Level 9 Team, New York State Championships." She always looks up at it when she talks to us during a team meeting. That one's from five years ago. We haven't come close since then.

Standing next to the vault table is my coach, Matt, engaged in intense conversation with a man I don't recognize. Matt looks exactly the same: spiked dark hair, dark eyes, black T-shirt filled out with muscles that are ready to catch us when we fall, which for me was frequently. I have a rush of what I can only call first-day-of-school jitters; what if he's pissed that I've shown up out of the blue? And who's this other guy?

When Matt sees me, his jaw drops. "The prodigal returns!" he calls, and the man next to him turns.

"New coach?" I whisper to Emery. What else has changed since I've been gone?

She shakes her head. "I don't know who that is."

As we approach, I eye the man's red and blue jacket. *The State University of New York, College at—*

"—Owego," Matt says as the coach shakes Emery's hand. While Matt's clearly surprised to see me, his tone remains professional and controlled. "One of the top programs in Division III, placing second at Nationals this year. Six All-Americans and five second-team All-Americans."

I hadn't dallied with looking at Division III schools. No athletic scholarships. No primetime prestige with thousands of fans cheering them on. Small potatoes. It'd been go big or go home in my college search.

Ponquogue sends a few intrepid graduates to Owego each year. As far as I know, the school, nestled between farms and more farms upstate, is a magnet for blizzards, ice, and general misery. The city that never sleeps, it isn't, unless you count the frat parties.

"This is Savannah Gregory." Matt turns to me with an obvious question in his eyes—*where have you been and why are you back?* "She's a senior and a Level 10."

Was a Level 10. "Savannah, fantastic to meet you!" Coach pumps my hand. I underestimated his strength. And enthusiasm. "Jeff Barry, head coach at Owego State. Are you interested in intercollegiate gymnastics?"

"Sure." What else am I supposed to say?

Coach laughs very hard at this. "Great, great! Your father said the same thing."

"My father?"

"Yep! He emailed me."

"My...father..."

"Said you'd blown out your knee but that you planned to make a full comeback."

I'm still stuck on *my father.* Making threats to have me return is one thing; attempting to manage my future is another. Was I staring at my phone, waiting to hear from Cassie, while Dad glanced furtively over his shoulder and typed out an email to this man? What was he thinking?

Oh, and *what full comeback?*

Coach completely misunderstands the expression on my face. "Injuries are no fun, that's for sure. Just have to keep a positive attitude, right?"

I'm holding my knee brace. I could swing and hit him with a satisfying clatter of hard plastic on bald head. Instead, I give a sort of sickly smile.

"He said that you're an honors student at Pon... Pon..."

"Ponquogue."

"Ponbog, right."

"Ponquogue." This man. My God.

"Exactly. Must be great growing up right on the ocean, huh?"

As soon as he blinks, I escape to a corner of the floor.

The younger girls sit in neat rows with legs straight, toes together and pointed. A couple of them wave at me with big grins, but it's clear that Vanessa has commanded them to be silent *or else.*

She scared the crap out of me when I joined the team, even though she's four-eleven and always has a perky ponytail. Nothing's ever good enough for her. Your legs are never straight enough, your toes not pointed sufficiently, and God forbid she catches you cheating on your push-ups. If by any chance you do perform to her standards, you earn a nod.

I stretch with the remnants of South Ocean's upper level team, which consists of Emery and the twins, Nicola and Erica, who are thirteen and still wear *I Heart Gymnastics* T-shirts. Bless them. I used to own one of those.

"You guys were, like, fetuses when I last saw you," I say.

Emery gives me a sassy look that clearly says, *That's what happens when you disappear.*

"Is Coach Barry here to watch you, too?" asks Erica, sitting on her knees and placing her palms on the floor to stretch her wrists.

"Seriously? With this beast?" I pull the brace over my right foot. In a matter of moments, the brace twists sideways with my foot stuck between two straps, neither one an exit. I could use some directional arrows.

"I think it makes you look cool," says Nicola, copying Erica's wrist stretch. "Like a warrior or something."

"I'd want you on my team," Erica adds.

Trust the twins to make anything seem positive. So young, so eager. Wait until they enter high school.

By the time I've wrestled the Beast into what appears to be its rightful position on my leg, the team has begun basic tumbling across the floor. I hide behind Emery, except I am now even more vulnerable to Coach Barry's gaze. The man doesn't miss a movement.

"Great extension on that handstand," he says to Emery. "Wow, look at that shoulder flexibility!" he calls to Tiana across the floor. Tiana's only six and she looks at him blankly. Vanessa nods in her stead, taking the compliment. "Excellent heel drive—both of you!" he says to Erica and Nicola, who look alike even in their gymnastics.

As the team splits into two corners of the floor for more advanced tumbling, I step to the side. Not that it bothers me that the Level 4s and 5s, none older than ten, are running across the floor and flipping with ease. Or that Nicola, who's learning a double full—one flip, two twists—keeps landing awkwardly, her ankles and knees bending at uncomfortable angles. Yet she walks away from each attempt ready to try another.

I want to put my hand over my knee to protect it somehow. Instead, I practice leaps on the side of the floor, staying out of everyone's way.

But not out of everyone's notice. "Great range of motion." Coach Barry walks over. "What are your jump combinations? I bet you're killer on beam, too."

I'm saved by Emery's tumbling pass. She lifts into the air, pulls her knees to her stomach, flips twice, lands with a satisfying thud. Then she walks back to the corner, face expressionless. I know that look.

She's focused, contemplating her next turn and how to improve.

"She's working double layouts onto a pit landing," Matt says to Coach. "Full-ins, too."

Coach nods vigorously; he likes this news. As I'm about to sneak toward my water bottle, he turns to me. "Are you an all-arounder?"

"Yep." Although I hate vault. Well, sometimes. However, I don't hate vault as much as I hate uneven bars. You'd think that a knee injury would have forced me to improve on bars. Instead, my decision to quit *might* have been a little bit influenced by the fact that my gymnastics would have come down to two round, wooden, unforgiving bars with lots of chalk. I've always enjoyed balance beam, probably because when I began the sport, everyone else hated it: suede-covered wood four feet off the floor, four inches wide. It was the uncool thing to like beam, so of course I did. And floor was always my favorite until April.

"How's the comeback going?" Coach inquires.

Matt looks up when he hears this question.

"It's, ah, all right." *Real convincing, Savs*, Cassie would say. "Good days, bad days. You know."

Coach chuckles and pats my shoulder. "I sure do." I'm not sure if I'm supposed to feel inspired or patronized.

Matt grins at me like we're all in on the same friendly joke, but his eyes say, *What the hell is this all about, Savannah?*

An excellent question. I haven't stepped foot in the gym since April, and here I am, bothering to lie to this guy instead of telling him the truth.

From what I can see, Emery has a terrific practice. She swings beautiful pirouettes on bars and lands her first vault on her feet. She is all elegance—sharply pointed toes and legs glued together, perfect posture that makes her regal. After that, Matt engages Coach in a long discussion of the merits of forward-entry versus back-entry vaults, I think so that Coach doesn't notice that Emery isn't doing any other attempts. I spend my practice on trampoline, gradually bouncing higher and higher until I'm brave enough to flip.

I launch into the air, tucking my knees to my chest, close my eyes, and roll over myself like a tiny moon in orbit. Again and again.

It feels good to be upside down. Amazingly good, if I'm being honest. Up here, everything that's tethered to gravity—Cassie in the hospital, Marcos with that smile—feels far below. It's something I can conquer later. No quick burst of joy can extinguish the fear, however. If I lose focus, if I stop listening to the creaks of the brace, something can happen.

Coach pumps Matt and Emery's hands in farewell. He uses the word "great" at least twice per sentence. I'm staring at the banners when he says, "Keep in touch, Savannah. I want to hear about your progress. It was great meeting you!"

The entire right side of my body moves with the force of his handshake. With a wave and several more "great"s, he's gone.

"Jesus Christ," I say.

"I liked him." Emery pulls her bag onto her shoulder. "He was kind of endearing, like a weird uncle you only see at Thanksgiving."

Radio and lights off. The electrical hum goes silent. The only soundtrack to my first night back at the gym is the squishing of the mats under our sneakers.

Under the amber emergency lights that bathe the nearly empty parking lot, we wait for Matt to lock up. "I know they're not Division I," he's saying to Emery, "but if you want an in-state tuition option, you can't beat them."

Lucky Emery, courting her college suitors. Turning down the paupers at her leisure.

"Savannah."

I knew this moment was coming.

Matt folds his arms across his chest. "What gives? Not a peep from you, and now you're here and ready to go?"

Here, yes. Ready to go—up for debate.

I choose honesty. "I missed this," I admit. "Although I'll probably need to be pushed around in a wheelchair tomorrow."

"You know," Matt says as he pulls out his keys, "Barry has a reputation for taking the broken and restoring them to full glory."

Is this the part where the *Rocky* theme starts playing?

"He likes comeback stories. He's big on gymnasts who have gone through injuries." Matt pauses. "Also, your dad told him your GPA."

He would.

"Can I borrow a few points?" Emery grins.

Matt's still looking at me. "What are your plans?"

"I'm applying to schools in the city." I ignore the lump that manifests itself in my stomach. I'm supposed to be letting go, not feeling something as stupid as longing.

"So glamorous," Emery says. "I'll be visiting."

My coach is undeterred. "What happened to Ocean State?"

"Don't let that assistant coach with no sense of humor scare you off," Emery adds quickly. Kind of adorable for her to act like I'm still in this thing, when the last e-mail exchange I had with Ocean State was telling them the doctor's diagnosis. The rest, as Hamlet would say, was silence.

"Too bad, you know," Matt continues casually. "If you were considering it, I'd say that the Golden Leaf Classic would be an excellent goal. December 10. I know, right, it seems a little sudden."

"There's no—"

He holds up his hands, and I shut my mouth. I'm the delinquent who left the sport without a goodbye; the least I can do is hear out my coach, although I'm 99 percent certain that he's out of his mind. "One event. Your choice. Of course, only if you were really serious about it."

I imagine a girl standing on the beam in our gym's silver-and-blue competition leotard. Arms over her head with her chin lifted, exuding confidence. But she's not me. She's Emery. She's one of the twins, smiling at the judges and in love with the sport.

I don't try to deny his ploy. "That's so soon."

Matt shrugs. "Come every day. I'll let you in on Sundays during birthday parties if you want."

This is absurd. A wide-open invitation to break myself afresh.

I came here tonight to...I don't know. Say "how's it going?" Say goodbye. Get out of the house. Stop thinking about Cassie for a little while. Gather myself before committing to a Middle-earth immersion with Marcos. Whatever. I didn't sign on for this.

For the first time since my road test, jitters of excitement launch down my arms and legs. This is the kind of adrenaline that I used to thrive on. At the same time, the now-familiar sickness rolls in my stomach. No, no—

The rip in my knee. The waiting room. Every afternoon on the padded bench at South Shore

Physical Therapy, watching my bone-thin right leg struggle to lift a five-pound ankle weight. I'd sworn to myself that I would never find myself in physical therapy again. Not if I could help it.

"If you want to compete in college, now's the time to get going," Matt says.

"Ocean State's dead and gone," I mutter. My empty inbox is a testament to that.

"Ocean State wanted you as a specialist," he reminds me. "At a school like Owego, you could be doing all-around."

True; I had sent Coach Englehardt video updates of my skills on all four events. "We're going to have a hole in the floor lineup next season," he'd replied, "and I think you're the perfect candidate to fill it."

"Not bars," I say automatically.

Matt's getting to me. I didn't do much tonight—just the basics—yet everything I did felt controlled, well-executed, and capable of being kicked up a notch if I can get used to the feeling of that bulky brace knocking around.

"Are you in?" he says.

I wonder if he asked Monica, Jess, and Ally the same question. If one by one, they all said no.

I see that girl again on beam. The large knee brace forces her legs apart but she's still standing, waiting.

"Okay," I say. Immediately Emery's arms are around me and she's shouting into the night, Matt's grinning like he might actually tear up a little, and I'm torn between abject terror and a tiny voice, that Cassie voice, telling me to just go out there and do it.

CHAPTER FIFTEEN

"**A**RE YOU OKAY?" Dad asks at seven in the morning.

"Yes, why?"

"I didn't realize you owned clothing besides sweatshirts."

"It's too warm," I say. Incorrect. I'm freezing. My fitted purple top and dark blue jeans leave me defenseless against the wind, and my straightened hair blinds me on the journey to the car. At least I'm not wearing make-up. That would be a blatant signal: *Savannah is actually trying today!*

It has nothing to do with a potential tutoring session at lunch. Nope.

"How is Cassie?" Dad asks.

I wish I knew. "Hanging in there," I say.

I don't want to talk about Cassie because I don't know what to say. Unfortunately, I've been fielding that question every day. That is, when I'm not shuffling through synonyms for "fine" as I answer endless questions about how school is, how my classes are going, how I feel about dinner.

Part of me can't really blame my parents; in the actively-doing-gymnastics days, I wouldn't shut up about the details of practice and my emotions toward every skill in all of my routines. (On the tough days, there were plenty of emotions to go around.) After I quit, I didn't have much to say about other topics, no matter how hard they tried.

"How about you?" Dad continues. "Everything okay?"

"Yep."

After seeing that he won't get much more out of me, he switches tacks.

"How was the gym last night?" Dad asks while we wait for the light on Quail Creek. He and Mom were both in the kitchen when I walked in last night in all my chalky glory. I hadn't given them a real answer then– "It was fine," I'd mumbled through a peanut butter-and-banana sandwich–but I also didn't miss the look they'd exchanged. The one that said, *Told you so.*

There's a good chance that when he parks at school, I won't be able to stand. Simple motions like turning my head or lifting my hand to block the sun make everything ache. I have never felt a soreness so encompassing. "I'm not applying to Owego, thanks."

"Why not?" Dad taps the steering wheel in time to the staccato clicking of the signal. "A gymnastics team, an honors program, all the snow you could ever hope for."

"The part where you e-mailed the coach and told him about me? Not cool, Dad. Really not cool."

"It's called recruiting." Dad smoothly cuts off a white Jaguar. "Every NCAA team does it. Sometimes, they just need a little nudge."

"He won't stop emailing me." To be fair, the Owego Coach emailed me twice. Last night, it was an enthusiastic "GREAT TO MEET YOU" followed by asking which major interested me. I responded with the single word "Kinesiology." (All of those injuries should be good for something, right?) His second email contained links to the kinesiology department, exercise science, sports science, fitness development, research published by faculty members, and study abroad programs available for these programs. Doesn't the guy have a team to coach? "Who's even heard of Owego, anyway?"

"It'll be an excellent option for you. Three of their top beam workers graduate this year. You could be a replacement."

Are we ignoring the fact that I haven't done real gymnastics in months? "I'm moving to the city with Cassie. Final answer."

The car turns so sharply into the school parking lot that my head knocks against the window. "Do whatever you want." The tone of voice for math class delinquents. "Give up gymnastics. Stop trying for your license. Get drunk at beach parties with Cassie." He sees my face. "You think I don't have students trying to get on my good side by telling on you?"

"It was only one party!"

"Don't pretend like you didn't fail your math placement test last June on purpose."

Move over, Owego Coach. My father's the one stalking my life.

"Mr. McMahon said he couldn't believe that a girl as bright as you could do so poorly. 'It's a shame. She'll have to take precalc instead of AP,' he said."

"I was upset about my knee. I couldn't focus."

"You didn't want to be in my AP class. You didn't want me as your teacher."

Can you blame me?

"What kind of girl are you?"

"You think I don't hear about you?" I shoot back. "Do you know how many dirty looks I get after you give a test? Do you know how many people won't talk to me because of you?"

That hits a mark. Dad pulls into a parking spot. My fingers wrap around the door handle, waiting for him to unlock it. Finally he says, "You know, I was going to let you start driving to school."

Great. The *I was going to* speech. Soon to be followed with *unfortunately, your behavior has shown that...*

"Unfortunately, your behavior has shown that you're not mature enough." The driver's-side door opens. "Enjoy your day."

....

I LEAN AGAINST the Dashing the Dolphin statue and call Cassie three times, feeling desperate when she doesn't answer. She's been out of school for four days and that's four days too long. I have to vent to somebody about my father's ridiculousness. I have to know what she thinks about me returning to the gym and agreeing to compete again. I'm actually looking forward to the teasing when she finds out that I kissed Marcos. Hopefully it'll make her laugh.

She's in therapy, she's sleeping, she's watching silly reality shows. I recite the litany of possibilities, make them into a mantra as I enter the building and pass the display case, where Cassie's photographs hang periodically. Today they're dedicated to a freshman art exhibit on Ponquogue Pride.

Service sucks, Cass texts during AP Lit. *Food is worse. Therapy's not so bad. How's school without me?*

Marcos. Gymnastics. Mr. Raia turns toward me, so I keep it quick. *Eventful,* I write back. *Papa Gregory's on the warpath.*

When isn't he? Cass replies with a smiley face. *I'll be out of here in a couple of days. I'll spice up that stupid place.*

A couple of days feels like a lifetime.

When the bell rings at the start of sixth period, I shoot Marcos a text: *On a mission. Might be late.* If there's a trail of bread crumbs I've missed that led to Cassie driving down to the bridge early that morning, then Juliana knows the way.

If she doesn't bite off my head first.

"What?" she says when I call her name by the library entrance, then whirls around to see me. Her face is tight, nostrils flared, firing on all cylinders. "Oh. Hi."

Don't step away. Don't back down. My dad's pissed about my feelings toward Owego, Emery's been too removed from the loop of my life, and my mom means well, but I don't want to add to her burden of worry. If anyone understands, it's Juliana. "Do you have a second?"

She checks her phone. "I gotta see if the doctor calls back about the twins, but okay." Younger brothers, I think.

No time for bullshit. This won't be easy, especially if she knows more than I do. "Did you have any clue that Cassie was thinking about killing herself?"

It comes out wrong—too harsh, almost accusing—and Juliana straightens up immediately. "You think I knew and did nothing?"

"Between the two of us, we could have figured it out."

"I told her that taking herself off the pills was a crap idea." The second she says it, she looks around to see if anyone's overheard. "You're not supposed to play around with those."

I blink once. Twice. Did I hear her correctly? "What pills?"

"Antidepressants. I saw her staring at them when we were on break over the summer," Juliana says. "She wanted to flush them down the toilet."

It feels like I've just slammed my ribs against the beam. I didn't know about any of this. The depression. The medication.

"I told her that shit was too expensive to waste and that she had better take it the way the doctor said to."

Tough love. That's what Juliana is to Cassie. I can see that for the first time. The girl made of steel who won't be moved by Cassie's whims.

I'm supposed to be the one she knows the best, the one that she spends silences and loud moments with and everything in between. How the hell didn't I know this? Why did she feel like she couldn't tell me?

"She talked about her parents." Juliana looks down briefly, the hint of a crack. Then she's staring back at me, daring me to ask more. "She felt pressured. Like she didn't belong here."

I knew that, yet I'd chalked it up to extreme senioritis, to conversations with her parents that would cease once she graduated and moved to the city.

"You should have told me," I say. "I could have convinced her."

Anger sparks in my chest. If I'd known the whole story, I could have stepped in sooner. When did Cassie begin to parse off her secrets?

Juliana tugs her hair back in a ponytail, quick and irritated. When she looks at me, though, it's with confusion. "I thought you already knew."

CHAPTER SIXTEEN

WHEN I FIND Marcos at the end of the day, I say to him, "Math or Middle-earth?"

His eyebrows scrunch up like this is a true debate. God, I could kiss him right now if I wasn't stuck on being the worst best friend known to mankind. "I want Middle-earth," he concedes, "although I know I should do math."

"Great. We're going to your house." He hustles to catch up with me. "Just make sure I'm back by four so I can get to the gym."

Judging by the growl of the engine, Marcos's car hails from the 1980s. I sink into the gray passenger seat, which feels like it may drop to the pavement at any time. The vehicle, however, is impeccably clean, besides empty boxes of cereal stacked in the backseat. It smells like it's been vacuumed so many times that the vacuum gave up and burned the fabric.

I'm still processing what Juliana said. I've spent enough time alone in my room trying to work through the riddles leading up to Cassie's suicide attempt. Marcos, the one who pulled her from the water, might have some insight of his own.

As we idle at the school's stoplight, I sense it before I see it—a window rolling down in the car next to us.

"Looks like we have spectators," Marcos says dryly, his finger tapping out an erratic rhythm against the wheel.

I turn to see Tommy Brown's freckled face a foot away from our window. His mouth moves but the bass from his car thumps too loudly for me to make out anything. In the passenger seat, Max Pfeiffer leans over for a closer look. The sunlight gleams against their sunglasses.

This is breaking news, I guess. Savannah Gregory riding in cars with boys.

I offer them a thumbs-up and Max disappears from view, but Tommy's sunglasses stay focused on me until the light turns green.

"Assholes," Marcos mutters under his breath. "Sorry about that. Tommy and Andreas had some words."

"Andreas seems to have a lot of words with people, huh?"

He offers a half smile, one dimple creasing. "That's a good way of putting it. They were pretty much neck and neck for first string. Andreas beat him out before the Galway game and Tommy hasn't let him hear the end of it." Then he glances at me, his smile relaxing. "Sorry, that's right; you think soccer is boring."

"'Boring' is a strong word," I say. "I enjoyed eating cookie dough bites with Cassie at my brother's games, does that count?"

He checks the rearview mirror. "How's she doing?"

"Better," I tell him. "Thanks to you."

"Good, I'm glad to hear it." He clears his throat and shifts in his seat.

The car rumbles through Ponquogue's main drag, a collection of boutiques with Thanksgiving cornucopias and pilgrim decorations in the windows.

First Pav's Place, the purple and orange walls whizzing by, followed by Wok and Roll Chinese food, always with the door hanging open even on cold days. The *Ocean Beaches* sign remains crooked and warped.

From here I'd turn right at the fork by 7-Eleven to go home. Marcos signals left at Main Street's one traffic light. Pine Needle Street.

The shops peter out, giving way to buildings with *For Rent* signs. The shack on the corner looks ready to collapse and give up on life for good. *Bienvenidos al Pueblo*, it might as well say.

"You wouldn't be able to handle it," Cassie had said.

Marcos's fingers take up their tapping again.

The sidewalk cracks until it's hidden by high grass. These houses were summer beach bungalows once. When people rich enough to buy mansions up on the hill left them behind, their exterior paint cracked, bleached by sunlight for too many years. Gone are the small grassy yards with swing sets and trampolines from the Ponquogue I know. Freshly painted porches, sturdy plastic mailboxes, the sound of a lawnmower and the hiss of a sprinkler—my normal.

From one of the windows, thick drumbeats flow out. Salsa music, maybe? I don't know. Then the *click-click-click* of bicycle chains, not smooth and oiled like my father's trail bike, but worn and choppy, skipping beats and catching others. Three kids with spiky black hair circle in and out of the road in figure eights. They don't react to the car until the last instant, swerving out of the way.

We pull onto a gravel driveway that slithers between two sagging chain link fences. To the left: a small white bungalow, chipped paint, shades pulled low. To the right: a small white bungalow, chipped paint, upside-down wheelbarrow in the yard.

"Here we are." Marcos shuts off the engine and the car exhales. He wipes his hands down the front of his jeans and attempts a smile.

I'm already halfway out of the car.

You wouldn't be able to handle it.

There's nothing to handle. I'm standing here while people all around are living their lives. I'm trying to figure out my own.

"Do you have snacks?" A dog barks from down the street, followed by the sound of a chain yanking against a fence.

"Excuse me?"

"Small morsels of food, preferably eaten between meals?"

Now his smile is real. "Since you asked so nicely, yes."

We step through a gaping hole in the fence toward the house on the left. He opens the screen door, stained with rust, and beckons for me to go first.

The walls are yellowed and the floors tired, curving under my sneakers. The kitchen and den blend into one, hosting a sturdy couch and a small TV. No photographs, knick-knacks, useless contraptions anywhere. Not like our house, dedicated to photos of Richard in uniforms: Ponquogue soccer, Notre Dame soccer, and US Army. I'd hidden all of my gymnastics pictures, leaving only a series of school portraits. Boring and safe.

A man in the kitchen looks up. He has Marcos's eyes and arms twice the size of my head.

"You must be Victor." I extend my hand. "I'm Savannah."

Victor sizes me up. He does not seem impressed. Suspicious, a little confused—yeah, I'd give him both of those. Has he heard anything about me? Well, I'm here now and I'm not going anywhere until Marcos says so.

"My charming brother doesn't function well before four o'clock," Marcos says.

That earns a smirk from Victor. He wipes his hand slowly on his jeans and then extends it. "What brings you to our neighborhood?"

"Helping your brother get a scholarship."

Our hands meet, his shake firm. "Good luck." While Victor's voice isn't exactly friendly, it's not sending me out the door. He's evaluating me with eyes like his brother's, except flecked with amber. "He needs all the help he can get."

"What would you like?" Marcos opens the refrigerator, causing Victor to fall into the counter. "We have cheese, bread, ketchup–"

"Cheese is expired." Victor propels himself onto the ledge.

"I had it for lunch. It was fine."

"I'm not driving you to the hospital for food poisoning," Victor says.

Marcos takes a deep breath. I bite back a smile as he fights to keep his composure. "Okay. Revised. We have bread and ketchup–"

Victor opens up a cabinet and hurls a bag of potato chips at me. I catch it with one hand. "They might be expired, too. Great date, *pendejo*. Way to plan ahead."

Marcos's face matches his red shirt quite magnificently.

"It's cool," I say. "I love ranch-flavored barbeque chips."

Victor's eyes widen with surprise. "No way. Have you ever tried–"

"Bye, Vic." Marcos nudges me toward a doorway.

His bedroom. My heart thumps as we sit down on the pale-blue bed. It's pressed against three walls, with one slim window overlooking it.

I take a breath. It smells like fresh laundry, and the cottony scent immediately calms the sudden onslaught of nerves. "Behave yourselves in there, children," Victor calls.

"God, Victor!" Marcos shuts the door in exasperation. "You are not allowed to speak anymore."

Through the wall behind us, an alarm goes off. It's loud enough to feel like it's in his room, urgent and angry. I jump.

"The neighbors." Marcos nods to the wall. "In the next apartment."

So this tiny place is split down the middle. "Where does Victor, you know, sleep? Do you share this room?" Meanwhile, Marcos is lucky he isn't any taller, because his feet would probably hang out the door when he lies down.

"Victor has slept on the couch for the past six months," Marcos says. "He thinks it will toughen him up for the military life."

"Correction. I *am* tough," calls Victor. The screen door wheezes open and closed. No privacy whatsoever.

"You know, my brother's an officer in the army," I say.

"The soccer player and *Lord of the Rings* fan?" Marcos picks crumbs off of the bed. Larger ones first, then infinitesimal ones. If he ever encountered my leotard drawer in its heyday, he'd be dabbing at chalk particles for days. "That's what Vic wants to do when he graduates from college. *If* he graduates. He's not one for going to class."

He pulls out a textbook and then turns to me. His gaze is piercing, commanding. "Can I be honest with you, Savannah Gregory?"

Everything feels magnified in this pale-blue room. Sound. My heart rate. The way his dark eyes probe mine for an answer, although I don't know what he wants to be honest about or why.

"Yes?" I squeak.

"I don't waste my time."

I ball my sweating palms into fists. "Uh-huh."

"I'm not like the assholes you read about in the papers getting DWIs and stealing shit. I'm no Roberto selling weed in the bathroom, although I have to admit that his business skills are impressive." Where is he going with this? I nod anyway. "I'm going to get this scholarship, and I feel like you're the best person to help me."

My PSAT success came from a fire that has since been reduced to embers. It was all for Ocean State Buccaneers gymnastics, not because of my love for academics and the pursuit of standardized testing.

"You work hard," he's saying now. "You know what it's like to focus on a goal."

I do, except that the things I once wanted wound up as fleeting as the early morning fog that rolls in off the ocean.

"Also." He shifts so that we're touching, his arm wrapping around my back, and now every part of me is warm. "Cassie is lucky to have you as a friend."

Yeah, right. But when I lean my head on his shoulder, I start to relax for the first time since Mr. Riley's assembly. "How about that math?" I say into his collarbone.

Outside, the dog keeps barking. Car doors slam shut, engines rumble up and down the block, and once in a while, someone laughs. No police sirens or the sounds of, I don't know, fists connecting with bones. The looks from Victor and Tommy Brown feel like they happened months ago. Whatever the hell Cassie was trying to imply about what I could handle, I'm not seeing it. The place is alive, that's all.

Marcos reaches up with the other hand to scratch the back of his neck. "I've learned all of this before, but I can't stay awake in class."

"Why's that?"

"Work." I feel the word against his throat. "Too much damn work. Gotta pay the bills."

It occurs to me that a senior Castillo might walk in and ask what the hell I'm doing in here with his youngest son. "Where are your parents, by the way?"

His shoulder tenses. It's like asking about soccer. It's something that he'd rather not share. I'm about to tell him it doesn't matter when he surprises me by answering. "My parents don't live here." Absentmindedly, he begins rubbing my side. "They're in Mexico."

I wasn't expecting that. At *work*, sure. *Permanently in Mexico*, no. I try to fight back the waves of warmth so I can focus on asking coherent questions. "It's just you, Victor, and expired cheese?"

"Pretty much."

"Do you visit them?"

He shifts, uncomfortable. Looks like Marcos is better at being the interrogator than the interrogated. "Too expensive. Hopefully after I graduate."

The dog finishes barking. The television through the walls shuts off.

I cough.

He clears his throat.

I cough again, willing Marcos to speak. For once, the boy doesn't have any questions. *You first, buddy.* He's not budging. He's waiting for me to make a move. One of his eyebrows quirks up as if he's inviting me to change the subject, or make out with him, or... anything besides sit here.

I could do that, I guess. Toss aside the textbook and the still-neglected bag of chips and...what? Pin him to the bed? Apparently I'm okay with kissing Marcos in front of the eight hundred or so students of Ponquogue High School, but not in this small room where we are clearly alone, all angles accounted for.

This goes on for five minutes. Okay, ten seconds. "Practice is going to kick my ass later," I announce without any noticeable trigger.

"Yeah?" He sits up a little straighter.

"We have a competition soon that will be a spectacular failure." To put it mildly.

"Impossible. I can see it now." He nudges me playfully with his shoulder, a motion which makes the bed creak and my heart flip. "Lights, cameras, Savannah Gregory on the still rings."

I glare at him. "You didn't say still rings."

"I may have."

"Boy, do you know anything about women's gymnastics?"

There's no tension in his shoulders, no tapping of his fingers, just a mischievous look in his eyes. "Enlighten me."

So I do.

Marcos doesn't stop me as I discuss the different levels, explaining that while being a Level 10 is solid, ahead of most gymnasts, it's not the same as elite, the Olympic-level gymnasts.

He shakes his head when I finish my spiel. "As far as I'm concerned, any kind of flip is death-defying."

I demonstrate a few jumps in the space between the bed and the wall, ignoring the way my muscles groan. Besides last night, this is the most I've jumped since physical therapy. The thin strip of wooden floor vibrates beneath me. Close enough to a balance beam. "If you do them in combination, you get bonus points," I tell him as I transition from a split jump to a tuck jump three-quarters. *Stuck it.* "But if you wobble in between, forget it."

He stands next to me, tugging up his jeans preemptively and shaking out his arms. "All right, all right." He pauses from his silly warm-up, exhales, cracks his neck once. "How do you do the goat jump?"

"Wolf jump," I correct him with a grin. He's so eager, so genuinely ready to try despite the fact that his neighbors are probably wondering what the hell the stampede is all about. "No goats allowed." I do it again, jumping into the air with my legs up to hip level. One leg straight, the other bent.

Although we're in his tiny bedroom on a warm fall afternoon and none of what I'm doing is for a coach or a judge, I can't fight the confidence that fills me each time I explain something, demonstrate something else, and he watches with approval.

He takes a dramatic moment to gather himself and then jumps with surprising agility. I applaud. "You've officially qualified for the Olympic Trials. Just gotta work on pointing those toes."

A neighbor bangs against the wall. "Knock it off," a voice calls.

"Say I'm a seventeen-year-old gymnast with wolf jumps and Olympic dreams," says Marcos, undeterred by his irritated neighbor. His hands rest on his hips like we're taking a brief water break before the next segment of practice. "Who do I have to talk to in order to make the team?"

"If only it were as easy as showing up and talking to someone." I'm off and running again, Marcos following along like we're on a grand adventure.

I never knew I had this much to say to anyone until he asked. I'm used to everything being implicit, to Cassie already knowing what I'm thinking after I've spoken half a sentence. To my teammates, who could watch my routine and know by my facial expressions whether I was pleased or disappointed.

"Why did we never talk before Senior Cut Day?" I'm a little winded. By this point, the textbook's on the floor, completely abandoned. I knocked it down when an attempted press handstand went awry. (Bet the neighbors loved that one.)

He scratches the back of his head, making his shirt ride up. *Focus, Savannah.* "I guess we run in different circles."

My former circle: gymnastics, Cassie, and more gymnastics. "Cass is friends with Juliana," I remind him. "This should have happened sooner."

His eyes crinkle. "Yeah? What's this?"

"This, uh..." I'm good at explaining cotangents. Hand me an on-the-spot emotional moment, though, and I'm reduced to waving my hands around, my cheeks heating up the longer I stumble for the words. *Tutoring*—except we've done none of that today. *Prelude to making out again*—perhaps, if we weren't so busy pissing off the neighbors with our frolicking. "This training session," I finish, and that's enough to make him chuckle. Time for a change of topic. "What are you going to do with your scholarship?"

"It'll cover two years at Suffolk. I want to be an environmental engineer, but my math grades are pathetic. Get the GPA up, hopefully get a scholarship somewhere else. Are you training for college gymnastics? Are coaches beating down your door?"

"Not so much." I know I should be excited about Coach Barry's e-mails. Flattered. The truth is, though, in November of my senior year with months off from the sport, I'm a recruiting spinster. Leftovers. Coach Barry's probably looking for someone to ride the bench in case someone's injured.

Owego State, however, is irrelevant. I'm going to do the Golden Leaf Classic and officially say farewell to gymnastics without a catastrophic fall as my last competition memory. That's it. "I want to study kinesiology, possibly physical therapy school after." His eyes have that *go on* look and once again, I can't resist. "I'd love to work for a sports team and help athletes with recovery."

"See," he says like I've made a point, which I'm pretty sure I have not, "you want to put things back together. I want to create from scratch."

"Sure, something like that."

He leans over, forcing the bed to sink, and pulls a lime-green Pav's Place T-shirt from his drawer. The thing's bright enough to stop traffic at midnight. "Juliana and I work at Pav's twenty-five hours a week. She wants to work to survive, help out her mom, and that's fine," he says. "It's not right for me. I have to feel like what I do will have more meaning."

"Yes!" I bounce in place, causing Marcos to windmill his arms for balance. Oops.

....

"SORRY I TOOK up your afternoon with my life story," I say when he pulls up in front of my house.

"We should do it again sometime," he says, not sarcastically, and leans forward just as I lean around for, I don't know, a hug or a high-five or something that inexplicably involves my left hand leaping in front of me. Which leads to the sides of our faces colliding, like those fake kisses on the cheek you give to your relatives where lips don't touch skin. All in all, quite sensuous.

"Hmm," he says.

"I'll talk to you later." I stumble out of the car. *Gracefully done, gymnast.*

CHAPTER SEVENTEEN

"ON A SCALE of one to ten, how pumped are you for today?" Emery says as we pull into South Ocean's lot.

"Eh, a solid two," I say. "Three points for seeing you, three points for the twins, and minus four points for the ache in my back." By "back," I mean "everywhere."

"Excellent." She offers me a whack on the shoulder, which helps nothing, and tosses me a protein bar. "See you out there, champ."

"She's back! She's back!" Tiana leaps into my arms as soon as we enter the gym. She can't weigh more than forty pounds, and it's definitely all muscle.

"Told you I would be," I groan.

"Tee! Look at my new socks!" another tiny Level 3 calls, and Tiana jumps off me and goes running.

"Thank God you're here," Emery says. "It's tough being their one-woman jungle gym."

As the Level 3s sprint into the gym and cartwheel onto the floor exercise ("Girls!" Vanessa shouts, and that's enough to make them fall into an obedient line and start jogging), I think about the kids riding their bikes in and out of Pine Needle Street. My limited time in El Pueblo is enough for me to know that it's not the kind of place where parents have the money for their kids to do competitive gymnastics. Don't get me wrong; if I get into NYU, my dad sure isn't writing me a check and saying, "Have fun, sweetheart." However, the hundreds of dollars a month toward training–gym tuition, competition entry fees, coaching fees for said competitions–isn't petty change.

My parents are never going to get that investment back with a full ride, either. Not like they've said anything–sure, Dad tried to run analytics on my YouTube channel to see if he could tell which schools had viewed my routines ("You're getting hits from Alabama–Roll Tide!")–but neither he nor Mom made me feel that if I didn't get a scholarship, I'd be a black sheep.

God, I ache. Everywhere. If I say I have to go to the bathroom, I can hide out until this soreness passes.

"Savannah and Emery, you're leading stretches," Vanessa calls.

Great.

. . . .

DURING OUR WATER break, while Erica and Nicola argue over who took whose ankle brace ("You guys are the same size!" Emery intervenes, but to no avail), I surreptitiously pull out my cell phone.

NEWS! Cassie writes, and the subsequent texts appear like a news ticker across a TV. *Coming home tomorrow + no school just yet = life is better.*

"Oh, my God," I say.

"Savannah agrees, and she's nicer than me," Emery says to the twins. "You guys need to get a grip."

Nicola glares. "Gymnastics puns aren't going to fix this."

When can I come over? I text Cassie, then perch the phone on the edge of my bag as I drink my entire water bottle in one gulp. My heart's pounding faster than it did during the tiny bits of tumbling earlier. She's okay enough to be sent home. Halfway to recovery. There's so much to catch up on, like how she spent her days in the hospital and what her life will be like now. How I've not only stepped back in the gym but agreed to compete again, and that there's one college coach who hasn't forgotten my name.

"Savannah, come here," Matt calls from where he's keeping one eye on the Level 3s. They're taking turns flipping into the foam pit, which means they're one second away from landing on each other.

He saw me texting. Busted. Last year, he took Jess's cell phone (she who quit gymnastics for her unattractive boyfriend) and tossed it into the dredges of the pit. Lesson learned.

I stand next to him contritely.

"I wanted to make sure that we're on the same page," he begins, cringing as one of the girls dives headfirst into the pit. "Lexi, this isn't a swimming pool. Anyway, I don't want you to feel pressured. If you don't want to compete, that's fine. You're a senior; I'm sure you have plenty of stress already, and this can just be a fun place for you."

It'd be easier that way. I could tumble into the foam just like the little ones, leap on balance beam, and swing on bars without judgment. No chance of having another very public disaster. Ease my way out of gymnastics, since cold turkey hasn't gone so well.

Yet there's so much that I've missed. The "I'm going to pee myself" feeling of waiting for the judges to raise their hands so I can begin, the feeling of drilling a vault landing into the mat and hearing the crowd applaud, even wiping out in warm-ups and knowing that it doesn't count, that I'm still in this. To me, that was the fun.

I'm afraid of breaking myself again, absolutely. But I've never feared competition.

"I don't want Regionals to be my last meet," I say.

"Neither do I."

My teammates do deer runs down the vault runway—front leg bent, back leg straight. Erica plows into Nicola and they start laughing, the ankle brace situation forgotten.

"The thing is, if it seemed like you were genuinely done with gymnastics, that's fine," Matt continues. "Plenty of athletes don't make it to their senior year. They get injured, they move on, whatever." Like the rest of my teammates—new gyms, new boyfriends, new lives. "You? I'm not buying it."

He's right. Standing here is giving me the old antsy feeling, just like Baby Savannah jumping up and down on the springboard, waiting for her turn to mount bars. I want to follow the girls on the runway, then find my measured spot (72 feet, five inches) so I can vault next.

There's still something to address, though, and as the Level 3s scamper away for water, I take my chance. "About paying for practice and meets."

Matt's already grinning—*meets*, plural—but I bypass it. Freudian slip. "I was wondering if I could work here and count it toward my tuition."

"Mom and Dad cutting you off?"

My parents know I'm practicing. Competing again—that's a whole other beast. More money down the drain if I get hurt again. At least this time, it'll be mine. Couple that with the fact that if I'm footing the bill, Dad can't hold whether or not I return over me. I might not have a car (or hell, a license), but this is the tiniest sliver of independence that I can claim.

You work hard, Marcos told me. It's time to do so now, even if walking is a little too uncomfortable for my liking.

What's worse: being in pain for something that I love, or being sore from standing for hours on end at Pav's Place, whipping up burrito after burrito?

"Not exactly," I say now. "I just...I feel like I need to do this on my own."

"Well, consider yourself hired." He nudges me toward the runway. "Friday, 3:30. Four- and five-year-olds. Be ready to get sneezed on."

. . . .

"HOW WAS PRACTICE?" Mom asks in her I'm-trying-not-to-sound-excited-but-I'm-really-excited voice, picking up the leftover newspapers on the coffee table. She knows I'm skittish.

I'm sprawled on the couch, head sinking into the pillows and bag of ice secured to my knee. It's been a while—the initial contact of cold plastic against my skin makes me grit my teeth and hold my breath. A few minutes later, I can fully exhale. "Not too bad."

I catch the most recent headline: *FBI Rules that County Agency Mishandled Investigation in Immigrant Death.* No mention of activity overseas, though, so I suppose that's something.

My phone pings and I sit up so quickly that the ice slides down to my ankle, leaving a chilly trail in its wake. Most likely it's Cassie, and I hope it's all still good news.

My wolf jumps have surpassed my memory for trigonometric functions. Math for real tomorrow at lunch?

I fall back against the pillows with a smile. My mother goes to the computer, humming under her breath as she clicks around. The steady tapping on the keyboard, not rushed, means that all is well. Richard must have e-mailed her.

The stairs creak as my father maneuvers his way downstairs. School concluded hours ago, but he's still wearing pressed khakis. He takes in the ice on my knee, the phone in my hand, and perhaps the red shade of my ears.

Then he utters two words. "Marcos Castillo."

Mom's hands are still on the keyboard. If she was excited about me returning to gymnastics, then the mere insinuation that I might have a boyfriend will thrill her for days.

How much does my father know? Did Max Pfeiffer, a student in AP Calc, make a comment to him? Goddamn Dad's excellent poker face. He settles in across from me on the ottoman, stands back up, and then sits down again. Good. Someone else feels awkward here.

Mom breaks the silence first. "Who's Marcos?" She's trying not to sound eager. "Do you have a prom date you didn't tell us about?"

Prom's only a million months away.

"I'm tutoring him for math," I say evenly.

"Is that right?" Dad's already smirking. He knows. I'm screwed.

"All I know about the boy," he continues, "is that he's in Paul Andreotti's class." Right. Trigonometry. "I believe he's retaking the course."

In my father's eyes, retaking a course is positively criminal.

"He works a lot," I reply. "At Pav's Place. He's there twenty-five hours a week. So maybe math isn't on his priority list."

The smirk slips. "Hmm. That's proactive; I'll give him that."

"Also"—why am I defending Marcos? We've shared one (pretty excellent) kiss. It's not like we're life partners— "his brother wants to join the military." The perfect response that causes Dad to shake his head and Mom to say, "Wow, how about that?" No doubt it'll cause them to murmur tonight in low voices, not quite arguing but neither conceding, hoping I confuse the sound with the distant waves.

"It sounds like you know him pretty well." Of course my father manages to make an innocuous statement sound ominous. "Just..." His eyes shift left and then right. Oh, this is not good. Something super uncomfortable is about to be unleashed, like when he walked into my physics class last April to tell me my MRI results.

A cough, one ink-stained fist to his chest. "I know how kids these days think they know all about each other because of social media. Please don't make bad decisions."

So he heard about El Pueblo, too? Well, I've obviously lived to tell the tale. "Like what, Dad? Please elaborate." If the man thinks he can smirk, then as version 2.0, I've perfected it.

For perhaps the first and only time in history, my dad's cheeks flush. That doesn't stop his eyes from latching onto mine with the steely resolve he reserves for kids that he's about to send to Mr. Riley's office. "Surely you remember health class?"

Oh, shit.

That's what this is about.

My dry lips part and then close because what the hell do you say to that?

"Rich, I think you're tired," Mom interrupts. Bless her. Bless her so much. "You've graded too many exams today."

Dad rises from the ottoman, ankles cracking the way mine do. "Be careful," he says like it's a mandate, his eyes carefully skirting away from me.

When I make it up to my room on creaking legs, I call Cassie. There's no way I can miss hearing her reaction to this.

Hey, mates, you've reached Cass's phone. Her recorded voice giggles. We were in her room when she recorded the message, experimenting with fake British accents. It was during our British-boy-bands-are-way-better-than-American-ones phase. *Looks like I've got something better to do. Leave a message.*

I call again. *Hey, mates–*

Four calls later, I bury the phone in a mound of pillows.

She's asleep, she has poor service, she needs her rest so she can come home tomorrow; I know all of this, yet as soon as I turn off the lights, I can't shut my eyes.

What if she changed her mind tonight?

She seemed happy enough, at least through her typed words, but if I've learned anything, it's that I can't read Cassie the way I thought.

I watch each digit on my clock glow. 1:01. 1:02.

It's the way we wait for Richard when a week passes without a word. Mom tries to examine every possible angle, printing out maps and smoothing them on the coffee table to mark what she's inferred from news stories, while Dad and I have always retreated. A need-to-know policy only.

Otherwise, there's too much awful possibility in every moment of silence.

CHAPTER EIGHTEEN

"**D**O YOU WANT to come with me?"

"Do I want to what?" Juliana's still pissed from the last time we talked. That much is evident by the way she yanks thick strips of hair into a single braid. I wince at each tug.

"To Cassie's. After school."

She continues to braid with less force. "One of the guys owes me for covering his ass last week." I suppose that's her way of saying yes.

That's how Juliana, Marcos, and I wind up taking a field trip.

"If Andreas cries to me one more time about the season ending too soon, he's gonna get a punch to the nose," Juliana calls over the rumble of the engine. She'd slid into the backseat as I wavered by the passenger-side door, uncertain about the politics of car seating arrangements with your (possible) boyfriend and his (definite) ex-girlfriend.

When Marcos doesn't respond, she turns to me. "How's your friend from the bonfire?"

"Emery?"

"Yeah, Galway Beach girl. She was funny."

It figures that Juliana has known Emery for point-five seconds and already likes her better than she likes me.

"Ugh," says Marcos. "Don't bring up Galway Beach in my car."

"What's your problem?" She leans between our two seats. Marcos's sharp avoidance of the Main Street pothole isn't enough to shake her.

Marcos's eyebrows are pinched together. His thumb taps rapidly against the wheel. "Did you forget Nelson's?"

"What about Nelson's?" Juliana says.

Nelson's. The summer party Cassie had gone to, the one that made her warn me away from Marcos.

"What those idiots were saying?"

Juliana's lips twist in contemplation.

"That guy?" Marcos tries again.

"Oh." The two words make her cringe. "Yeah."

"Then Cassie up and—" He stops short at that. "Sorry. Going too far."

I know that Marcos punched a guy. I know that Cassie was shocked while Marcos viewed it as defending his best friend. Cassie having any kind of hand in this—now that's new.

Juliana manages to slide up further so that her face is even with my shoulder. She looks at me, then seems to remember that I wasn't there that night. Frankly, I'm starting to feel glad that Cassie didn't invite me, either. "What Marcos is trying to say is that he was *shocked* when Cassie peaced out because our hero here decided to start an MMA career on the spot."

Marcos exhales a short, quick breath. "Didn't she drive you there?"

Juliana shrugs. "So?"

"Then she up and left."

"I walked home. It wasn't that big of a deal."

"I sure as hell wouldn't leave my friend behind."

Leaving in the thick of things—that doesn't sound like Cassie. She loves the excitement, the voices that pick up momentum and collide.

Juliana rolls her eyes. "You do a lot of things that nobody else would."

The car jerks to a halt. Both Juliana and I buck forward. The seatbelts catch and squeak.

Tension ripples off of Marcos. He doesn't remove his eyes from the rearview mirror as he says, "I did it because Andreas was in over his head, and I wasn't going to wait until someone called the cops."

"It wasn't that bad." Nothing about Juliana wavers. Not her stance, not her tone, and definitely not her scowl. "Nobody was gonna call the cops."

"That's because the cops don't care." He balls his fist against the wheel. "You know that."

Do they remember I'm still here?

"I got more important things to worry about," Juliana shoots back. "Believe it or not, some of us forget when a jackass runs his mouth."

Marcos hits the gas and the car rumbles forward. "Well, good for you. I don't."

A stormy silence settles over the car.

Thus, with all the happiness and good vibes that, say, a funnel cloud would bring, we pull up to Cassie's house.

Her pale face presses against the window. In the next instant, she runs outside in bare feet. It's a flash of the girl who would grab my hand as we sprinted over the sand on summer days, hair flying free behind her. My heart leaps at the manifestation of the mantra I told myself last night. *She's okay.*

"Where are your shoes?" Juliana scolds as Cassie leaps into her arms. Then it's my turn, Cass nearly crushing my face against her shoulder. I inhale the lavender and cinnamon, the steady scent that hasn't been changed by hospital beds and ice cold water. The wind whistles over us, and I hold her tighter. Then she's gone, out of my reach, tucking hair behind her ears only for it to loosen again in the wind.

When she approaches Marcos, they're both subdued until Cass says, "Thank you, Marcos," and squeezes him so tightly that he takes a surprised step backward. "Shit, it's cold," she says, releasing him. "Get inside, kids. My mom has leek-and-tofu soup just for you."

Juliana catches my eye. *What the heck?*

Welcome to the Hopeswell house.

We settle around the kitchen table, Marcos and I on one side with Juliana and Cass facing us. I automatically reach for a bamboo napkin holder and roll it to Cassie. "How's everything going?" I say. Juliana sniffs the air, grimacing like she's about to choke. Incense burns thick in here, and with the bubbling and hissing of water boiling on the stove, it's like inadvertently entering a witch's lair.

Cass pushes the napkin holder back to me. "Tiring. It's not easy wowing your doctor, resident, social worker, nurse practitioner, and nurse every day."

"Whoa," says Marcos under his breath. Her words, though, make me feel hopeful. If five medical professionals approved Cassie's release, then she has to be improving.

"They said I'll need to be home for the next week or so. Once they all agree that I seem stable enough, I can go back to school." She smiles faintly. "I'm sure that my academic output is missed terribly."

"Hell, yeah, it is," says Juliana, missing the reference. Cassie's eyes meet mine. Sarcasm without any despair. She seems steady. I relax a little more.

"Of course," she continues, "Mom thinks burning a shit ton of incense will be just as helpful. I smell like the love child of frankincense and myrrh."

I roll the napkin holder back to her. Juliana's eyes track it. *Just between us, Juliana.*

"Why the incense?" Marcos shifts his weight and the chair creaks. Like Juliana, it's evident that the smell's getting to him, too.

I open my mouth to answer. Juliana beats me to it. "Her mom ran a pharmaceutical company and thinks all the drugs are bullshit."

"It smells good." I fight the burning in my throat from the overload of smoking spice. "Uh, soothing."

Cassie rolls her eyes. "Shut up, Savs, you don't need to lie to me. Never helped before, did it?"

She's smiling; the bamboo circle's already on its way back to me. So why do I let the napkin holder wobble and tip over without making a move to catch it and push it back?

When she turns to Juliana to ask what she's missed in photography class, I'm left staring at that circle, decorative and just as useless as I feel.

A strong arm loops around my back and gives me a little squeeze. He noticed, too.

I expect him to pull away. I'm not used to being held by anyone besides Cassie, functioning as her anchor. Marcos stays put, however. His fingertips gently rub the place just below my ribs and send undulations of warmth rolling through my bloodstream.

Cassie's eyes are ice-blue fire.

"When did this happen?" She pushes back her chair to circle around us like we've got something hidden on our persons.

Unfazed, Marcos keeps his arm in place. Hopefully he doesn't feel me sweating from the way Juliana crosses her arms and glances between us. Of course she knows (heck, Richard Gregory, Sr., knows), but the way she's scrutinizing me—well, it's not exactly a look that says, *Wow, so thrilled for you two!*

Cassie realizes it the moment I do and whirls toward Juliana. "You didn't tell me, either. What the heck, guys?"

"You've had a lot going on," I say honestly. *You haven't told me everything, either.*

She stands up tall enough to block the sunlight streaming in through the window. "This is major news!"

"It's not like we're engaged."

Marcos snorts.

"What does Papa Gregory say to this union?" she persists.

Oh, just super awkward allusions to The Talk. Passively judgmental comments about Marcos's math coursework. The usual.

Marcos saves me with a chuckle. "I haven't officially met him yet, so that remains to be seen."

There's a *yet*, as in this boy plans to shake my father's hand and tolerate stupid jokes and scrutiny of his academic performance?

He doesn't know what he's getting himself into.

Cassie's on the same page as me. "Yeah, good luck with that one." She cracks one knuckle on the table.

Juliana cringes at the sound. "Gross."

Cassie ignores her, moving to the next knuckle.

We descend into silence to the soundtrack of Cassie's knuckles and the soup simmering on the stove. The onion-y smell of the leeks combined with the incense makes Juliana exhale heavily as she picks at her short nails. Even I'm starting to get lightheaded.

Cassie leans back in her chair, daring one of us to speak first.

Marcos takes the bait. "You have practice soon, right, Savannah?"

Unfortunately, it's the wrong thing to say. For the second time today, Cassie's eyes drill into me. "Let me get this straight. Gymnastics, this..." She waves her hand between Marcos and me. "You shredded your knee," she continues in her I'm-two-weeks-older-and-infinitely-wiser voice. "I distinctly remember you saying that if you had to do more physical therapy, you would hang yourself with an Ace bandage."

"God, Cassie," Juliana exclaims.

My ears burn, but there's nothing I can say. She's right about all of the above.

Cassie pushes the napkin ring with too much force. "You seemed so much happier without gymnastics. Less stressed."

Although my body creaks and groans like a rusted door, I don't regret returning. Yet. I don't know where Marcos and I are headed, but with his arm around me, I feel like I'm part of a team again for the first time in a long while.

"I'm teaching little kids at the gym." Might as well put that one out there, too.

"Children. Demon spawn." Cassie's eyes widen comically.

Why is she taking issue with everything I've done? "I think it'll be fun."

"It's all fun and games until one of them gives you the flu," she says, and Juliana chuckles in agreement. "What about your Papa-Gregory-inflicted extracurricular activities?"

My return to the gym seems to have satisfied him. However, in case the Golden Leaf Classic goes as well as Regionals did, I'll need a back-up plan. "I might join spring track. I ran pretty quickly in flag football the other day."

"Wow," says Marcos. "You're really blazing the way."

"Like you would do better?" I elbow him and he laughs. "I'll join for real if you do."

Yes, this officially counts as the closest I've ever come to asking someone on a date.

"Whoa, whoa." His dimples are on full display, but do I detect fear in his eyes?

"Ha! Are you kidding me?" Juliana enters the fray. "Marcos can't walk up the tech wing stairs without sucking wind."

Marcos holds up his hands. "I had bronchitis!"

Cassie's watching us, an unreadable expression on her face. She no longer seems annoyed or indignant. She's not happy, though; I know that much. When Marcos finally concedes that, all right, he might be a little out of shape, she says, "Clearly I can't end up in the hospital again because who knows what you'll do next."

It should be a joke, the way she told me that lying never got me anywhere before. All the same, the words hit me with a sense of responsibility. *You should have been there.*

"Once you're back at school, everything will be normal again," I say. It's a hollow platitude, much like staring up at the posters at the gym that say "Everyone's a shining star!" as you fall during your tenth beam routine. I know as soon as I say it that Cass won't be convinced.

Sure enough, she looks up at me with the I'm-Two-Weeks-Older smile, except it's more wistful than usual. "Right, Savs."

....

THING IS, SAVANNAH, your life's like a hallway.

Cassie is wrong. Some doors are shut firmly against me.

"Let's go, Savannah." Matt claps twice. "You've done drills for an hour. It's time to put it into the pit."

No. "My hamstring's a little tight," I offer. Everything aches today. My knees, my wrists, my back. The euphoria of flipping upside down comes with more than gravity: reality.

Matt stalks away, shaking his head with frustration. The two of us that remain from the original five aren't exactly putting on a model performance for our younger team members. Emery's not up to par either. She starts from a deep lunge at the end of the runway, jogs, picks up to sprint—and sprints clear past the springboard. "I'm sorry," she says each time, hands pressed to her forehead. Matt sighs deeply.

What's the point?

Emery will go for the vault eventually. If she doesn't, Matt will tell her to go home, and she'll get angry and go full-force at the table, like proving Matt wrong is paramount. Which, for the moment, I suppose, it is. So what if she never goes for the vault? What does it matter?

Emery can do anything she wants without trying. Or, in the case of vault, with a little bit of effort. She doesn't have irrational fears of landing in a foam pit, like I suddenly do. She can show up at the gym and be stunning, and not think about knees and friends giving out. Must be nice.

"How's that hamstring, Savannah?" Behind Matt, Emery runs down the runway and past the springboard. He doesn't look. "Let's make a deal," he says before I reply. "A full into the pit. No rush on the double. Okay?"

"Okay," I say.

"I'm not hearing much confidence in that answer."

"Okay," I say, louder.

Matt studies me. I pretend to adjust the Beast so that I don't have to look at him, but if anyone's accustomed to reading me throughout the years, it's my coach. "Are you all right?"

Emery saves me from replying by slamming into the table. She groans and staggers onto the springboard. The little kids gasp. "Do you need ice?" Tiana calls.

"Either you go next time or you go home," Matt says without turning around. If anything's guaranteed to piss him off, it's making a stupid mental error in front of the little kids.

Emery's eyes meet mine. She looks about as good as I feel, which is total crap. "I'm sorry—"

"You're too good for this, Emery. How many times have I told you? Let your mind work for you."

"It's not—"

"Stop. The more excuses you make, the more you're overthinking. One."

"I'm not—"

"Two."

Matt doesn't need "three." Emery goes. She sprints with long, purposeful strides and as soon as she hurdles, I know it's going to be a good vault. Her feet hit the springboard and her back arches as her hands touch the table. She pushes off, flips and twists once with her body straight, lands with an extra step. I should be happy for her, but it was all inevitable. Matt will shake his head when I don't go for the full tonight into the pit. But for now he won't push me as much as he pushes Emery, because neither of us knows what will happen after I lift into the air and twist. That's the part I'm not sure I want to know.

CHAPTER NINETEEN

MY PHONE BUZZES. *Picking you up in five minutes,* Cassie writes. *Be ready.*

I've spent the last week running to her house after school. We'd go up to her bedroom and sit on her bed, surrounded by the blanket from Peru, the carved wooden statues from Switzerland, and the creepy stuffed animal rat that her father brought back from Australia. She'd ask me stories about school and tell me about her doctors and nurses. While it's all surface-level—"the doctor was convinced for, like, a full day that I was fishing and I was too out of it to correct him"—I'm glad she's speaking about it. She doesn't ask about gymnastics or Marcos, and I don't bring them up.

With all the zeal she saves for end-of-the-year essay-writing binges, Cass has convinced her team of medical professionals that she's ready to return to school, the place she hates most. The place that I'm pretty sure was a huge contributor to her stress.

I'm going to wow them, she'd texted me after Juliana, Marcos, and I had left her house, rumbling away in Marcos's car. *I don't want to be left out of anything else.*

Has enough time passed? Is she really ready for this? There's no opportunity to ask, to express my concerns, because not a minute later, I hear the music approaching.

It feels right to sit beside Cassie on the deep-blue fabric seats, pushing aside the various trinkets she's collected over the years. The car chimes until she tugs on her seatbelt, the other hand tuning the radio. "Cass, I can do it," I always say, and she replies as usual, "I got this."

The radio's too loud, a cup of iced coffee rattles in the center console, and the only indication that anything's at all amiss is the slim stretch of eyeliner she applied to each of her eyes. She never wears makeup to school. She says the place isn't worthy of it.

I wonder where the note is now; if Marcos took it and flung it into the water, or if he's still carrying it with him. "You're okay to go back?"

She swings out into the road after the briefest pause at the stop sign. "Okay as I'll ever be."

Not exactly reassuring. "I have the chemistry and precalc notes," I tell her. "We can go over them together."

She kicks up the volume with her pinkie finger. A guy with a super-strong Long Island accent shouts to us about "Anthony's Pizza, Great to Meet Ya!" over the radio. "Oh, good. Let's invite Mr. Riley."

I roll my eyes, although I have to say that this Cassie—turning up the radio, loading up the sarcasm—feels a lot more familiar than the Cassie at her kitchen table, looking at all of us like we'd conspired to betray her. "How's therapy going?"

She flips to the next station, then the next, then the next. "Can we talk about something else? I'm sick of talking about myself. It's all I've been doing." She half-smiles. "Turns out I'm a little fucked up. Who would have thought? So, you and Marcos. Has your dad looked up his GPA yet?"

No, she's not shaking me off. I'm tired of filtering in bits and pieces from Juliana and Marcos. "What did the doctors say?"

A long, slow exhale. Like if she does it for long enough, she won't have to answer. "Which one? I guess this is what it's like if you commit a crime. You talk to different people all day long, telling them the same stories."

Stories about what? Her fingers tremble slightly as she reaches for the iced coffee, and if I wait long enough, she might tell me something real. Something she's been avoiding.

"Everyone's been...really nice. Not judgy." She hits a song she likes and switches away again. I've distracted her. "I had to promise not to try to self-medicate again. Or not to *not* medicate. That was part of the problem."

That was the part Juliana had known.

"They called the guidance office and my teachers are going to hold my tests for now. Praise Jesus."

My sneaker nudges the stress ball rolling around on the floor. Instantly, my ankle cracks.

Cassie winces. The sound's always grossed her out although she's the one who cracks every single knuckle, ten in a row. "How the hell did you go from zero to sixty in one practice? What's this noise about competing again?" She's switched the subject too quickly for me to wrangle it back. "I think this is too much for you."

It's the first time she's asked me about myself since the afternoon Marcos, Juliana, and I went to her house. The questions make me grip the passenger-side door handle because I know that no matter what

I say, I'm going to have to defend it. "Like El Pueblo?" I say sarcastically.

"How was that, by the way? See any drug deals?"

"Is that what you say to Juliana?"

She leans on the brakes so suddenly that it's a wonder we both don't end up with whiplash. A truck swerves from behind us, honking, and the car rocks from its speed. "Cass!"

She stares at me, ignoring the truck. There's hurt in her eyes. How did the conversation escalate so quickly? Why can't I just let her laugh about Mr. Riley and leave it be? "You're a tiny girl out of your comfort zone, Savs. Is it wrong that I'm looking out for you?"

"What do you think is going to happen?" *Back off, leave her be, she's too fragile for this.* No, I need to know. "Marcos told me that you walked out of Nelson's party during the fight."

"Hell, yeah, I did," she says without hesitation. "This Galway Beach–Ponquogue turf skirmish, it's nothing like what I saw on the news at the hospital." She pauses, gathering her words. "A migrant worker from El Salvador was waiting at the Montauk train station, and a bunch of teenagers stabbed him to death. Guys our age. That guy who sits outside of 7-Eleven every day—he was our age once. This is how it starts."

It's true. Someone in our school wrote on the lockers. Being an anonymous racist idiot is one thing, though, and crossing the line to physically hurting someone—that's another.

"Well, it's not going to stop me from hanging out with Marcos."

I don't have to look at her to know she's just rolled her eyes at me.

"What, do you think I need someone to hold my hand?" I say.

"Look, Savs, I support whatever you want to do. You and Marcos? Totally cool. Gymnastics? Go ahead. Hell, maybe you should take your road test again."

"Okay, Dad."

She smiles. "Never thought you looked to me as a father figure, but okay. I just want you to go into this with your eyes open. That's all."

Was that how she'd walked under the bridge, eyes open and fully aware?

I push away the thought.

. . . .

OUR ENTRANCE INTO school elicits more whispers than the red carpet. Fingers freeze mid-text and conversations halt.

Cassie pauses, looking a little seasick. All of the bravado she had in the car while doling out life advice is gone. "They're judging me. They think I'm crazy."

I grab her arm, the way she always does to me. It does the trick; she looks at me with nervous eyes. "You're not crazy. You're going through a tough time, and you're getting help."

I can tell she's itching to crack her knuckles, except I'm holding her one hand away from the other. "I'm here for you, okay? I'm not going anywhere."

Her eyes survey the lay of the land. The new photographs pinned up in the glass display case; the thicket of sophomores who look at her nervously; Jacki, who peeks her head around the bank of lockers and squeals, "Oh, my God, Cassie! It's so great to see you! So, so great!"

"Okay," she says, barely loud enough for me to hear her.

I give what I hope is a reassuring squeeze before releasing her hand. "You got this."

We didn't see eye to eye in the car. Right now, though, in front of everyone, we do what we do best: we stick by each other's sides.

The first person to greet us isn't Juliana or Marcos. There's a quick twitch of limbs, a hop from the left foot to the right, and then Andreas Alvarez plants himself in front of us.

"I'm offended," he says immediately. "I heard there was a shindig at your house last week and what, no invite? C'mon, Cass, show this guy a little love."

Cass offers him a small smile.

"All right, all right, I'll take it!" He turns to me. "I hear you're tutoring Marcos, eh? Wanna hook a brother up?" He pokes me with an elbow.

"With Marcos? I'll put in a good word for you."

"Burnt by the Gregory!" He draws back as if he's in pain, still laughing. "Unbelievable, man. Absolutely un-freaking-believable. You're gonna eat those words."

"I'm terrified."

Cassie's smile has extended to something more real.

A wave of girls moves by, and Andreas points both index fingers, backpack bouncing against him. "Hey, Melanie, Janine, Alondra." He nods to each girl, smile widening at the prettier ones. "Steph, how you doing today? How's the basketball team shaping up?"

Despite the fact that he's clearly a man on a mission, he keeps pace with us on our way to Cassie's locker.

"Tough playoffs, huh?" I say, since apparently we're friends now.

Andreas nods, and his whole body moves with him, a rapid twitch. "Those punks up island." He rolls his eyes up to the holy heavens. "Coach made the fatal error of putting Tommy Brown back in the lineup."

I glance around. "You know he can hear you, right?"

"I don't give a fuck," Andreas says cheerfully. "You can bet your ass that I let him know it."

Cassie and I exchange a look. Somehow, I'm not surprised.

He loops his arms around both of us. "So Savannah, it's my duty to find out what your intentions are with my main man."

Cass actually laughs. It's a beautiful sound, and somehow that makes Andreas's grin even wider. How does the kid have so much energy?

"I'm helping him get a scholarship to Suffolk," I say. "How's that?"

He shrugs. The motion moves through his entire body. "I gotta tell you, Ms. Gregory, I'm pretty impressed. The kid takes freakin' years to let anyone in. Then when he finally does, he jumps all over anyone who crosses you. Even when it's got nothing to do with him." For a moment he stands still, as though weighing whether or not he should continue. "You want to know something funny? Marcos went for a run yesterday. All because someone challenged him to do track."

I look away quickly, except there's no masking the flush on my cheeks or the way that both Andreas and Cassie are laughing. "Kid was panting like a dog. You know, he's a kick-ass soccer player, but we could never get him to join the team."

"Why not?"

"Like, he works a lot and shit. We get that. I think it's something more. He's scared to belong to something."

"He trusts you guys."

"He does, but he only trusts us to a certain extent." Andreas exhales loudly. "Wow! Way too deep before school, man. Pretty sure I have a migraine now." He pokes me with an elbow. "Too bad you didn't wanna join soccer, bet you could have convinced him, too. See you later, *chiquitas*."

"Is it just me, or is your head hurting now, too?" Cassie says once he's frolicked down the hallway.

"For real," I say immediately. It feels good to agree about something again.

The bell rings and her small smile freezes.

"Let's go," I say, steering her toward AP Chem. "It'll be as fun as AP Chem can be."

Her steps are slow, reluctant, but they're still forward. That's the most I can ask for right now. "You know how I feel about rules, Savannah. I'm going to hold you to that fun business."

CHAPTER TWENTY

I FINISH MY run to find a text from Marcos. So I *know it's Sunday and you're probably busy...*

Yes, busy running for a whole fifteen minutes. Actually, I'd almost zoned out for the last couple of minutes. Runner's high? Have I made it to that level?

There's a cool bite to the November breeze that feels welcome against my warm skin. I balance on my right foot, satisfied when my knee doesn't waver, and smile as I write back. *Are the triangles getting you down?*

Cassie attended every class this past week. She didn't love it, that's for sure, and I can't say that the "fun business" was achieved. She stuck it out, though, leaning over to ask me about what she'd missed. "The doctors advised me to do my best to be present," she'd said. "I know it sounds stupid, but it feels better coming from them, you know?"

"It's not stupid," I'd said immediately.

Can neither confirm nor deny, Marcos replies. *I have a fried avocado taco with your name on it in the fridge. Pick you up in fifteen?*

Between helping Cassie catch up after school and practicing, I haven't had any time alone with Marcos. *Sounds great!*

Then again, I'd rather not ruin the good flow of this week by witnessing Marcos and Dad having their first awkward handshake. *On second thought,* I write back, *pick me up at the corner.*

When he pulls up ten minutes later, I'm at the old bus stop that Cassie and I waited at in elementary school. He honks, and I bound over to the car.

When I slide in, he pulls me to him and kisses me so hard, I forget to breathe. His lips, his hands, his breath, everything's warm against my cold skin, and I want to press against him, gathering up more of that flame.

So I do.

"Sorry," he says when we finally break apart, the dimples revealing that he's not sorry at all. "You looked so happy."

I *am* happy. It's not the off-kilter euphoria of being drunk off Cassie's hot chocolate-and-mint concoction; it feels more like nailing a beam routine with the most difficult elements. Making sure Cassie stays afloat. Improving in the gym. Carving out a future. Marcos. I just have to find a way to keep everything together, no wobbles.

"How were the kids you coached on Friday?" he asks.

"Out of control," I call over the rumble of the engine. "Super cute, though. One clung to my knee and cried when it was time to go home. And one kicked me in the eye."

"Sounds about right. Andreas and I used to be volunteer coaches for the elementary school soccer league."

Is it wrong that the idea of Marcos shepherding children on the field is adorable? Must be how he learned to be so absurdly encouraging.

"Of course," he adds, "Dre was pretty much one of the kids."

When we drive onto Pine Needle Street, the same trio of boys on bicycles refuses to get out of the way until the last moment. "C'mon!" Marcos calls out the window in exasperation, leaning on the horn.

The effect's less than ominous, as the horn bleats like a dying goat. The kids laugh and scrape their sneakers along the road, balancing on the bikes. There's a woman across the road who hangs laundry despite the chilliness, dressed in pastel blues and pinks. Dreaming of warmer places, possibly. A man, perhaps her husband, sits on the cracked steps with the newspaper. He waves at Marcos when we pass.

In a house before Marcos's, music pours out the windows. "Merengue?" I say and he confirms it, pleased that I knew, although it was a shot in the dark. Through the kitchen window, I see a woman sashaying near the counter, arms and hands twisting up to the sky and back down again. "Laura Morena," says Marcos. "She dances all day. She makes great empanadas, though."

We spend an hour with the pen scratching over the paper in the living room, our heads close. He'll laugh when he makes a silly mistake, his warm breath brushing my cheek, and as he crosses out a mistake in firm black lines, his elbow knocks against mine and remains for an extra moment.

He's the one working hard; each problem must be solved and resolved until there are no more cross-outs. "Let's do number two again."

"We finished it," I say.

"I want to do it on my own this time, know what I mean?" He nudges me playfully. "No cheating."

Victor roams around the kitchen. The cabinet doors swing open and closed, a metal lid reverberates against the counter, and the microwave begins to hum.

"You want any, Marc?" he calls.

Marcos shakes his head, causing him to smudge an acute angle. That'll be another three-to-five minutes of him redrawing it to perfection.

"How about you?" Victor says to me, elbows up on the counter and dark eyes watching me closely. Measuring. The black ink of a tattoo slips into view from under the sleeve of his shirt.

I watch him right back. "Got any more of those chips?"

The screen door wheezes open and in an instant, my palm is stinging from an Andreas high-five. "Ladies, gentlemen, put your books down," he announces like a horserace caller, "we've got the Miami Heat to watch."

Victor groans and replies in Spanish. Andreas shoots back, switching to English to add, "A man's gotta do what a man's gotta do!"

Marcos has not glanced up once from his redrawn angle. I bet it would align precisely with a protractor. "Victor's hated basketball ever since Andreas scored on him last summer," he tells me. "It was truly David and Goliath."

Apparently Andreas wins this round, too; he plops onto the floor at our feet and turns on the TV. "Savannah, how you doin'?" He offers me a large grin, all white teeth. "I invited all the boys. You'll love 'em."

"You know this isn't your house, right?" Marcos says sternly.

Andreas waves his hand and settles in at a spot just under my knee. "Details."

After ten seconds of microwave beeping, Victor plops down next to Marcos and the entire couch sinks.

He eyes Marcos's notebook over a steaming bowl of chili. "Looks boring," he announces.

As the door opens, I smell the cologne. It reeks of inexperience and optimism, much like when Richard used to bathe in the stuff before heading out on a date. They arrive all at once and Andreas turns up the volume so that their greetings don't drown out the game. Muscular guys dressed impeccably in tight T-shirts and jeans, short hair gelled into pointy tips. Are they juniors, seniors, or even from Ponquogue at all? I don't know. Marcos stands up, embracing them with the weird manly half hug. Then they see me.

"This is Savannah," Marcos says, dimples on display as he grins, and it makes my ears redden but not in a good way. Because there's the suspension, the lull before one of them says, "How's it going?" and gives Marcos a wink. The others nod at me and then look at each other, their heads moving together as they settle on the floor near Andreas. They mumble to each other, a steady thrum that goes beneath the cheering onscreen and Andreas's enthusiastic shouts as he tries to remotely coach the players.

I'm used to being judged. Gymnastics will do that for you. You're never good enough, and even in the rare times that you are, there's no guarantee that you will be again. Couple that with Dad teaching at school, and I've accepted that the occasional side-eye and dropped voice is part of my life.

Tiny girl out of her comfort zone.

My fingers fumble for my phone to text Cassie. I'll invite her here, ask for a ride home, anything. We'll take the awkwardness side by side and she'll charm them or whisk me away. Preferably both.

You wouldn't be able to handle it.

Victor's watching me out of the corner of his eye as he spoons bites of chili. Is this all a test to prove that I don't belong here?

My phone chirps with an e-mail notification. Coach Jeffrey Barry.

Savannah!! Great to meet you!! Just wanted to confirm you received the links to all of the great academic opportunities Owego State has to offer!!

I'll give it to the man; he's got great timing. I spend an inordinate amount of time typing out my response– "I did, thanks!"–and hope that by the time I look up, something will have changed.

Nope. Marcos leans against the counter, in earnest conversation with one of the guys. When he switches to Spanish, his voice turns deeper, smoother, gliding up and down the syllables instead of skipping through them.

I'm about to text Cassie. Instead, I do something completely different. It might be the testosterone flowing as the boys make drumroll sounds on the floor when the player onscreen goes for the layup. Perhaps the mere thought of texting Cassie brings out the more spontaneous side of me. Either way, I open up a new draft.

To: englehardtmichael@athletics.osu.edu
Subject: Savannah Gregory—Return to Competition

Dear Coach Englehardt,

It was great meeting with you last season. I've recovered from ACL surgery and will be competing next month at the Golden Leaf Classic as an event specialist. If possible, I would love to speak with you about opportunities for next year on the Buccaneers gymnastics team.

Sincerely,
Savannah Gregory

Before I can talk myself out of it, I hit Send and it whooshes off into oblivion.

My heart pounds like I've performed a floor routine for Coach Englehardt instead of sending him a peppy e-mail. Instead of waiting for a score, all I have to look forward to is when he inevitably writes back with, "We've filled our roster. Sorry."

"Oh, come on!" a guy next to Andreas yells as the Heat's center tumbles to the floor and the whistle blows. "What is this bullshit? The refs are fixing this."

"I don't know, he plowed right into that guy," I say. "Looks like a flagrant foul to me."

The quick hush again. Victor's spoon dangles between his chili and his mouth. The guys on the floor stare at me, bewildered, but now I'm not sure if it's *Who brought this girl?* or *She's talking basketball?*

Andreas recovers first. "Damn right that was flagrant!" There's no hesitation in his eyes as he squirms around to high-five me. I could hug the kid right now.

Luckily, someone else takes the spotlight. "Andreas Alvarez, what in the holy hell are you doing with your sneakers on the floor?"

Andreas hastily tugs off a shoe. "Sorry," he mutters.

I didn't even hear the door open.

Rena Garcia takes the open seat next to me, shaking her auburn curls vigorously. "You better be." A curl whacks me in the face. "So sorry," she says, her eyes crinkling as she smiles at me. "Oh, Savannah, hi! I love your dad. He's the best teacher I've ever had." From livid to buddies, just like that. It's downright unnerving. "He's so funny, too."

She's got the wrong guy.

"Andreas's girlfriend," Marcos whispers as he bends down behind the couch, and my mind starts replaying that kiss in the car and calculates how soon we can repeat it. "She's a junior."

"He hits on anything that moves," I say.

His shoulders brush mine as he laughs quietly. "He says it 'keeps his game fresh and zesty.'"

Rena keeps up a steady stream of chatter: the players' uniforms (unflattering), Andreas's hygiene (TMI), the smell of Victor's chili ("like a sewer, just not as good"). Marcos perches himself on the arm of the couch, and when Rena says something particularly ridiculous, our eyes meet and he's holding back laughter as much as I am.

On my way out, she hugs me. "So good to see you, girl," she says genuinely, like we're friends, and I can't deny that the warmth makes me feel good. Wanted.

. . . .

I LEAN AGAINST the chain-link fence while Marcos ducks inside for his wallet, watching the leaves spiral down over the driveway.

Well, I did it. I survived a whole gathering of strangers without Cassie and lived to tell the tale, and I didn't need to be drunk to do it.

Down the road, an engine sputters as tires grind on gravel. The sunlight has already started to fade, which will mean driving to gymnastics at dusk and leaving in the black of night. No hope of sunset, not like the summer days at South Cross, but it's an exchange I'll have to make.

"Hey."

There she stands. *La reina*, Juliana, poking her head out of the window that happens to belong to the apartment attached to Marcos's. Her black hair, long and wet, streams over her neon green Pav's Place shirt. You know, no big deal that she's probably in the bedroom adjacent to his and heard my entire boring life story (not to mention gymnastics jumps) through the inch-wide walls. Or that she can slip through the screen door and cross the house in an instant to Marcos's bedroom if she wants. I bet she has—

"What are you doing here?" she says.

"Just, you know, stuff. Things."

"Right." She looks at me full on, which she rarely does. She takes in the jeans that I've worn since ninth grade and the old green hoodie that Cassie donated to me a while back and the spiky dark-blonde hair that won't stay in a ponytail, no matter how much I fight it.

"Juliana!" a voice whines inside. "He won't let me play!"

"Liar!" another voice declares. "He broke my crayons!"

With a sigh, she closes the window. Not angrily. Just naturally. Maybe that's the true Juliana. The girl who works brunch at Pav's on Saturday morning while her classmates wake up with hangovers. The girl with purple bags under her eyes, helping to raise her kid brothers. I'm the one contemplating sunsets while she has things to do, real things. I can leave. She must stay.

"You ready?" Marcos appears at my side.

"Just chatting with your neighbor."

"You didn't know she lived next door?" He grins. "She chewed off my ear about all of the gymnastics."

The ride home is quiet, yet it feels comfortable. Marcos catches me as I'm about to leave the car. I turn to him for an instant, and his callused hand slides up the back of my neck. Those soft lips are on mine. They're warm, slightly chapped. I can smell coconut and hear the kids across the street crashing in the leaves, and dimly I hope that they don't notice us.

He rests his forehead against mine. "I've been waiting to do that again all day."

"Me, too," I say with a voice way too breathy to be mine.

He pecks my nose. "Flagrant fouls. So what else don't I know about you?"

That I can't think about flagrant fouls at a time like this? I unbuckle my seatbelt, slide as close as the center console allows, and kiss him again.

When his tongue slips into my mouth, gentle but not shy, I follow its languid path. I lift a tentative hand to his shoulder and he presses closer to me, his thumb whispering against my neck. We touch and move away and touch again. We dance in slow circles until the garage door rumbles open.

My father. His bicycle. Two words: yellow Spandex.

"I should go start my homework." In the rearview mirror, my eyes are half-crazed and my ears are on fire.

"Okay." His calm gaze meets mine in the mirror.

"Thanks for the ride home. I'll catch you later," I say in a way that I hope is cool and awesome and nonchalant.

He laughs and kisses me on the cheek. My ears are sending up smoke signals. I bet they're visible across the Atlantic. "See you tomorrow, Savannah."

CHAPTER TWENTY-ONE

"**M**AKE FIVE ROUTINES," Matt tells Emery, Nicola, and Erica at Monday's practice. "Show me the sixth."

They nod. Nicola fastens and unfastens her grips, the leather straps that cover her palms. Velcro. Unvelcro. Peel. Unpeel. Finally satisfied, Nicola sprays her grips with water and rubs them in the chalk bucket, a garbage can with the lid flipped upside down. When Richard came to my first gymnastics meet, he asked Dad, "Why is there parmesan cheese everywhere?"

As long as there are nervous gymnasts, there will be chalk. Magnesium carbonate for the hands to help you swing on bars again and again. A thin white line on the beam to mark your feet for your dismount. A circle at the end of the runway to wipe your feet and hands before you vault. It absorbs moisture on those sweaty palms. It wastes time. It offers direction. It provides a sense of purpose.

"Savannah, let's do tap swings, and if you're up to it, do a few dismounts."

Landing. On a real floor, bending my knees to absorb the impact.

I was afraid he'd say that.

. . . .

IN THE FIRST rotation of Regionals, I was the first gymnast up on floor. It's usually considered a disadvantage to be the first girl competing, as the judges seem less willing to give out high scores right away. That day, I was convinced it wouldn't matter.

The violin music began. I swept my arm over my head and grinned at the judges, fully aware that my dramatic music didn't merit cheesiness. I'd place in the top of my age group, wow Coach Englehardt – who was sitting right up front – and go onto Nationals, where even more college coaches would be watching.

I sprinted for my second tumbling pass. Hands to the floor and off again out of the roundoff. I launched into the air and pulled my fists to my left shoulder. Twisted so fast that I couldn't see the floor or the lights or anything, had no idea how much I'd spun until my feet struck the floor and everything in my right leg shattered.

I screamed.

Couldn't breathe. Couldn't see. The burn ripped up and down my leg and into my lungs, and as I'd lain there clutching my knee to my chest, the music played on until someone shut it off.

Strangers had rushed over with ice packs and checked the color of my fingernails and asked inane questions like, "Does it hurt?" and "Rate your pain on a scale of one to ten," while Matt was above me saying, "Don't shut your eyes, Savannah. Squeeze my hand if you need to, okay?"

The crowd had applauded as I was carried out. I'd mustered a smile.

I'd wanted to die.

"The good news is that you almost threw a triple full," Dad had said in the emergency room waiting area. "When did you get that?"

"Are you serious? Cass, did you get that on film?" My knee already felt better, although I couldn't really move it. I'd placed my foot on the chair next to mine and let the back of my knee extend. A little swollen, sure, but nothing unreasonable.

By the time we'd made it into the examining room, I could walk gingerly. The pain of impact was already fading. Hopefully Matt would be able to petition me into Nationals, wow them with a sob story.

The doctor had nodded politely as I glossed over describing the incident and told him that I felt recovered already. He'd placed one hand above my knee and one under, lifted the lower half of my leg up, then down, and wiggled it from side to side. I had to bite my lips. Not excruciating, though. Not like earlier.

"I have like a billion Ace bandages at home," I'd said. "I'll wrap it up and ice it."

He'd performed the same motions on my left leg.

"Lots of ice," I'd added, hoping that if I spoke loudly enough, it would drive away whatever he was looking for.

"I'll write you a prescription for an MRI," he'd said to me, looking at my parents. "I'm highly suspicious of an anterior cruciate ligament tear."

No.

"That's super serious," I'd said, panic bubbling up my throat. "My knee doesn't hurt that much."

The doctor had sat down on a wheely stool and scooted over to the counter, where he wrote on a pad. "It's most common in activities that involve jumping and twisting. Some patients experience a high degree of pain. Others feel a popping sensation and minor pain, and they can walk after."

A popping sensation, like champagne uncorked. Nothing like the rip through my entire body.

"I need to go to Nationals." My lips had trembled.

"Next season," he'd said.

He'd taken my good leg in his hands and performed the same trick. "This is the Lachman test," he said. Then he moved to the other leg. "See how this leg feels looser? There's a good chance that your ACL is no longer attached."

I hated him. Hated Lachman, too. And my body, which didn't let me have any say in this. And that my parents were sitting right there and didn't say anything. Didn't question the doctor and demand that we see a real one on the spot, not this kid who was barely out of med school and probably quoting WebMD. That the first thing my father had said was not a question, but a statement: "She'll need surgery."

In the waiting room, Cassie had put her arm around me. I'd buried my face in her shoulder so that nobody would see me cry.

....

THE UNEVEN BARS creak as my teammates swing up and over, again and again. The high bar rattles as Nicola releases it and swings toward the low bar. Her hips rise above her head as she twists, catching the low bar in a handstand.

"Awesome, Nic." I'm genuinely impressed. She was nowhere near that skill in the spring.

"Are you all right, Savannah?" Matt turns to me. "Do you need a spot?"

"No, no. I got this."

With the steadiness of a toddler, I crawl up on the low bar and push myself so that I'm standing. I teeter back and forth before jumping to the high bar. Chalk flies into my eyes and I blink it out as quickly as I can, eyes tearing up.

Swing forward. Swing back. This is a rhythm I know well: give and take. Out of my periphery, Matt and the girls have paused to watch.

This won't be pretty.

I let my toes rise in front of me, let go, close my eyes and pray, and flip over to land on my feet. A burst of stars in my eyes, but no pain.

"Savannah, you're amazing!" Tiana shouts from across the gym, and everyone giggles at her exuberance.

Amazing, no. The flyaway, though, is safe. A second flyaway, stretched out this time—also safe. Excitement rises in my chest like a giggle. I'm upside down again and living to tell the tale. As long as my feet hit the ground first and don't budge, I am all right.

．．．．．．．．．．．．．．．．．．

ON NIGHTS LIKE tonight, after a practice that felt good, I feel like I'm in the process of surviving something. Nothing dramatic, mind you. Not like near-death. Still, a story that's becoming my own. Depending how this Golden Leaf fiasco goes, one I might be proud of someday.

When you climb into Level 8, 9, 10, you still have the small perky girls scampering up the podium. At the same time, you see the taller girls, a little heavier, moving more slowly. They have braces around their wrists and ankles. The bars bend under their weight. They're here because they've survived. Not everyone can handle the transition from cute and light to awkward and not so light. In the beginning, you burn to run around the gym and flip until your head is dizzier than your tired legs. Then the burning settles into ankles and shoulders and your coach saying, "No, no, that's not right." For most girls, it turns to smoke. Carried away by a gust of boyfriends or other sports or the promise of free time.

Not for all of us. We're still here.

Did you always want to go to Suffolk? I text Marcos when the lights are shut off, my miscellaneous aching joints iced and rubbed and wished upon.

"Stairway to Heaven" starts playing and the screen flashes brightly in the darkness of my room. Incoming call.

It's Marcos, and he's laughing. I want to hear it in person, feel his breath against my cheek. "Yes, Savannah. As a young boy in Texas, I dreamed of the day I could attend community college in New York."

"You lived in Texas?"

"Yeah. What's going on?"

I want to know more about Texas, but the *yeah* is clipped. "Did I wake you up?"

"I just showered and still smell like guac, so no, you're fine." I bet he smells like coconuts now, not fake and trying-too-hard like the guys at his house on Sunday.

"How was work?"

He groans. "One customer said the other guy stole from him, push came to shove, cops had to be called. All they did was tell the guys to stop being dicks and left."

Yikes. As long as he stayed out of it, though—

"So, Suffolk? Thinking about applying?" I can hear his smile.

I take a breath. "I told you about moving to the city with Cassie, right?"

"Yes."

"I...don't think I want to do that anymore."

"Why not?" There's no shock in the question, or an accusation, or anything that implies *You're making a terrible mistake that you will regret.* He's curious. Open.

"I don't think I would be happy if I didn't give gymnastics a shot. I could walk onto a team next year. Or I could sit on the bench for three seasons and compete once as a senior. No matter what, I can't do any of those things if I'm in the city." I'm rambling now. "A wise person once said that he thought I was afraid of failure."

He groans. "I'm sorry about that."

"No," I said, "I think I'm more afraid of *not* trying."

The sound of creaking in the background. I wonder if he's lying back on his bed, looking at the pale-blue walls. "It sounds like your decision is made, then," he says, but I can't stop there. I tell him about Richard, Ponquogue's soccer golden boy, who managed to chase both of his dreams, one of which was one we knew he wanted and the other was one he'd never told us.

There's more that I don't say, like how seeing Juliana react to her brothers calling her name made me realize how lucky I am that I don't have anything to hold me back. Except myself, and the body that's determined to make me question this every step of the way.

"I'm inspired by you," he says, and I laugh. "Seriously! The thing is..."

We're quiet. This is vulnerable territory. With the lights out and a few miles between us, it feels safe.

Finally, he says, "I'm real good at talking myself out of things. Like trying out for the soccer team. I've always been better at being a spectator."

"Why?" I think of what Andreas told me. *I think he's afraid to belong to something.* The last thing he wants to hear about is his best friend and me discussing his psyche, though. I have to hear it from him.

"I give myself a million excuses. I have to work, I'm too tired, there are jerks like Tommy Brown." I nod although he can't see me. "I think about college and I wonder if I'm too poor or if some guy is going to tell me one day that I only got a scholarship because I'm Mexican, not because I worked my ass off. Then I see you going after what you want, and it makes me want to do it, too."

"You can still try out for track," I say, and now it's his turn to laugh.

"Only if it's in the spring," he teases. "Juliana wasn't lying—I need to get my ass in gear so you're not ashamed of me."

That ass looks plenty fine to me.

"What's stopping you?" he says. "You sound worried."

There's the tiny matter of my best friend, who's hanging onto the slippery ledge. "Cassie," I say. "There are no schools with gymnastics teams near the city. If I do this, I can't live with her."

He's silent for a moment. "If you can tell off that drunk douche from Galway Beach, you can be honest with Cassie. What if you suggest somewhere else?" There's shifting in the background, followed by an electronic ping. "Name me a US city, and I'll see if I can find a gymnastics team."

I stare at my phone as though I can see him on his laptop. "By the time we're done," he says, completely serious, "I'll know more about collegiate gymnastics than anyone."

My grin is so wide that my cheeks hurt. He believes in me. He really thinks I can do this, regardless of the huge disadvantage I'm at. "When did you get so wise, Marcos Castillo?"

"I was taught well in the halls of Rivendell."

I snort so loudly that I immediately bury my face in my pillow. The last thing I need is to attract my father's attention.

"Let's go," he says. "Fairbanks? Los Angeles? Little Rock?"

No, yes, maybe. I imagine Cassie's reaction to me saying, "Let's move to Arkansas," and by the time Marcos hits Nebraska, I'm cracking up because it's so not New York City that Cass might actually spring for it.

The phone burns hot against my cheek, beeping at me that the battery is running low. Hush, you thing. I don't know how long we've been talking, but I do know that I don't want to stop.

CHAPTER TWENTY-TWO

AS RICHARD GREGORY, Sr., once told me on the cusp of failing my first road test, "You can flip over a four-inch-wide beam. Any idiot can drive."

If I can get my ass back in the gym, I can be upfront with Cassie. I've avoided the topic for the past couple of days, but now that the calluses on my hands are hardening, so is my resolve. I'm armed with a Marcos-inspired list of college teams across America that has been Emery-approved. *You're taking the nation by storm!* she'd texted me.

What about all of the fetuses who verbally committed when they were 12? I'd replied.

In a sport where girls typically peak in their teens, I've heard of gymnasts making verbal commitments at age thirteen or fourteen. Even Emery, as good as she is, is in limbo waiting for an official offer. As I know too well, anything can happen between then and senior year.

They've got nothing on you, she'd written back.

On the car ride this morning, Cassie was distracted by our impending AP Chem quiz. "I memorized the entire periodic table thanks to this stupid song I found on the Internet," she'd said, and then proceeded to sing it before I could protest. Now that the quiz is done, she waits for me by her locker with relief on her face.

No better time than the present.

"What do you think about Rhode Island?" I say.

"Chilly." She picks a piece of lint off of my sweater. "Lots of wind."

"How about Rhode Island School of Design?"

She shrugs. "I've checked it out."

Not a flat-out rejection. "Would you want to maybe move to Providence?"

Her locker shuts. Our smiling summer photos vanish. "Did the coach call you?"

"No," I admit. "I e-mailed him."

She clucks her tongue like I've admitted to returning to an ex-boyfriend. "And?"

"And...nothing. Yet!" I say as she shakes her head, willing me to stop. "He might be more interested after I compete."

She tilts her head and considers me. "You were so excited when we went to Regionals." It *was* a "we"— she took the trip, too—but the way she says it makes it sound like we had both put in the work to qualify. "Then that jackass couldn't be bothered to send you a 'get well soon' card. Don't give me that nonsense about NCAA recruiting rules. He could have said something by now, right?"

"Yeah." I avoid looking into her eyes, because if I do, I'll see that she thinks my hope is foolish. That I'm working up my body and soul just to crumble to the ground again.

I want to feel as invincible as I did when I stepped onto the floor at Regionals, knowing that I couldn't have been more prepared. On that day, I knew that I was good enough, that all of those inspirational posters at the gym about hard work and opportunity weren't a ruse to make us stop complaining during conditioning. Although I've been surgically repaired, I want to feel like that girl again.

And I want Cassie to believe that I can be.

She hesitates, and then pulls me in for a hug. "Stop looking so sad, Savs." She smells different today–laundry fresh, but lacking the lavender. It doesn't feel quite Cassie. "I'll do a little research on the art scene there, okay? You want to go for the gold. I get it."

I return the hug for real, and she laughs. "Okay, how about letting me breathe?"

I can't wait to tell Marcos he was right. Cassie gets it. While it's evident that she doesn't love the idea, she supports me. I'll be able to have both a college with a team and an apartment with my best friend.

When I see him at his locker, my heart skips as I take in his faded jeans and the way his green shirt clings to his shoulders. I'm already smiling as I approach him. "Good morning, sunshine," I call.

He keeps his eyes forward until the last possible second. When he finally faces me, I gasp. His bottom lip is cracked. Deep blue and purple bruises swell under his right eye. "What happened?" My heart hammers. "Did you get in an accident?"

Marcos shuts his locker instead of answering. Okay.

"You look like shit," says Juliana from the other side. Couldn't have said it better myself.

Andreas skids to a stop as he approaches. "Crapballs, did Victor use you as a punching bag?"

"What did you *do*?" Rena squawks. Her ringlets swing furiously as she shakes her head. "If your mama was here, she'd whoop your ass. I'm tempted to do it myself."

"It does look pretty bad," I say.

His back retreats down the hallway. "Really, guys? I had no idea. Thanks."

Juliana rolls her eyes. "Good luck with that stubborn ass," she says to me. She means it.

He slows down just enough for me to walk beside him. "You want to talk about it?" I say.

"Not really," he grunts. "I'm gonna be answering questions about this all day."

"You could start with me."

That stops him. He leans against the glass Homecoming Court showcase, arms crossed. Reluctance and pain radiate off of him. "You're not going to like it," he warns without meeting my eyes. "Cassie's gonna jump all over it."

A fight.

I swallow back the worry. Marcos only fights when he thinks there's a good reason. He's not afraid to get physical when other people do. He's loyal. He doesn't trust most people, according to Andreas. He thinks Galadriel could beat Elrond in a showdown, he eats cereal for lunch because he can't stand the smell of cold cuts, and he can argue endlessly with Andreas about the merits of Real Madrid versus FC Barcelona.

I might not like what he's about to say, but I can handle it.

"Marcos, oh, my God! What happened?" Jacki Guzman halts, her cheeks flushed. "You know, my mom's a nurse."

Marcos flashes her a reassuring smile. It's not the real one that reveals the crooked tooth. "I tripped. I'm not as coordinated as this one here."

Once Jacki has walked away with several promises to provide him with homecare tips from her mom, he says, "My boss got into it with some guys at work last night."

Immediately, I recall the night he said he'd called the cops. According to him, they'd done nothing. But he'd stayed out of it that night.

"They came in saying that all the goddamn Mexicans need to get out of the country and that they're sick of seeing signs in Spanish because this is America. Meanwhile, they think we can't understand them. My boss tried to kick them out, but that just made them angrier. One of them pushed him."

He checks to see if I'm enraged on his behalf. It reminds me of Always Late Nick's words down at the beach, kicked up a vicious notch. I wait to hear the climax, the part that Cassie's going to jump all over.

The long exhale. "I kind of pushed the one guy back."

There it is. "And he punched you."

He nods. "I slept at Dre's because Victor would beat my ass."

"As he should."

"Thanks."

"I'm serious." I look him in the eye and try not to wince. It's a shiner, all right. "That's what the police are for. You don't have to be the beacon of justice everywhere you go."

"The police don't care," he says vehemently. "When they came to Pav's the night those drunken idiots were there, they told them to knock it off and went home. What's the point?"

"Wouldn't that still be better than this?" I gesture to his face.

He gives me a sad half smile. "You don't get it. I don't want to be that guy who stands around and does nothing if someone's about to get hurt. I've been that guy for too long."

"I do happen to think it would be beneficial if you stayed out of jail, didn't get into situations where multiple guys could beat you up, and otherwise didn't jeopardize your future," I say. "Oh, yeah, and wasn't there a scholarship you really wanted? So maybe I don't get it. Sorry."

He sighs. The beginnings of a sheepish smile creep up. "When you put it like that—"

"You're welcome," I say. "Let's get some ice on that."

. . . .

"OH, NO, YOU don't," says Cassie as I approach the library doors at the start of sixth period. "You're all mine."

She hugs me, and I'm momentarily buried in her tangerine-colored scarf woven with gold threads. "This is going to blow your mind. I have a math question that I legitimately want to know the answer to."

"I'm impressed." My voice is muffled under the scarf. I shove my way out of it.

"My dad's been sitting at the kitchen table every night with this chem textbook he ordered from the Internet," she says. "He doesn't say anything, just looks at me like a puppy who wants a treat. He's clearly begging for me to ask him for help. It's obnoxious yet kind of cute."

She looks and sounds like the old Cassie, the one who wasn't afraid to walk into school. She holds her head higher, her voice confident and infused with a touch of humor. She seems normal, and that's what worries me.

Her eyebrows knit. "You're looking at me all weird."

Is this Cassie when she's normal? Or is this the façade she puts on to hide the Cassie who clung to me when we walked into school on her first day back? The one who was scared, confused, hurting?

I shake my head. "You should throw your dad a bone. He just wants to help you."

So do I.

The library door creaks open and Marcos stands in the entryway, backpack on his shoulders. Despite the ice pack pressed to his eye, his swollen and cracked lips are still too visible. "I was wondering where you were," he says around his wrist.

Cassie's arm tightens around me. "What happened to you?" It sounds like an accusation.

Marcos's jaw clenches. His good eye turns to me—*told you so.*

"You know what, Savannah already told me."

I flinch at the lie.

She draws herself up taller. "Let me tell you this, Marcos Castillo."

Oh, God. This sounds like Cassie on the phone with Beth O'Leary the day of Regionals. The tone that spells fire.

I attempt to distract her. "What was your math question, Cass?"

It's like throwing myself in front of an oncoming train. She whooshes straight over me, unstoppable. "If you so much as *think* about getting my best friend caught up in your vigilante nonsense, she will end this faster than you can throw a punch."

My jaw drops.

Marcos takes a step back and bumps against the door. "Savannah can think for herself."

"I'm looking out for her," Cassie shoots back. "I don't need to beat people up to prove it."

Marcos pulls down the ice pack, revealing the deep bruising and swelling around his puffy eye. Cassie lets out a small gasp.

"Guess that's what you were doing when she fell into the water on Senior Cut Day, right? When you stood there watching her?"

Cass grips my shoulder so hard that it'll bruise for sure. "You mean when you wanted to act like the hero?"

"Cass, stop." I wriggle out of her grasp. "First of all, *Savannah* is standing right here and can hear all of this. Second of all, you both need to simmer down."

My words have the opposite effect. She looks at me with that same fire. "You're choosing him over me? Is this why you're all gung-ho about forgetting about the city?"

I reel back. "What are you talking about?"

"I'll leave you guys to it," Marcos mutters, retreating back through the doors.

I want to follow him, try to explain that Cassie's just overprotective, but no excuse in the world can hide her angry words. She meant everything she said.

I stay put, because when your best friend accuses you of choosing a guy over her, you don't run after him.

"Why didn't you tell me?" Cassie says. "Are you covering for him?"

"We had precalc," I say. "I didn't have the chance to tell you."

"Uh, hello, modern technology?" She taps her cell phone. "He's going to get you both in trouble one day, Savs. I don't want him to bring you down."

"We talked," I say. "He agrees that he could have handled it better." His heart's in the right place, even if the execution is misguided.

She rolls her eyes. "Of course he'll say that. He's trying to get in your pants."

"Cassie!" What the heck has gotten into her? I thought she'd be happy for me now that I have a boyfriend. I expected teasing, lots of elbow nudging, jokes about my dad meeting him. Instead, I have the two of them staring each other down in front of the library. If there's some sort of jealousy, well, she could walk down the hallway and find at least ten willing suitors. She's never been hard up for guys wanting to date her. "He saved your life."

"I know that!" she snaps, and her voice cracks. "Did I ask him? Did I get on the phone and say, 'Hey, Marcos, you wanna be the hero today?' He was there at the right time and in the right place, but that doesn't mean I have to trust him."

"Aren't you glad he did?"

My question dangles in the air. All of Cassie's fire vanishes. Her rod-straight back slouches and she drops her eyes to the floor.

"Yes," she says quietly. "That doesn't mean it's not as hard as fucking hell to get up every morning. Sometimes I think it's harder now."

"Why?" I step closer to her, expecting her arm to loop around me.

She keeps it pressed to her side. "Before, I could keep it all in. Now everybody knows. They all look at me differently. Even you."

"No, I don't," I say. Sure, ever since the three of us visited Cass at her house, it's been a little bumpy. That's friendship, though. We find a way to navigate everything together. We always do.

"*Especially* you," Cassie replies. "God, the way you look at me. It's like you think if you turn your head, I'm going to jump off something. You look at me like I'm broken."

My stomach drops. "I don't think that. Not at all."

She shakes her head. "I don't want to talk about my feelings all day. I don't want to hear about your life secondhand. I just want you to be my best friend. Can't you do that?"

For someone who railed on Marcos for using his fists, she might as well have punched me. It would have hurt less.

CHAPTER TWENTY-THREE

I'VE LEARNED ONE thing from Cassie. At the front desk, I sign myself out with a shaking hand. *Sports event*, I write as my excuse.

I text my dad as I walk outside into the blinding sunlight. *Matt has another college coach visiting, and he wants Emery and me to come in early. She's picking me up.* I'm done with the message by the time I reach the traffic light.

My legs know where they're going before the rest of me does.

I follow Main Street and step over the cracks in the cement. The stores are already decked with garlands and red ribbons for Christmas. There's almost no one on the sidewalk, just a few women with strollers, several migrant workers by the bus stop, and me. I pass the sign for Pine Needle Street and instead cut through the alley behind Pav's and onto Ocean Avenue. Around here, all roads lead to the ocean.

It's too long of a walk; my scar tissue lets me know with each crack. Too cold.

I continue anyway as the stiff winds of the bay slap my hair against my face like sails. It's a hissing wind, a little nasty, promising worse to come if you proceed. The bay sparkles so brightly under the sunlight that I shield my eyes. The waves are whipped into tiny whitecaps that will surely be swells on the ocean side. The bridge stretches in front of me, steel and concrete arching up so high that I can't see down the other side until I reach the apex.

Nowhere to go but up.

My quadriceps clench with every increasingly steep step. Cassie and I walked up here in the summers before Cass had her license and when we were too cool to ask our parents to drive us. "This sucks," she'd say in cadence to her footfalls. This. Sucks. Still didn't stop us. We'd get honked at, and she'd throw up her middle finger. "What if we *know* them, Cass?" I'd say, giggling at her audacity.

Halfway up, I'm already out of breath. As though I'm climbing a direct road to it, the sun's so bright that I feel a headache coming. I take heavy gulps of the salt air. A seagull swoops overhead, lands lightly on the railing, and then flies off.

Beneath it, the bridge makes room for boats and beach parties at its base and girls slipping into the water in November, not intending to come out.

When I finally reach the top, an American flag flaps against the railing. My cheeks burn from the exertion and the sharp wind. I force myself to lean over and look straight down. Maybe I can figure this out.

Because you can't know until you've been there.

Below me, the deep-turquoise water churns. She could have jumped from up here, right at the heart of the arch. She could have ended it easily.

Instead, she chose the more difficult way, letting herself get cold until she couldn't feel anything. The car still hummed in the background in case she decided to run out and sprint back in, peeling out of the parking lot like death was chasing her.

I follow the bridge down to the tiny strip of sand where the bonfire was. It's the kind of place that's abandoned in the early morning, save the early-riser fisherman or a boy with a metal detector who was up before school that day and went looking to see what people had left behind.

Under the bridge, the tide churns around the concrete supports. I listen to the steady lapping against the pillars. Bits of ash and bottle tops still rest on the shoreline, out of reach of high tide. Out in the water, plastic soda rings, the kind that you see in anti-pollution ads wrapped around cute turtles, bob along meaninglessly.

When Richard became scuba certified, Mom wouldn't let him dive here. She said you had to know the tides here to a T because they shift so quickly under the bridge. It was a fact I didn't expect Mom to know. That's how Cassie intended to go. Down, down. Maybe this bridge is one arching tombstone.

If I yell under the bridge, will it echo? Or will it be silenced by concrete?

Was there a moment when she wanted to turn back before the cold took her, but she couldn't move? How could the girl who gets bored so easily sit for so long in these currents, waiting for the dark?

I watch the water until I have the urge to wade in. Put my face down, spread my arms, and float. See how it feels. Watching the water, it doesn't feel so unreasonable. It doesn't matter that we're in November. The water is probably warmer than the air. Mom said that, too. Mom and her nautical knowledge. What was it like, Cass? How did it feel to start losing yourself? Were you scared? Did you want it to hurry and be done with already?

Did you see anything?

Did you think of me?

I think of sinking.

I think of relaxing my limbs and ignoring the ache in my lungs that points me to the sky. Of relinquishing the struggle.

Then the image stops.

This is the difference: I cannot let myself sink.

I'm running now. I cross Dune Road, fly through the parking lot, and don't stop until I reach the rocks, heart pounding. Sand whispers through the tiny spaces in my shoes. In the summer I'd be barefoot by now, leaving divots in my wake as I sprinted to the waves. I climb up the rocks and make my way over to the smooth, cool surface of the one I'd done a handstand on. The white caps hiss, the waves curl and crash onto themselves, the tide floods over the rock and immediately soaks my shoes, and I don't budge.

I always have to fight back. If Marcos hadn't jumped in after me on Senior Cut Day, I would have found my way out, or tried my damnedest to do so. Cass was right. I don't need him. I want him, though.

There was no way I could have gone back into the gym with Emery to "say goodbye." I had to see if there was still a shot that I could flip again. I'm still testing. Part of me has been fighting this retirement for months now, and finally, that part is breaking the surface.

I might not ever be able to fully understand what Cassie tried to do, but I have to help her fight, too.

Ping-ping-ping—my phone erupts with texting tones. I've caught the lone bar of service down here. With my eyes on the water, I pull the phone from my pocket.

NEW HAMPSHIRE IS GIVING ME A FULL RIDE I'M SO EFFING HAPPY I JUST CRIED IN CLASS WE NEED TO CELEBRATE.

It takes a moment to process. Words like "great" and "amazing" and "awesome" should come forth right now, but they feel distant. Somewhere back on the bridge above the tides.

HE SAID HE LOVED MY VAULTING ABILITY HE MUST BE DRUNK I DON'T EVEN CARE.

"Congratulations," too, the obvious one, flat as the plastic rings under the bridge.

I CAN'T WAIT TO SEE THE LOOK ON VANESSA'S FACE.

Vanessa. Matt. Erica and Nicola, bickering with each other yet always in sync. My old teammates who left the gym. Tiana and the little ones, who move through the day at the gym or on the monkey bars of a playground, jackets dangling over their heads. Little girls who don't feel anything but the sting in their hands after a long practice on bars or the heaviness of the first gold medal around their necks. Nothing but joy.

STOP BEING A NERD AND ANSWER MY MESSAGES.

THAT'S SO AWESOME CONGRATS, I finally respond.

Sorry for all-caps. But we need a serious FIESTA!!

Fiesta. Just as far away as the playground.

A second message. *Srsly couldn't have dealt with all the stress this fall without you. You have no idea!!! Xoxoxo.*

I haven't helped with anything. I've let Emery drive me to the gym and she let me do conditioning next to her. As if being a friend is that easy. Simple participation in the same space.

If I had answered the phone, would Cassie have been jolted awake from the dream?

That's what you're supposed to do as a friend. You support the dreams, the good ones, and you shake your friends out of the bad ones. Bad boyfriends, bad haircuts, bad decisions. I was too caught up in forgetting my old dream, competing for Ocean State, to help Cassie out of hers.

I need to be awake.

Not just for Cassie. For me, too.

. . . .

AS I CROSS the dunes, the reeds bent in the breeze as if bidding me farewell, I call the first person I trusted. Not Cassie, not Emery, not even my parents.

"Savannah?" he says when he answers, sounding out of breath. That makes two of us. The connection's staticky and unclear. I'm so grateful and relieved that he picked up that I start rambling.

"Slow down, kid, I can't hear you!" He laughs. "How's the old man? Driving you up the wall yet?"

"You have no idea," I say. Since whenever we talk to Richard it's usually interrupted by him needing to run off, I get to the point. "Do you have a minute?"

"For you? Of course."

I grin. Richard did his share of teasing me as a kid, but with the six-year age difference, more often than not he was the one babysitting and driving me to the gym if our parents had to work late. Haltingly, I tell him about Cassie.

"You have a boyfriend now?" he asks when I finish. "Has Dad printed out his transcript yet and hung it up on the refrigerator?"

"Richard!"

"I'm kidding. Well, I hope I'm kidding. Anyway, sounds like you've had a hell of a fall, kid. I'm sorry to hear about Cassie." He sighs. "I wish I didn't relate. Unfortunately, I do. We lost a guy over the summer to suicide."

"I'm sorry."

"It happens, I'm sad to say. That's the thing: you don't always know. Some people can seem like the happiest and most well-adjusted guys you'll ever meet, and the next day, they put a gun to their heads."

I shudder.

"There was nothing you could have done to stop her. You're doing your best, kid. Just keep being there for her. Keep being you."

His words are simple, yet they make me feel so much lighter. When we hang up a few minutes later, I make my way up and over the bridge again. I hear the steady cracking of my ankles, the quiet soundtrack under the wind.

. . . .

MATT CLAPS. "GATHER around, ladies. Make her as uncomfortable as possible."

The little ones giggle and squeeze next to each other on the high beam. Their skinny legs kick back and forth like they're sitting on a swing. And yes, I'm nervous. Failure's embarrassing enough, let alone in front of children. It's like watching them realize Santa isn't real. I've been enjoying their hero worship, hearing their applause ring out whenever I get an old skill back. They don't know anything about my life outside of here or why I left, really. To them, I'm just Savannah, the older girl with a brace that's almost as large as some of them.

I raise my arms straight above my head in a salute. It's required to do this at the beginning and end of your routine. If there were judges here, they would give me a token smile. As it is, I'm looking straight at Vanessa, who already does not seem impressed. "Let's see what you've got," she says.

I start my routine as the girls hiss and shush each other. They are silent as I hold the handstand. A few clap as I lower myself to the beam. *I am awesome*, I tell myself, the way Matt always advised. *I am beyond awesome. I am so—*

Slippery.

My left hand slides over the beam. I crash down on my armpit, then nose, and wind up dangling underneath, still clinging to the beam with my right hand.

Gasps.

Then:

"Oh, my God, that was, like, so cool," says Tiana. "Can you do that again?"

"Coach Matt, can that be in my routine?" asks another little one.

"No fair!" a third chimes in. "I was gonna ask that!"

It will leave a bruise. My nose tingles and my shoulder and neck don't feel so great, not to mention the armpit, which has left a minor sweat mark on the beam. Delicious.

Matt makes a motion like he's going to check up on me, but I know what to do next. I crawl my way back onto the beam and continue.

The beam is my bridge. As long as I stand on the bridge and not under it, I am awake.

CHAPTER TWENTY-FOUR

AT 2:33 IN the morning, Cassie calls. "I'm sorry, Savs. I was mean this afternoon." Her voice is somber, and I wake up fully. "I promise I won't butt in with Marcos anymore."

"It's okay." I stretch my arms so far back that they crack. They're tired, heavy, hinting how much they'll ache when I wake up for school. "I know you're worried."

"I hung out with Jules and she assured me that Marcos wouldn't do anything to put you in danger," she says. "You know Juliana—she doesn't pull any punches." She pauses. "Shit, too soon?"

I grin in spite of myself. "I think the only way to properly apologize will cost one dollar and sixty-one cents."

"Lucky for you, that's exactly how much I have in my wallet," she says. "Also, I'm outside."

. . . .

WE LINGER IN Cassie's car, listening to some truly awful men on guitars while the harsh lights of 7-Eleven illuminate the dashboard. "Cats in heat sound better than this," I say.

She takes a noisy slurp through the straw before handing the drink back to me. "My roommate at the hospital said they're the shit, so I gave them a whirl. You're right, though. They're just shit."

She punches off the radio, and the car plunges into silence. "Am I allowed to ask if you want to talk about anything?" I say as I sip the slushy blueberry concoction.

Her head rolls back against the seat. "No," she mutters, but she's smiling. "My doctors had a field day when I told them about us playing Manhunt as kids. They found all sorts of metaphors about me hiding from my feelings. I tried to explain that we were two weird kids who liked getting dirty and winning."

Despite the cold drink, my heart feels warmer. "You talked about us?"

"Of course I did." She turns to me. "You're a hell of a lot more fun to talk about than my parents."

"I'm honored." Although I say it sarcastically, I mean it.

"Which way?" she asks when she pulls out of the parking lot.

I should say home. The Slurpee has cooled my better judgment, though. "Right," I decide.

We wind up the hill. Fog dampens the windshield and her wipers slide against it. Once we've reached the apex, she kills the lights and we stare past a tremendous mansion to the black water below. Under the crescent moon, the foam rolls in thin lines beneath the distant bridge.

I'd called her crying the night after she passed her road test. "Please come get me."

She showed up at the curb two minutes later and asked the only question that mattered: "Where to?"

"The beach," I'd said, and she'd blasted my favorite song as she drove so quickly up the bridge, it felt like we would take flight. She'd stood beside me as my feet sank into the smooth sand at the shoreline.

"We were talking to him on Skype and the connection cut out," I'd said. I didn't have to tell her who "he" was. "My mom turned on the news. There was an insurgent attack."

Her arm had locked around me. "He's fine," she'd said confidently.

"How do you know?" My voice had cracked.

"Richard probably had all of their countermoves memorized before they even knew what they were going to do," she'd said. "The government will make a special exception for him to be commander in chief."

I'd blown my running nose on my sleeve.

"I bet," she'd added, "that he doesn't even have a speck of sand on his uniform."

Her description of my overachieving brother had made me smile, and sure enough, when she dropped me off, Richard was back on Skype alive and well. She'd turned the unthinkable into the bearable, and, somehow, her confidence had made it reality.

Cassie's voice breaks the quiet. "I'm gonna miss this when we're in the city." Her eyes are on the stars. "As much as this place sucks, you can't beat that view."

I don't want to fight about this by bringing up Providence or another college city, so I just nod. Sitting up here above the fog and under the stars feels right.

....

WHEN THE LOUDSPEAKER announces another assembly, I freeze. Around me, everyone talks and laughs at the normal pitch, and I remind myself that it's not low tide. It's not a disaster.

"Yay, Diversity Discussion Day. Can't wait to learn about how we all need to love one another." Cassie yawns, leaning against me. "I could use the nap. These damn pills make me feel like passing out all of the time."

At 3:00 this morning, she was clicking through the pictures she and Juliana had taken in Southampton. When she'd dropped me off, the radio was on a dance music station. Six hours later, she's blinking and rubbing her eyes. "You should go to the nurse," I say.

That's enough to earn a smile that turns into another yawn. "She's going to ask if I have pink eye, give me a rice cake, and tell me to lie down." True; this is the typical medical response at Ponquogue High School.

Andreas slams into the lockers ahead of us.

I almost laugh—a stunt to make the girls roll their eyes at him and giggle, of course—until he rebounds, face red, and shouts, "Is that the best you can do?"

I catch a glimpse of Tommy Brown's freckled face, eyes narrowed and cheeks flushed, and then everyone swarms at once and he's blocked from my view. There's no mistaking the slamming of skin on skin. Bodies move in and others push back, fast and hard, until a shoulder drives into mine and rushes forward.

I catch the tips of his T-shirt but can't hold on long enough. "Marcos, stop!" I call.

There's no use.

He yanks Andreas back, but Andreas, disoriented and shouting, swings at him and connects with his cheek. Marcos stumbles and pins Andreas to the floor, the crowd jumping back as they fall, and then Dimitri shoves into the middle, picking up Max Pfeiffer by the collar. "You mess with my friends, you mess with me," he yells in Max's face.

Right then, the crowd parts on an unspoken cue. Every motion ceases as Mr. Riley strides in. People back away until it's just Dimitri in the center, sweat dripping from his pale shaved head, panting like he just made a drive down the soccer field. Slowly, he releases Max from his grip. Max slumps to the floor and groans.

"Who would like to tell me what happened here?" Mr. Riley's voice is pure iron, but there's something else in his eyes. Real fights don't break out in the halls of Ponquogue. Maybe some push and shove, a single punch until someone pulls the two parties apart. Nothing like this.

"It was—" Andreas begins, rubbing his jaw.

"Me," Dimitri interrupts. "I'm sorry, Mr. Riley. This jerk said a racial slur to my friend, and I got carried away." He looks down at his long blue sneakers.

An immediate flurry of whispers.

Mr. Riley gives all of us a long, hard look. Everyone around me steps back, eyes down. "Alvarez, Brown, Pfeiffer, Bondarenko, Castillo. My office, now. Everyone else, get to the auditorium. Diversity Discussion Day is starting immediately."

Marcos looks at me as he follows the assistant principal. I stare back at him. I don't know what to think. He bailed out Andreas again, and what's it going to cost him? Suspension? Worse?

Under the whispers, I hear hushed comments from voices too low to be recognized. "That's what happens when you let dirty Mexicans into this country."

Cassie stiffens beside me. Her mouth twitches like she's about to say something. I wait for her to let them have it, the way she unleashed her fire on Marcos, on Beth.

Instead, she stays quiet until the crowd disperses. Juliana keeps casting nervous looks in the direction of the office. "They're going to get suspended," she says. "There's no way Riley's going to believe it was only Dimitri."

A suspension will jeopardize Marcos's shot at the Suffolk scholarship, if not ruin it altogether. Frustration burns in my chest. He should have let Andreas handle it, yelled out to Mr. Riley himself, *something*. Whatever nonsense Tommy and Max said to set Andreas off isn't worth risking his future for.

I finally find my voice. "Why did Dimitri take the fall?"

"His mom's on the school board," Juliana says. "He'll get out of it. Everyone else, I don't know."

When I turn back to Cassie, her chapped lips form one big O. The bell rings, but none of us makes a move toward the auditorium. "You see what I mean?" she says finally.

I do. Unfortunately.

We stand in the back as the speaker talks in earnest about mutual respect and open dialogue. Throughout the whole presentation, there's the rumble of whispers, of fingers typing text messages, of teachers muttering to each other about what happened earlier.

The thing is, I don't believe that one assembly with good intentions will be enough to change anyone's mind. Even Cassie, the most fearless person I know, looks at me and shakes her head.

If it happened once, what's to stop it from happening again? And what's Marcos going to do next time?

....

DURING SIXTH PERIOD, Marcos is still missing along with the rest of the crew taken down to Mr. Riley's office. I turn into enemy territory: the math and science wing.

My father looks up from grading when I drop my bag on a free desk. His eyebrows lift in surprise that I've chosen to visit him during our mutual free period. This has happened a total of...never. As soon as the surprise shows, it's replaced with the Smirk. "What college was that coach from, by the way?" he says.

"New Hampshire," I say. "They just signed Emery." The truth of the latter statement keeps my ears from burning.

"Wow." He looks impressed. "Did you give them your contact information?"

I'm not doing so hot on that front. Coach Barry has been quiet, and Coach Englehardt has yet to reply to my e-mail. I've considered resending it, imagining it got lost in a spam folder somewhere. "Can I ask you a question?" I say instead.

He shuts the laptop. "Shoot."

"There was a fight earlier today," I begin.

He nods. "If I'm not mistaken, your boyfriend was involved." His expression is unreadable, which is about as good as I can hope for.

"There are problems between guys on the soccer team." This is hard. Since the injury and the end of discussions about my future and which programs would be the best fit for me, I'm out of practice when it comes to having real conversations with my father. I clear my throat. "One of the guys has been making racist comments to Andreas Alvarez, and it reached a breaking point today."

"Right." Again, unreadable.

"I wanted to...get your perspective, I guess." My palms sweat. "What do you think about all of this?"

Dad's hazel eyes scrutinize me, analyzing the question. The longer he pauses, the more my heart rate accelerates. I'm afraid he's going to say something that aligns with the guy sitting outside of 7-Eleven, holding his *Secure Our Borders* sign, something that means my timeline of having Marcos meet Dad will change from "ninety years from now" to "never."

"It's complicated," he says finally, and I let out a tiny breath. "I won't lie when I say that the influx of immigrant students has put a huge financial strain on the district. It means more staff and more space is needed, and of course that means finding money in the budget."

"Right," I say. "Isn't the budget always a problem?"

He smiles a little. "This is true. It's also a problem in Galway Beach, Southampton, East Hampton, the rest of Long Island, Texas, California—you ask ten different people and they're going to give you ten different answers about what they think the federal response should be."

"What's your answer?" Without meaning to, I'm wringing my hands like Mom waiting for Richard to call.

He doesn't hesitate. "As an educator," he says, "my goal is to help all of my students be the best they can be, regardless of where they're from and how they got here. I understand the difference between choices that their parents made and choices that their kids make. Not everyone in this building feels the same way. That's my philosophy, though, and I'm sticking with it."

I consider running over to my father and hugging him. A tiny freshman knocks tentatively on the doorframe, though, so I just offer up a sincere, "Thank you, Dad."

"You're welcome. Also," he says on my way out, "when are you going to let me meet this guy?"

CHAPTER TWENTY-FIVE

NO SUSPENSION, THANK God, Marcos texts me as I walk into the gym. *I almost cried. Dimitri is a saint.*

The fight is still on my mind as Emery and I heave mats into the pit. Every step and tug plunges me deeper amid the blue and red foam blocks. The little kids "help" by running, jumping, and sliding down the mats into the foam.

"If you don't get out in the next three seconds, you have one hundred push-ups!" Vanessa calls. "Three, two—" Children scramble and an errant pit block flies up, hitting me in the nose.

Emery, the twins, and I mark our spots for tumbling. Nicola goes first, running down the strip of floor, taking off, and landing on the stack of mats. She has so much power that she bounces off the mat and rolls into the foam, earning a round of applause.

Okay, I can do this. The landing will be squishy, easy to absorb.

"You can go first," I tell Erica, who's whispering to herself as she draws her arms close to her chest and twists. If you're prone to overthinking, gymnastics is an excellent athletic pursuit.

"You can go next," I say to Emery, who's in the middle of fixing her hair. She blows a stray chunk out of her eyes and takes off.

"Nic, did you want to go again?"

"Savannah," Matt calls. "Sometime today?"

Dammit.

I step forward to my mark, take a breath, and stare down the next twenty feet or so of my future.

Just a warm-up, I remind myself. *One skill at a time*. Except as I start running, my mind's skipping ahead already: single full, double full, two-and-a-half, knee snapping upon landing–

I run onto the mats.

"Do you want a spot?" asks Matt without sarcasm, which makes me feel like more of a wimp.

"You got this, Savannah!" Emery calls too loudly as I resume my starting position, and the rest of them take up the chant. The little girls stand on the beams and face me, eager to watch this train wreck.

The day I performed my beam routine in front of them, I felt confident again. The old competitive Savannah who would fight her damnedest to stay on was back. The one who, no matter how much she liked her teammates, would set her jaw and do her utmost to beat them. Today, that Savannah's hiding in the pit as my palms sweat copious amounts.

Enough's enough. I extend my arms, point my left foot forward, and take the first step.

I feel better the instant I move forward. Stronger, powerful, not a shadow of myself but the same girl I was.

Do it.

Hands down for the round-off, feet snap together fast, back handspring, punch–

You got it–

My foot crumbles.

The pain is sharp, sudden, and I've rolled enough ankles to know that this isn't anything worse; it'll be fine in a couple of days.

Doesn't make it sting less, though.

"Do you need ice?" someone calls, and when footsteps thud toward me, I think for a moment that one of them is about to land on me. Instead it's Emery racing over with an icepack, Matt following close behind. Emery's green eyes are worried as she sits down next to me, something that our coaches never condone. "Get back to work," they'll tell the other gymnasts when someone goes down with an injury. The message is clear—maintain focus, even when things are crumbling around you. Matt says nothing to her now, which means he must think something's really wrong. Great. I swallow back the anxiety rising up my throat. I could be wrong; after all, I'd thought I was okay at the Springfield hospital with my knee, hadn't I?

Matt makes me point my foot in all directions—up, down, left, right, "north by northwest," he says and Emery chuckles, so I finally offer up a tiny smile to make him quit trying to make me feel better.

The little ones walk on their toes across the beam, arms held high above their heads, still staring. "Focus, ladies," Vanessa snaps as one wobbles. Erica whispers to Nicola, who shakes her head. Even though they weren't at Regionals that day, I know the question is on their minds. On a scale of one to broken, how bad is it this time?

I smile wider, ignoring the throb in my ankle, until they look away.

When Matt's finally satisfied, I'm left alone with the blue gel icepack. Amateur status. Give me plastic bags of ice cubes. That's the way to numb this.

By the time my teammates leave the floor and swing through their bar routines, I'm still icing. When I try to stand, Matt gestures for me to sit back down.

Great practice. Glad I took a chance and failed, the way I always do. Whatever resolve and belief I'd mustered at the beach seems to have drifted away with low tide.

The chains holding up the bars rattle as Emery releases the bar, flips twice, and lands with a large lunge. And winces. She nudges off her grip to examine her palm, and I can see the blood from over here. "Boo. Party foul."

Nothing better than having a callus explode. My hands have pale-yellow circular scars marking the places where the skin has torn open.

"Let me see!" Erica runs over.

"Erica, you're so gross," Nicola groans. Emery flicks the flap of skin in Nicola's direction, making her squeal.

When it comes to rips, you wrap up your hand with tape and get right back on the bar. Rolled ankles, you wait a little longer. Torn ACLs, that's a whole other kind of waiting.

"Hey, Matt?"

I look up because although I'm not Matt, it sounds as though Emery's talking to me.

She toys with a roll of tape in one hand, her lips twisting as she contemplates her next move. "I know we still have half an hour left but I have this huge midterm tomorrow..."

"Go ahead," says Matt. "Savannah, you take care, okay?"

I smile. I wave. I hop away on one foot, shooing off offers of help. I am the model of good injured behavior. Even Vanessa cracks a smile when Tiana runs over to hug me good-bye.

I want to hide in a corner and never come out.

. . . .

WE SIT ACROSS from each other on the stiff McDonald's plastic chairs, a veritable feast in front of us. "To Vanessa." Emery holds up a French fry. I brandish one of my own.

"To the diets of champions," I say.

"How's your ankle, for real?" Emery mumbles between bites of cheeseburger.

I've got my foot up on the adjacent chair. "Not that bad."

"But." She twirls a fry, gesturing for me to continue.

"I know it'll be fine by the weekend."

"But." The fry comes dangerously close to my face.

I bat it away. "But...it sucks." I drop my eyes and examine the swelling under the fluorescent lights. A little puffy around the knob of my ankle and a little bruised.

She pokes at my cheek with the fry. "Before you came back, I almost quit."

"Why the hell would you do that?" I all but yell. "You're God's gift to South Ocean."

She laughs so hard that she nearly knocks over the tray. "Can I use that on my college applications?"

"You're powerful, graceful, good at competing– you've got everything." Everything that I'd once had.

"Shut your mouth, Gregory. You've got it backwards. Did you know I cried when they took you to the hospital at Regionals? The judges had me go last on floor because I was a mess."

"Then you won." *Of course.* It's my turn to jab her with a fry.

She rolls her eyes. "Then I went to Nationals, came back, and half the team was gone. Don't get me wrong, the twins are darling, but they're kids. We did two-a-days three times a week. Worst summer ever. Plus *someone* kept saying she'd stop by and never did." This French fry of choice is smothered in ketchup. "Mom kept suggesting that I switch to Express."

"No," I protest. "She knows better than to send you to hell itself."

There are some things in life that change. The robot army of Express Gymnastics, with identical hair and identical perfect toe points and leaps, is not one of them. After every competition, I'd stand nearby as Emery's mom hugged her and said, "Watching all these skinny kids makes me crave wings," to which Emery would answer, "How hot and where?"

She nods in agreement. "There's no way we'd be able to afford a gym like Express. Also, I love Matt and even Vanessa's kind of a real person when you're alone with her at a meet for long enough."

"Who would have thought?" I swipe the fry before she can jab it at me again, popping it in my mouth with one bite.

"Then I saw you flipping on trampoline, not caring that Coach Barry was grilling you the whole time," she says. "You were doing it for you, and even though this college bullshit is going to give me an early death, I've been thinking about that ever since."

"About that." I poke at the bottom of the cardboard container for the burnt bits. "I e-mailed Englehardt from Ocean State."

"You did?" She nearly launches herself from her chair. "Was he pumped to hear you're back in action?"

"So pumped that he can't put it in words."

"Oh." She slides back down. "Shit, I'm sorry. I'm telling you, his assistant coach? No sense of humor. None. What about Owego? Barry was all about you."

"You mean he was all about *you*. He probably wants me to bait you to go to Owego." It's not supposed to sound bitter, but the force of the words makes me clamp down on my tongue.

Emery tugs out her phone. "They have some awesome vaulters. Honestly, I'd think about it if there was even a chance they could offer me money."

"What about an academic scholarship?"

"Ha! Hilarious. Unless you want to lend me some of your GPA."

We lean in together as Emery's zebra-painted nails type in the search query and the video loads. The first girl barrels down the runway, does a round-off onto the springboard, back handspring onto the table, flips over completely stretched out, and sticks the landing. In the background, Coach Barry leaps into the air with his fists pumping. "Great!" he bellows over the sound of the team cheering. Surprised, I am not.

"She's their leadoff," Emery informs me.

"That was pretty damn real," I agree.

Side by side in the chairs that spin halfway and then send you back, we work our way through Owego's roster. "This girl was the North Carolina state champion on beam."

Cassie would laugh, call me a stalker with a teasing grin, but this is the kind of sleuthing that I loved to do. Emery doesn't get bored, either; she finds videos of the Ocean State girls with their stone-faced assistant standing in the background, not reacting to anything the athletes do. She replays one of the videos until it becomes hilarious, adding her own commentary, and as we laugh I realize that my ankle hasn't so much as twinged in the past half hour.

"This was fun," she says when we pull up in front of my house. "We should get food tomorrow night, too."

"Perhaps we should add a leafy green to our meal next time."

High beams flash twice.

"That sad-ass pickle was totally a leafy green." Emery flashes her high beams in response. "It looks like you've got a stalker out here."

"Oh, that's Cassie."

"Cass! Tell her I say hi," Emery says heartily. "Is she really friends with that kid Nick from my school?"

"Always Late Nick?" I say automatically. "We know him from working at the beach."

"He's the biggest douchecanoe I know. Text me about your ankle tomorrow, okay?"

As I limp over to Cassie's window, she leaps out of the car. "What'd you do?"

I roll up the leg of my sweatpants to show her the damage. "The usual."

"Holy crap, Savs!" She squats down and pokes at the swelling, withdrawing her hand when I flinch. Her fingernails are bitten down to the quick. "It looks like a freakin' softball."

Irritation mixed with despair rises up in me. It's true that my ankle's huge, but it's a sprain; it's just how they work.

"You need to stop doing this to yourself." Her voice drops, becoming soothing. "You don't have to prove anything."

I *do* have something to prove—that I'm better than, braver than what happened at Regionals.

"You're going too far again," she says when I don't answer. I don't want to talk about this. I want to wake up tomorrow and have all of these aches and warning cracks be a memory. "Like when you'd research those girls from all over the country. You were so worked up over things you can't control. It took over your life."

"I know."

She rubs my shoulder. While it's a gesture I feel stupid offering up, she does it expertly. I've required a lot of shoulder rubbing in our years of friendship. "All I'm saying is, if you want to stop, nobody will judge you."

I *will*, a tiny voice says. She's right, though. She's cheered for me when I won the all-around and sat beside me in the emergency room. If anyone has a well-rounded outside perspective, it's her. Emery's biased—her body hasn't turned against her—and Marcos, well, he encourages me but does he really get it?

"What are you doing here?" I bite down on my bottom lip to fight off the radiating pain that increases with each step.

She wraps an arm around my back, hoisting me up. "I had a craving for lab reports and Slurpees. Mostly Slurpees."

Once we're inside, my mom rushes over with an ice pack. "We can take you for an x-ray tomorrow," she says, eying my foot like it'll display a list of what's wrong if she stares long enough. I grit my teeth.

"It'll be okay, Mrs. Gregory," Cassie says. "Savannah said it's already feeling much better." I shoot her a grateful look as my mother, with a final concerned glance, leaves the room.

Cass sits next to me with her laptop, analyzing the data we collected during lab. "These things are pointless," she says while typing approximately three thousand words a minute, all correctly spelled. "It's so obvious what results they want you to find."

Deep within the recesses of my gym bag, buried under chalk, grips, and the limbs of the Beast, I dimly hear "Stairway to Heaven" playing. I take a peek. *Marcos.*

It feels right to sit here with Cassie without bickering or cold words. If I answer, Cass is going to get worked up all over again.

So I let it go to voicemail.

CHAPTER TWENTY-SIX

"**H**ERE COMES THE hero," Juliana says dryly as we stand by Cassie's locker.

Marcos arrives with Andreas, Rena trailing not far behind. I see an apology in his eyes. Then he sees Cassie, and the look hardens.

A ball of tension settles in my stomach. No better feeling than to have a boyfriend who doesn't get along with your best friend, despite the fact that he saved her life. I expect him to stay where he is, safely across from our semicircle, making sure that Andreas doesn't fall over. Andreas is clearly hurting this morning; he has a swollen jaw that makes his smile look like he's been injected with Novocain. "Mornin', ladies," he manages. Rena whacks him gently without missing a beat.

Marcos crosses the circle, leans his chin on my shoulder, and wraps his arms around my waist. I'm immediately engulfed by the warmth of his embrace, the feeling of his heart beating through his thin navy-blue shirt against my back. At the same time, nerves shoot through me. Cassie was right. He didn't listen to me in the hallway, when I cautioned that jumping in after Andreas could ruin his shot at a scholarship.

Cassie's eyebrows shoot up. Andreas's lips twist in a painful smile. Juliana, however, is all business. "You shouldn't have gone in there yesterday," she chastises Marcos. "One of these days, somebody's gonna get into real trouble, and at this rate, it'll be you."

His Adam's apple moves against my shoulder. "Tell Andreas to stop getting in over his head."

"It's not just his fault. We all remember your black eye."

"I already apologized." Andreas presses an ice pack to his face, shoulders slumped. "Hey, Savannah, can I come flip around in your gym?"

"No," Rena and Juliana say in unison.

"You guys have no sense of adventure! Come on, you know I'd be a natural." He raises a bandaged hand. Not so convincing.

Two juniors bump into Cassie and don't apologize; they're so caught up in their conversation. Whatever Cassie hears, though, makes all of the amusement leave her face. She crosses her arms, shoulders rolled forward ever so slightly. They must be talking about her.

When she meets my gaze, I raise my eyebrows. *Everything okay?*

She shakes her head slightly then looks over my head at Marcos. What does that mean?

"You would snap your neck on your first try!" Rena exclaims. "Remember ice skating?"

"We had to sacrifice an entire night to make sure you didn't sleep through a concussion," Juliana agrees.

"Practice for nursing school, am I right?" He loops an arm around both of them.

"No art school?" I say.

Juliana snorts, yet there's the tiniest flash of wistfulness in her face. "I'm not spending all that money for stuff I can do on my own."

Slowly but surely I've become accustomed to spending time with Juliana. Sometimes she laughs at my jokes, although I can't quite shake the feeling that she doesn't like me, that I haven't been fully accepted.

"Tell you what, Andreas," I say. "If I make it through my competition, I'll teach you how to flip, okay?"

Cassie's gaze darts back and forth between us, like she doesn't know which aspect of this situation to address first.

The bell rings. "See you ladies and Marc later," Andreas says. "This ain't over, Savannah!" Even Juliana offers a wave, still laughing at Andreas. As they walk off, I'm bummed that we have to go our separate ways. All of them add something: Andreas's outrageous enthusiasm and ego, Rena's feistiness, Juliana's no-nonsense attitude (even when it's aimed at me).

"I'll see you later?" Without waiting for a response, Marcos spins me around and leans in. My heart starts pounding. I say a little prayer that Dad won't walk by and move to meet him halfway.

Over his shoulder, all of Ponquogue watches us.

Jacki Guzman whispers to Blake Rogan. Tommy Brown nearly gives himself whiplash as he does a double take. Roberto Aguilar and Preston Bolivar cease talking to stare at us.

Of course people know. Hell, my father knows. After yesterday, though, there's something beyond glance-and-move-on in their looks. In a flash, I remember Marcos's T-shirt sliding out of my grip, the way he kept moving despite me calling out to him as he ran into the center of the fight.

This is the last thing Marcos needs—all of these eyes on him, the whispers, the clandestine elbows.

My eyes flit to Cassie's, looking for support or confirmation or anything, really, but her eyebrows are straight up in surprise—*seriously, Savs?*

And I cough so that the kiss hits my cheek, not my lips.

....

"YOU HAVE TO talk to him," Cassie says as we run laps around the soccer field. In spite of the chilly air that turns to smoke each time I exhale, I'm not struggling to breathe. Praise heavens or some kind of injury karma I've built up for good behavior, my ankle feels better. "You're the only person he's going to listen to."

"I tried." Today Andreas is stuck on the sidelines. Marcos jogs in place to chat with him despite Coach Doroski blowing his whistle threateningly. "I told him to stop yesterday. He didn't."

"In keeping with my most-hated phrase, how did that make you feel?" Cassie's long legs take one stride for three of mine.

"Scared," I admit. The grass is slippery beneath my sneakers. We had frost last night, which has since melted into a glossy moist sheen over the field.

"I could tell. You had the same look on your face when he tried to kiss you."

I cringe. "Was I that obvious?"

"To me, yeah. Marcos, I don't know how well he knows you." For several strides, she's quiet. "You need an ultimatum."

I don't like the idea of an ultimatum. It feels heavy, like other choices I'm not willing to make.

"People like Marcos see what's immediately in front of them," Cass continues. "As soon as he sees someone in trouble, he doesn't slow down to think about what his options are. You have to give him options."

As we come down the straightaway, Andreas calls, "Looking fine, ladies! Keep it up!" Marcos rolls his eyes and extends his hand for a high-five. I slap it on my way past him, both of us smiling.

"You guys are adorable; I'll give you that," Cass says when we turn the next corner. "He's going to be devastated when you dump him."

My stomach drops. "Who said anything about dumping?"

Her Wiser-Than-You voice is back in full force. "Either he keeps you, or he keeps up his misguided hero act. He can't have it both ways."

"Why not?"

Cass sighs, emitting a long puff of smoke. "I know you really like him, but this is for his own good and yours, too. Wouldn't you feel better knowing he's not going to fly off the handle because Andreas gets caught up in dumb shit of his own making?"

I don't want to end things with Marcos. The thought makes my heart hurt. On the phone with him as he scrolled through gymnastics programs all over the country, his genuine excitement at trying the jumps I showed him, the way his breath caught and his jaw clenched just before kissing me in the car...

Then my mind flashes to Marcos cringing as he placed ice on his swollen eye. Hearing Andreas's hand connect with his face as he mistakenly swung at Marcos. Being convinced that Marcos was suspended with his shot at the scholarship blown. I don't want that, either.

"You see what I'm saying?" Cass says when I've been quiet for too long.

I swallow hard. "Yeah. I do."

CHAPTER TWENTY-SEVEN

THE STEADY POUNDING on the front door is enough to rattle my bed, I swear. I close my eyes and press the pillow to my ears, but the pounding persists.

Why isn't Mom answering? What time is it? Should I be at school? The gym?

I race down the stairs in pajama pants and a Level 8 State Championships sweatshirt. The person at the door could have something to do with Richard—

I throw open the door to find not a military man with a somber face, but Marcos. He's wearing an orange Texas Longhorns sweatshirt and jeans, and as soon as I blink at him with bleary eyes, he smiles. "Good morning. What time do you need to be at the gym?"

"Uh." I look down at my shirt to check for toothpaste stains or drool. Marcos's gaze drops, taking in my get-up. I feel my ears heat up under the scrutiny of his eyes, the way his smile slowly spreads. God, what time is it? Mornings have never been my forte. "Eight forty-five."

"Great, so we have plenty of time."

"For?" The breeze blows cold and I wrap my arms around myself.

"A driving lesson," he says cheerfully. "Once you pass your road test, you won't need anyone to drive you to school or the gym."

"We couldn't have done this at a normal hour?"

"I work a double today." His smile slips. "I'm sorry. I thought it would be fun to surprise you."

"No, this is awesome," I say hastily. "Let me, um, get shoes or something."

When you're not desperately wishing you were warm and sleeping, you find Ponquogue kind of beautiful in the morning. There's so much light, and it comes in at angles you've never paid attention to. And you're a little less nervous about driving, even though you're next to your boyfriend who may like you a lot less if you crash his car, and in fact you're not nervous at all, because you can easily convince yourself that you're still asleep.

There's no music or conversation. Only the groan of the engine and better yet, no traffic. Marcos doesn't flinch when I stop short, barely missing a jogging couple in matching green Spandex. Once in a while he'll offer encouragement. "I think if you speed up a little here, you'll still be good, know what I mean?" he says when I cruise by Ponquogue Elementary School at five miles per hour.

After an incredible parallel park behind a Mercedes (I need to do this sleep-deprived driving more often), I feel empowered. "Bagels? On me. If you win the scholarship, you'll owe me one."

"If you insist," he agrees. "If I win the scholarship, I'll owe you anything you want."

We walk into Bayside Bagels, Marcos all fresh and crisp with his hair smelling like coconuts and me in the running for a Ponquogue version of The Bachelorette in my pajama pants and sweatshirt. In my smoothness at the counter, I drop my bag. Marcos bends down and comes up with my driver's permit in his hand. "'K.S. Gregory,'" he reads. "Have I met her?"

"I'll take that back now, thank you very much."

He holds it out of reach, using the few inches he has on me to his advantage. "Katherine? Kara? Karma?"

"Marcos I-Don't-Know-Your-Middle-Name Castillo, put the permit down and nobody gets hurt." I take a swipe at it.

"Marcos Alonzo Rodriguez Castillo." He wheels around. Andreas was right—the boy does have athletic skills. "Kelly, Kristina..."

We've attracted onlookers; an older lady with her fleece sweatshirt zipped up to her chin inspects us, and I brace myself.

"Can you believe that?" she says to her companion. "Kids up early on a Saturday? Who would have thought?"

Momentarily distracted, Marcos lowers his arm, and I snatch the card from him. "Kaitlyn, by the way."

"Kaitlyn." He says it with an unreasonably large grin. "What's wrong with that?"

"I like 'Savannah' better."

"So if I call you Katie—"

"How about you help me pass my road test, and then you can call me whatever you want, okay?"

"It's a deal." He offers his hand and I shake it, both of us pulling back slowly without letting go.

We sit next to the window and watch the baymen gather their nets and lines, tug on thick boots, and make their way down the docks. From here, they look unafraid of the biting cold water. The breeze ruffles the long hair that sticks out from under their knit caps. The red and blue buoys bob in the bay, waiting, riding the white curling tips of waves.

"How was work yesterday?" Marcos adjusts the salt and pepper shakers so that they line up perfectly.

I launch into the story of a child's elbow colliding with my skull and he laughs, drawing more glances from people leaning over coffee and newspapers. The looks are fleeting. Caffeine and bold-typed headlines are more concerning than us.

Nobody at Bayside Bagels cares.

My feet swing under the chair and once in a while I look up from my sesame seed bagel to find Marcos watching me. He smiles each time I catch him, dimples widening.

Seven forty-five a.m. Does this count as a date?

....

WE PULL UP in front of my house at eight fifteen, which gives me another fifteen minutes to locate a leotard and attempt a power nap before Emery picks me up so I can teach (and *she* can nap) before practice.

"What were you and Cassie whispering about yesterday?" Marcos asks.

The golden rule of best friendship: be at odds with one another, but always stand united against the world.

You need an ultimatum.

My stomach twists. How can I do that after he showed up at my house this morning with a smile on his face, ready to let me get behind the wheel and possibly endanger him?

"Cass had some stuff on her mind," I say evasively. Technically it's not a lie.

"Did it have to do with the dirty look she gave me when I high-fived you?"

I snort. *Subtle, Cass.*

"Now we're getting somewhere." Marcos straightens up.

"I gotta get ready for the gym." My fingers slip around the handle. "Thanks for the driving practice."

Before I can tug open the door, he says, "I don't mean to offend you, but you're different around Cassie."

Don't mean to offend means that I am already halfway to offended. "How so?"

"It's like you wilt when she's in the room."

"Thanks." One swift tug, and I'm out of here.

"Stop. Let go of the handle."

I don't. "Is there more?"

Marcos spins his hands in the air, looking for the words. "When Cassie's around, you're watching her the whole time. It seems that everything you say has to be approved by her, and God forbid it isn't. Like that night you told off that douche from Galway Beach and she pulled you away."

"Thank you."

He doesn't stop there, because surely I haven't heard enough. "I feel like you're so worried about what Cassie will say or do that you won't let yourself go for what you want."

What I want is to not break myself at the Golden Leaf Classic, for Coach Englehardt to e-mail me back, to feel confident that I've made the right decision in returning to the gym. None of that has to do with Cass.

"I've known Cassie for a million years. I am more than fine with myself, thank you."

"You see?" Marcos calls as I storm down the walk. "You're being the real you."

I flip up my middle finger.

As the car rolls away, I hear him laughing.

CHAPTER TWENTY-EIGHT

THIS HAS TO be the best Saturday practice I've ever had. The limbs-are-still-dreaming feeling disappears in warm-ups. I do a series of back handsprings down the floor. Instead of feeling shocks through my wrists and ankles, my body rebounds into the next and the next and the next.

The sun trickles through the windows as I raise my arms for my back handspring-layout step-out series. "Make ten flight series on the line," Matt had said before he turned to the girls on beam.

In Level 10, you're required to perform two skills in a row in which, at some point, both your hands and feet are off the beam in flight. Or for me, "in fright."

Out of the corner of my eye, Erica lifts off the beam for her back tuck. Her feet separate as she tries to land. *Bam*. She straddles the beam and gets bucked to the ground. "Oww," she moans, limbs in a heap.

Oof. I cringe in empathy. We've all been there. The shock of that pain never feels any better, no matter what level you are. Straddling the beam, faceplanting, taking a step back and discovering that there's no more beam behind you—all of the joys of operating on four inches. "What kind of sport is this?" Cassie had demanded after a meet when I'd missed my layout

step-out and slid down the side of the beam, earning
a huge burn from the friction of skin against suede.

Matt doesn't give Erica so much as a glance.
"Tighten up those connections, Nicola," he says
instead. "No weight on the heels." I wonder if Nicola
feels the twinly pain, if she wants to get down on the
floor and see if her sister is okay. Slowly Erica stands
up, shakes out her legs, and climbs back on the beam.
What else can she do?

Emery practices series after series. Front aerial,
back handspring layout step-out, stuck. Layout step-
out, tiny wobble. No matter the outcome, she puts her
hands up and kicks forward without waiting. She is so
focused, so deliberate, that I can't imagine how any
school could overlook her.

"How's it going over there, Gregory?" Matt calls.

Oops.

I imagine the competition beam. There will be
judges to one side, notebooks open and pens ready.
Matt will stand on the other side, arms folded. He'll
mutter under his breath as I move through each skill,
saying things like, "Come on, come on, hang in there."
It's the end of the meet, the last rotation, and if I nail
this now...

I don't know what the imaginary payoff will be.
Even so, I reach my hands as far up as I can, until my
stomach can't suck in any tighter. Then I swing my
arms down and back past my head. My toes lift off the
floor, my legs snap over into a split as my hands hit the
line, feet back on the floor, punch up, flip once, land
on the line.

The little girls on bars clap.

It's just the floor.

But still.

....

DURING OUR WATER break, Emery looks down at her phone and her cheeks bulge out like a squirrel's. She waves her free hand frantically.

"Are you choking?" I exclaim. "Can anyone here do the Heimlich?"

Emery manages to catch her breath, but her cheeks are still unnaturally red, and, frankly, I'm worried that she's still choking or having some kind of allergic reaction to whatever she saw on her phone. "Savannah, did you e-mail Barry?" she demands.

Okay, that's definitely not what I expected this ruckus to be about. "No, why?"

"This is a national emergency!" she shouts.

"Emery Johnson, is that a cell phone I see?" Matt calls.

"The press release on Owego's new assistant coach," Emery says. I shake my head. "You're kidding me—you don't know? Get thee to the Internet, my friend. ASAP."

"Oh, my God, it's Angela Cardena?" Nicola squeals then claps her hand over her mouth.

Am I hearing them properly? I did wake up much earlier than usual, after all. I might have returned to a dream state between balance beam and now.

Emery brandishes her phone in my face. "'The State University of New York at Owego is proud to welcome—'"

"'Olympic uneven bars champion Angela Cardena,'" I read. "Emery. Emery!"

"Savannah!" she yells.

"What the heck is she doing in Owego?" This can't be real. Internet hoax, highly authentic-appearing?

"The quote from her says that her boyfriend is there for grad school."

"What the heck is he doing there?"

"Who cares? If you don't choose there, I'm driving you up there and forcing you into a dorm room. That is a promise."

"*Emery*," Matt calls threateningly. "You have three seconds to put away the phone, or I will happily put it away for you."

She drops it like a hot potato, although not before Vanessa notices. "You girls are the ones setting an example," she calls from where the younger ones do pliés against the wall. Ballet with Vanessa is its own special kind of hell. "As a reward, you'll start strength early today."

We look at each other, all of us holding back groans.

The prospect of doing extra conditioning with Vanessa isn't enough to dampen the excitement, though. "I bet Coach Barry's gotten like a gazillion e-mails," Nicola says, tucking away her water bottle. "I wish I was old enough to go to college."

A *gazillion e-mails*. Gymnasts all over the country sit down at their desk, ponytails still perky after a six-hour practice. They open the laptop and the *Gymnastics 4 Life* background awakens, coupled with a photo of them winning Regionals. They begin: *Dear Coach Barry, I am very interested in gymnastics at Owego.* Gymnasts with knees unbroken by scars. Gymnasts writing with the subtext: *I deserve to be coached by an Olympic champion.* Gymnasts saying: *I am a champion.*

Emery's already been caught for using her phone, the stern words used, the punishment doled out. But

I can't stop myself from pulling out mine and typing the world's fastest e-mail. Cassie would be proud of my blatant bucking of the system. I can handle a few extra push-ups.

Dear Coach Barry, Thank you for the very helpful links to the kinesiology department. ("Very helpful" is a stretch, but whatever.) *I would be happy to update you on my training and competition results. In fact, I will be making my comeback at the Golden Leaf Classic, and I hope that my knee stays in one place.*

I hit Send. Then refresh. Refresh. In retrospect, adding a few exclamation points might have helped—

"Savannah!" Vanessa sounds both exasperated and surprised to catch me in the act. "Forget it. You girls are starting now."

....

FACE TO THE floor. Push up. Clap.

The quicker my nose brushes against blue carpet and then jumps back up, the less my arms shake. It's way too hot this close to winter. Isn't there a fan in here? *Thirty-four. Thirty-five.*

"You're on a freakin' roll, woman." Emery pants next to me. "Is your boyfriend afraid that you can beat him up?"

"Her who?" Nicola gasps like she's on the verge of an asthma attack.

"You have to see him, Nic; he's adorable. I hope he's attending the meet."

"Shut up, Em." My hands slap together.

"If you have enough energy to talk, you have enough energy for fifty more push-ups," calls Vanessa.

We're seventeen, not seven—

"I see that face, Gregory." Her small white shoes step in front of me. "You want another fifty?"

"Vanessa, this is getting excessive—" Matt cuts in.

"You can't baby her forever, Matt. Doing fulls into the pit all practice isn't getting her back to where she needs to be."

Okay, one second. That's been my decision, not Matt's.

"They had a hard workout today," Matt says.

"Why do you think the other girls left?" The shoes pivot and walk away. Nicola gulps next to me, trying to control her breathing so we can listen.

For as long as I've been at South Ocean, it's been the duo of Vanessa and Matt. Vanessa leads the younger children through the lower-level compulsories and passes them to Matt for the higher levels, though she's always watching, calculating, commenting, and punishing when she deems fit. Matt's quicker to encourage and joke with us when we're grumpy. They've always worked out the balance.

Until now.

"Why?" Matt's voice is quiet, bracing itself.

"They weren't being pushed to what they're capable of."

"Or they wanted to bone their boyfriends," Emery mutters. "Sorry," she adds with a contrite look at the twins, but they're too riveted by the exchange to notice.

Face down. Push up. Clap.

"Their parents want to know all those years of money and competitions and injuries weren't for nothing," Vanessa continues. "Division III gymnastics doesn't cut it."

The comment stings, though haven't I thought the same? Ocean State or bust?

Coach Barry and the ferocious pump of his handshake, his heavy abuse of exclamation points (heavy abuse of exclamations, period). Based on the videos that Emery and I watched at McDonald's, his team isn't hurting for talented athletes.

Matt's voice doesn't rise. He leans against a padded pillar, casual—like he's waiting for practice to start. Somehow he seems less offended than all of us, but I guess he knows Vanessa better than we do. "Just because it was that way for you doesn't mean that it's all about the scholarship for every athlete."

Vanessa walks farther away and we all hold our breath. "You could have her coach the little ones," she says quietly. "They look up to her. It would be an easy transition."

Nobody needs to whisper to confirm whom *her* refers to.

I signed on to teach a few classes of little kids. I didn't sign on to be in the gym at the same time as my teammates and *not* be flipping, because as I learned very quickly after blowing out my knee, the thought hurt too much.

I'm prepared to stand up and end these shenanigans once and for all when Matt speaks for me. "She wants to compete."

"*You* want her to compete. The girl's coming off ACL reconstruction. She's terrified of everything. It's all over her face."

First you give me an extra hundred push-ups, and then you insult me?

"Can't baby them forever, can we, Vanessa?" Matt claps once and we spring to our feet. "That's enough, ladies. Line up."

....

VANESSA ACCOSTS THE four of us in the lobby. I've jammed my feet into my shoes, brace still on, no pants or sweatshirt. I'm ready to get the hell out of here.

"I want to talk to you girls," she says.

The problem with Vanessa is that, up close, she's not so intimidating. You can see that her eyeliner's a bit smudged, that she still has holes pierced in her cartilage. Like we might have something in common.

"I'm not trying to undermine Matt or the work you girls have done." A boy cartwheels against Vanessa in his enthusiasm to run into the gym. She doesn't sway. "I want you to consider what your goals are and to find a way to commit to them for every moment you're here. If I didn't get the scholarship to Arkansas, I would have gone to community college. And probably nowhere after that. I couldn't afford it."

Emery's eyes are downcast. What would have happened if New Hampshire hadn't pulled through for her?

"Savannah." Vanessa's face reflects the concern she feels when one of us receives a score that she believes is too low: rare, but genuine. "I hope that you're in the gym because you want to be here, not because you feel obligated."

"Angela Cardena is coaching at Owego," Erica announces. "Savannah already e-mailed the coach. He's probably gonna be like, 'Can you start here this spring?'"

"Excuse me?"

Erica's face says, *I'm shitting myself.* But her eyes stay on Vanessa. "We saw it online."

"Barry thinks Savannah's the greatest thing he's seen since Angela Cardena's bar routine," Nicola joins in, and I want to hug both of them for being young and foolish and believing in me without any doubts.

"The knee brace sealed the deal," adds Emery, not to be outdone. Make that three.

We all hold our breath. Then Vanessa smiles. "Well, I'm glad to hear it." I can't tell if she's patronizing us, but the smile seems real.

....

YOU KNOW IT'S going to be a beautiful Saturday night when your parents have more exciting social plans than you do. They left the house all gussied up for the faculty's Casino Night. So far my biggest fashion move has been changing from sweatpants to pajama pants. I've checked my e-mail fifteen times. I've turned my phone's ringer off, telling myself that I don't need technology's interruption, and then immediately turned it back up. Either way, it makes no noise.

Cassie texted me again after I'd finished practice. *What are you doing later?*

Want to come over? I'd replied.

After several minutes passed, she'd written back, *Out with Juliana. Will let you know.* Hours later, that hasn't happened.

I know that I have homework to finish and limbs to ice. Even so, I feel a knot of irritation that, whatever Cass has planned, it doesn't include me.

Marcos had offered up a stream of text commentary from his night at Pav's. *Guy tripped over a salsa bottle; ambulance called.*

Andreas is here and trying to convince me to serve him beer. One drink and he'll be dancing on the bar.

Uh-oh. Just got slammed with teachers from the faculty Casino Night. Coach Doroski is doing shots. This is awkward...

Hey, your dad's here. Should I introduce myself? :)

Marcos's texts soon petered out—too many drunken teachers to deal with, I'd wager—and now I click on the Internet browser. There will be no e-mails. I am sure of it.

But instead of clicking on the e-mail tab, my fingers do something they haven't done in a long while. They navigate to YouTube and type, "Olympic gymnastics."

I watch Shannon Miller stick her first vault in the all-around final of the 1992 Olympics. Next video and there she is winning the gold on beam in Atlanta, eighteen years old and the "woman" of the team. Twelve years later, Shawn Johnson takes the beam gold.

By three thirty, my parents have long since returned and closed the bedroom door, and even Cassie, if she were out, would be finding her way home by now. My eyes are wide open, working through footage of the 1998 American Cup.

They land. They always land.

CHAPTER TWENTY-NINE

DID YOU TALK *to him yet?* I read Cassie's text from Marcos's bed, where I'm working on an essay for AP Lit while icing my knee. When I'd sat down on the bed and my knee had cracked, Marcos had vanished into the kitchen and returned with a plastic bag filled with ice cubes, just the way I like it. The fact that he automatically knew that without asking made my stomach flip, silly as it sounds.

We've made it a week without Cassie bringing up Marcos, without Marcos leaping to anyone's defense, and I've been able to focus my worrying on the meet tomorrow. I'd tricked myself into believing that the lull was permanent.

Just like my road tests, I don't know why I expected a different outcome.

"How's your knee holding up?" The door swings open and Marcos returns from the shower, mid-tugging a shirt over his head. I stare at his smooth tan chest until it's covered again with the shirt. Damn.

He grins. Oh, he knows exactly what he's doing.

"Living large." I roll up my jeans to show off my inflated knee. The three-inch scar, a dull pink, runs just off-center of the kneecap. "I'm going to get frostbite at this rate."

"You're dangerous," Marcos says, and I almost spit out my water onto my laptop from laughing. "I'm serious!" he protests. "Have you looked at your calf muscles lately?"

"One looks like a shriveled eggplant compared to the other. Obviously you're in this for my hot gymnast body."

Worst. Joke. Ever. Heat floods my ears.

"Sure doesn't hurt." With that, he moves across the bed to sit next to me. I tense immediately, equal parts *Take off your shirt again* and *I don't know what I'm doing!*

"I also like your laugh," he says, and the nervous part of me lets out a tiny exhale. "Your ability to explain the difference between secant and cosecant is pretty nice, too. The way you talk really fast when you're explaining a gymnastics skill, that's something to appreciate. And the side comments you make when you think that nobody is paying attention."

He slides closer, gently shutting my laptop and lowering it to the floor. "The way you stand up for what you feel is right, that's pretty attractive." His voice is low, husky, sending chills all over my skin.

"You left out my ability to fail my road test." I watch the flex of his forearms as he shifts to face me. He smells fresh, cleanly scrubbed with just a hint of aftershave splashed on. His jaw is completely smooth, unobstructed, and I want to run my fingers down the bone.

"Can't be good at everything. Wouldn't be fair to the rest of us mere mortals."

I roll my eyes—

And he's kissing me, fast and sweet. He leans back onto the bed and I follow him, our heads hitting the pillow side by side. He pulls away for a moment, dark eyes searching mine. The way he looks at me makes me feel like I can dive into frigid waters, flip and land on my feet and do it all over again.

This time, I lean in first. My hand slides up the back of his neck, catching his curls. His lips smile against mine. When I slide my hand across his jaw, feeling the way it tenses and flexes, he lets out a soft sigh.

Then the kiss slows down. His thumbs glide over my abdomen, down my back, press lightly on my hips in small, gentle circles. This is not the farewell kiss outside of my house. It's a curious kiss in a small blue bedroom with no one outside of the walls. It wonders what's next.

He's so close. So warm.

His fingers work their way under my shirt and brush against my back. A pause in the movement—*is this okay?*—and when I don't resist, his palm sweeps over my stomach, just under my belly button. My abdominals clench reflexively and he chuckles softly. "Abs of steel," he whispers into my ear, and I shiver. His hand glides up over my torso like a road through a mountain, curving around my back in long arches, and I freeze.

"You okay?" he says quietly.

I nod before I can psych myself out. It's not this moment that frightens me. It's the thought of the ones that may follow.

His hand slips away. "I didn't mean to make you feel uncomfortable—"

I trap his hand with mine.

"I'm—" he begins.

"Stop apologizing."

Our eyes lock.

"Okay," he breathes after a moment. His hand, cautious now, moves to the front and I close my eyes.

I want to be able to tug off that shirt and pin him on his back, relishing the look of surprise on his face. That's what Cassie would do in this situation. Take control, the way she does with everything, and make it her own.

But I'm the girl who hesitates, considers, takes days to write an essay. When his fingers slide, I blurt out, "What was it like when you found Cassie that morning?"

"Is that really what you're thinking about right now?" he says, eyes half-closed, breath brushing my lips.

"It popped in accidentally."

"Interesting," he says, moving in to kiss me again.

"What was it like?" I say.

"Cold." His lips hover just a moment from mine. "It kept running through my mind as I pulled her out of the water. It was damn cold."

Pale skin with the edges turned blue and purple.

And I had no idea.

"She survived." Marcos rests his forehead against mine. "That's what matters."

The Cassie I thought I knew walked out of her car and under the bridge. The one who returned spoke just like her, laughed like her, made the same rash decisions as her. But she had gone somewhere none of us had been.

"Warmer thoughts," he says, and cups my chin.

I close my eyes and see water.

The longer he kisses me, the sooner I don't see anything at all.

. . . .

WE FALL ASLEEP in his bed, and I wake up to "Stairway to Heaven" playing. I fumble for my phone, forgetting that I'm not at home, and hit him on the nose.

"Thanks," he mutters, opening his eyes and grinning at me. His eyes are sleepy, his curls stick up every which way, and I ignore my phone to lean forward and kiss him again.

"You make for a great alarm clock, minus the hitting thing," he mumbles, drawing me close to him and nuzzling my shoulder.

"Stairway to Heaven" starts up again. Marcos wears a look of concern usually reserved for challenging math problems and crumbs from Victor's snacks. "Do you need to get home?"

"I don't think so." I finally unearth the phone from under one of Marcos's sweatshirts.

Cassie.

Something must be wrong for her to call me twice in a row.

"Everything okay?" I answer. Marcos's arms wrap around my waist and my head falls back onto the pillow. I could definitely get used to this.

"Did you talk to him yet?" she says.

"I'm great, thanks, and you?" I try to duck away from Marcos so that he can't hear, but in this tiny space, that's damn near impossible. Juliana can probably hear from next door.

"You're avoiding the issue," she says firmly. Fleetingly, I think of getting up and running into another room, or pretending I have poor service and hanging up.

Marcos's arms go slack.

"Everything's fine," I say.

"It's not going to stay fine and you know it," she says. "I thought we agreed."

By now Marcos has pulled away completely, sitting up against the wall. His eyes are a storm.

"I gotta go." I hang up and toss the phone away with a shaky hand.

"Let me guess," Marcos says flatly. His relaxed sleepiness has completely shifted to rigidness, guardedness, and my palms sweat. "Cassie wants you to break things off with me. You agreed, if I heard correctly."

I lick my lips, still swollen from all of the kissing. "Yeah," I whisper.

"Let me ask you this." He leans forward, taking my sweaty hands in his. "What do you want?"

My head swims. Everyone thinks they know what's best for me. Cassie, Marcos, Vanessa, my father—

Who's right?

"I want to be with you," I say, and a small smile parts his lips. "But I don't like the fighting. You really scared me the other day with Andreas."

He runs one hand through his curls and takes a deep breath. "I'm sorry. It was stupid, and I'm grateful as all hell that I didn't wind up suspended."

This is good. We can work with this.

"I told you, I can't just watch the people I care about get hurt," he says, sounding pained. "Even if they've done something stupid to bring it upon themselves. So no, I can't promise that it won't happen again."

My heart sinks. "I don't think I can deal with that."

"*You* can't deal with it, or Cassie says you can't?" he challenges. "How do both of you feel about all the racist shit that's being said and done around here?"

"It's terrible," I say. "We both agree on that."

"Which one of you is willing to stand up and say something about it?"

"Me," I say automatically.

He lifts an eyebrow. "Exactly. While Cassie's the one who runs at the first sight of any trouble that she hasn't caused."

Anger flares in my chest. He tricked me into that answer. "That's not true! She's been going through a tough time."

"Don't we all?" He takes another long breath and exhales slowly, like he's my dad and I'm getting on his nerves. Which only makes me angrier. "If you and Cassie met today, would you be friends?"

"Absolutely," I say.

"You're a hundred percent positive?" He stares hard into my eyes, searching for a breaking point.

Cassie writing her last-minute essays while saving time for going on exploratory drives, talking with strangers, plunging into a new life in New York City without a plan. Okay, they're not the activities I've generally prioritized, but so what?

Taking the phone from me to tell off Beth, facing down Marcos outside of the library and warning him—a little over the top, sure, but she does those things because she cares.

"What about you and Andreas?" I counter.

"I'd probably want to punt him," he says, and that releases the tension in my chest for a tiny second. "Look, I don't agree with everything he does, but I would do anything for him. That's why I can't make you a promise. There are very few people I can say that for. Him, my brother, my parents, Juliana." He pauses. "You. Absolutely."

My heart swoops at his words, the anger temporarily muted.

"That's what kills me," he says. "I've only known you for a short time, and I already know I'd do whatever it took to get you out of a bad situation. Cassie would save her own ass before she saved yours. I guarantee it."

All of the warmth freezes. "Why are you so quick to judge her?"

He starts ticking off points on his fingers. I might actually kill him. "Nelson's party—she ditched Juliana without so much as a goodbye. You falling in the water. That asshole at the bonfire."

"All of those things turned out fine," I say.

"You were vulnerable," he says like he hasn't heard a goddamn thing I've just said, "and she's taking advantage of that. It's the truth. Don't get mad at me for that."

Too late.

I'm sick of everyone else's version of what my truth is. Maybe the real truth lies somewhere in the middle of what everyone thinks is best for me, but I want to be the one who claims it.

"You know what the problem is? This conversation." I shove my laptop into my backpack.

Marcos spreads his arms in the doorway so that I have to stop. "Can we talk about this?"

It'd be easy to wrap my arms around him. Let myself fall into the smell of coconut and the feel of his back muscles flexing and relaxing and the safety that his arms bring.

My phone rings again. His eyes harden.

This time she's texted me. *Can you come over? I need you.* She's never said it so blatantly since the suicide attempt. She'd rather try to laugh, cheeks pale, than talk about what haunts her.

Pick me up on Main Street in five, I write back. Marcos tries to read what I'm typing, but I slip my phone away and step around him. "If you'll excuse me," I say, "my best friend needs me. Surely you can understand that."

"You're not walking back," he says behind me.

"Savannah, slow down. I'll drive you," he says when I'm in the kitchen.

"When is your meet tomorrow?" he says when I'm on the steps.

"Is this what you want?" he calls after me, voice straining like it hurts him to ask the question.

My retreating back is the answer.

Except when I walk, I keep hoping that Marcos will follow me. My face stays ahead, but my eyes dart to inspect every car that passes. That damn dog that never shuts up barks incessantly behind me, and I wonder if I'll hear Marcos's footsteps soon, his hand on my wrist. His voice steady this time, not aching. I walk until the music fades and the grass becomes trimmed and orderly, the sidewalks filled in. I walk until I think I ought to feel better, but I don't.

CHAPTER THIRTY

TRUE TO HER word, Cassie scoops me up at the intersection of Pine Needle and Main Street. When she sees me, she slides over to the passenger seat.

I don't need Marcos. I don't need those afternoons of drawing triangles and jumping up and down on the wooden floor, kissing until my heartbeat drowns out the dogs barking and the music playing. I have my shaky attempt at a comeback. I have my best friend. I do.

I get behind the wheel and adjust the mirror the way I did the night we drove to the party at the beach, a night that had held so much promise but ended with angry words around the bonfire.

She doesn't give me a destination. In fact, she doesn't say anything. So I go.

Cassie stretches her long legs and closes her eyes with a heavy sigh as I turn onto a road off Main Street. "Thank you," she says. "It's been a tough day."

"What's going on?" I do my best to focus on her words, to take in her body language. She's exhausted, not clamoring to change the lite rock radio station.

"It's not so much things going on externally as it is things going on in my brain. You know? I could lie awake all night and experience a hundred emotions without ever moving a muscle."

"Yeah, I get that."

"Do you?" She's sitting all the way up now.

"I'm trying to." I'm also trying to banish any thoughts of Marcos's ugly words. Cass is finally opening up to me and I want to listen carefully. "The more you tell me, the more I can understand what you're going through."

She snorts. "You sound like my therapist. *Therapists*, I should say. I needed to get out of my own head for a while."

I make a right onto Salisbury Street. The engine whirs beneath us, creaking a little during the turn. It's not nearly as loud as Marcos's.

"How's everything going with your parents?"

A small shrug. "We're going to therapy together, which is so uncomfortable that it makes me want to scream. I think they're starting to get me, though."

"That's good, right?" I latch onto that. "They'll pressure you less."

She examines her nails. "They'll probably always pressure me in their special way. I think it's ingrained in them. Dad wouldn't be Dad if he didn't make some backhanded remark about how art is a hobby and not a career."

I frown. That doesn't sound helpful. "Maybe things will be better next year when you're not living with them."

"You mean when we move to the city?" Her lips quirk up.

Don't say it, don't say it—"Or Providence."

The tiniest crease between her brows. "I thought you hurt your ankle."

"It's fine," I say. "I did some research and RISD looks like a really good school."

"I'm aware."

"And there's this thing where the city sets the river on fire—"

"Okay." Her voice is clipped. Done with the topic.

"It sounds cool," I finish. "I think you'd like it."

"It doesn't matter where we go."

I can't feel elated by this admission the way I want to. She sounds as defeated as that morning she spent hiding in her bed as I tried to coax her to come back to school.

"Look," she says, "what I've learned from the doctors is that it doesn't necessarily matter what's going on around me, or how nice my parents are, or how much I love Mr. Riley. Which I don't, for the record. It doesn't matter if we're in precalc or on Mt. Everest. Sometimes I'm just going to feel like shit, and it's all because of my brain chemistry."

"That makes sense," I say. "Are the antidepressants helping?"

She tenses a little at the question. "They're all right. They make me feel blah, which is the worst part, but I guess that's better than feeling like you want to die, right?"

"Juliana told me about you taking yourself off the pills this summer," I say. *The ones I didn't know you were on.*

It's the wrong thing to say. Her blue eyes are immediately cold. "You guys hang out and discuss your crazy friend Cassie?"

"No." I hastily turn onto Towson Boulevard. "You know we don't think that. Hell, we don't even hang out."

"You and Juliana don't even like each other," she adds.

I think we kind of, slightly do now. There's a grudging respect. "I talked to her because I didn't know what to do or what to think."

"Why?" Her knees are drawn up on the seat.

"Because I felt guilty." My heart hammers in my chest.

She tilts her head, genuinely confused. "Really?"

"I felt like I'd missed something." I feel unburdened, finally telling her this. This might be what's been holding us back from truly being on the same page since she returned to school. If I can get this off of my chest, we can move forward together. "I felt responsible for not seeing the signs. If I'd known, I could have stopped you."

She sighs. "You're as bad as Marcos with the hero complex."

My fingers tighten on the wheel at the mention of Marcos. "What does that mean?"

"God." She's irritated. What did I do? "This is why I didn't tell you about the pills in the first place. You want to fix everything. You would have run to my parents and made sure they administered the exact dose at the exact same time each day."

"Why is that bad?" I'm trying not to feel hurt. She's finally being vulnerable—

She throws up her hands. "Because I don't want that! Juliana doesn't try to fix me. She's not about to give me a gold star because I did my lab report. She just lets me be."

How do you respond to that?

I drive faster down the tidy honeycombed streets with gold Christmas lights wrapped around the porches and electric candles blazing in the windows.

Underneath my shaky breathing and hammering heart lies the truth: I can't let it be. I am like Marcos, although I use my words instead of my fists. If I see my best friend hurting, I can't sit back and watch.

But Cassie won't let me be that person for her, and I don't know what else to do.

I drive until Cassie says, "All right, Grandma, you're putting me to sleep," although I'm going fifteen miles above the speed limit, and so I drive us to my house and drop myself off.

She hangs her head out of the window. "When's your meet?"

"Eight in the morning." I try to look at her and see the Cass who would twist my hair into intricate braids and perfect buns in the back of the car on the way to competitions.

"Ah, man. I have an appointment with some witch doctor that my mom wants to take me to." She rolls her eyes. "Good luck, though, okay?"

"It's fine." Another disappointment. She's never missed a meet.

She waits there for a moment, looking at me.

She's supposed to be the one who knows the right way to go, despite how many afternoons and nights we've spent driving down the wrong roads. She's always made the plans, offered unsolicited advice (plenty of that), told the stories.

For the first time I can remember, we have nothing to talk about.`

....

HOURS LATER, I can't sleep. I can't stop replaying our conversation in the car, the way Cassie pulled away when I pushed and struck back when I retreated.

That's not her. That's not us.

My ankles crack as I slip out of bed and pad over to the wall, where photos of us cascade like a slideshow of my life. There we are as little girls on the beach with soaked hair and sandy sunglasses, sipping Slurpees with blue lips. Next come the countless Halloween costumes, including our classic peanut butter and jelly get-up that included actual peanut butter and jelly (Mom was not amused). In those photos, we're unified. No hints of the cracks to come.

I look closer.

All right, there were the little things. Tiny jabs at my outfits and out-of-control hair that didn't stop after I asked her to. There was the way she stuck to my side at birthday parties and avoided my gymnastics friends, although they tried to talk to her. How she wouldn't speak to me for the rest of the day if she found out I was going over to someone else's house. By the next morning, though, everything was healed. She'd braid my hair on the bus, cheer me on at competitions, spend hours in my bedroom making bracelets.

Then Cassie began taking the photos, and with each passing year, the colors become crisper, the focus stronger. As the photos progress, we grow taller (at least, she does), my braces come off, we figure out how to put on make-up. There's Cassie tugging me by the hand to the shore. I remember the gray sky, the warning clouds promising thunder. We were fifteen, old enough to venture to the beach ourselves. Cassie wanted to swim, and the fear in my eyes is palpable.

"There's lightning," I'd said right after her camera clicked.

"Not yet," she'd said.

Her grip was strong, but I yanked free. "No."

For a moment she'd looked at me like she didn't know me. Like she was disappointed in me.

I'd held my breath. I didn't often say no to Cassie, but I swore that rumble in the distance wasn't a truck in the parking lot.

Then she'd set the camera down on the towel. Her hair billowed in the gusts of wind. "Whatever," she'd said. "Be boring by yourself." Then she'd walked off into the hissing surf without a look back.

Later, as we raced home through the pouring rain, I'd been the one who apologized. I couldn't stand the heaviness in my chest from her refusing to speak to me. Why she gave me the photo, I have no idea. But the next time she came over, she wanted to know why it wasn't up like all the other ones.

She's strong-willed. I know that. She knows what she wants and she's not afraid to grasp it, even if the way she holds on makes it hard to breathe. I'd take that over the stifling silence of her being angry with me.

Funny, I don't feel that incessant tug from Marcos or Emery. Instead, I feel it from within me: a natural desire to be around them, to laugh, to listen. It's an easiness I'm not used to.

I turn back to the photos. Of course my relationship with Cassie is different; we've known each other for so much longer. We have a history.

A non-Cassie photo: the sunset over silhouetted trees when I went camping the summer before freshman year with my parents. I'd texted Cassie whenever I found service in the woods. *Can we talk? I'm dying. So many mosquitos.*

Cassie was evasive: *Busy. Maybe later,* she'd texted.

I texted her as soon as we left the campground for the world of WiFi and full cell service. No response. I called and she didn't answer.

The next day, she wrote back: *Finally dumped Chris. The worst.*

Who's Chris?

The guy from Galway Beach. I told you.

No, you didn't.

Asking her in person elicited even less of a response. "It was nothing," she'd said with a shrug.

There's the two of us smiling in my front yard before junior prom. She wanted to go to a party after. I was too tired, went home, and didn't hear from her until the next afternoon. What happened? She wouldn't say. Another shrug, a smile that said *you'd know if you were there.* She stepped around me then, and she did it again today.

The same person who held me together through all of my injuries, through Regionals, through Richard's deployments, is the one pushing me away now. As much as I want to believe it's the depression speaking, not the Cassie I've known forever, I can't ignore the feeling that there's something more that I haven't seen. That I haven't allowed myself to see.

Push and pull. Ebb and flow. Which one is she? I stare at the photos until my vision blurs, and only then do I see the answer.

She's both.

This is Cassie. This is who she has always been, long before she walked out of her car with the engine running and slipped into the water under the bridge.

I don't know how to feel about that.

....

I WAKE UP Sunday morning ready to puke.

I move quietly in the bathroom so as to not wake up my parents. I've kept the details of the competition purposefully vague (that is, they know I'm attending one eventually and nothing more) because I want as few witnesses as possible. I tug on the deep-blue-and-silver leotard and smooth out the glittery mesh sleeves. Already it feels itchy. Strangely, it's reassuring that the feeling hasn't changed.

My eyes are puffy, exhausted, and the only kind of competition I look ready for is a sleeping one. I flip my hair over and stick it under the cold running water, then go about the business of spraying almost an entire can of hairspray and unloading a full pack of bobby pins on it. Monica would be proud. She'd go through a pack a meet. For a moment I consider texting a picture to all of my original teammates.

Instead, I have a joint text from Nicola and Erica. GOOD LUCK TODAY! WE LOVE YOU! They competed in last night's session, and if the online results are any predictor of the future, South Ocean will be well represented in the awards long after Emery and I graduate.

The steps creak as I move downstairs. I rummage through the kitchen and settle on a banana and a handful of cereal. I can't eat, though, so I sit on the couch and commence waiting for Emery.

There's a soft *thunk* on the door, followed by a car rolling down the street. Probably the newspaper delivery.

When I open the door and step into the cool dawn air, there's an envelope addressed to me in meticulous block letters.

I didn't think I could feel more nervous. I was wrong. I pick it up, open the flap, and take a deep breath as a wave of nausea hits me. I've never been this nervous in my life, not even for Regionals. That day, I couldn't wait to compete. Today, well, if Emery forgot to pick me up, I wouldn't be devastated.

From the envelope, I tug out a sheaf of paper. At the exact same moment, a text message arrives.

Marcos: *Hey Savannah, hope this doesn't wake you up. I'm sorry about how we left things yesterday and I know you're probably still mad. I wrote you this letter to show you where I'm coming from. Well, it was supposed to be a letter, but...you'll see.*

A second text. *Good luck today! I'm proud of you.*

I set down the phone without answering. If I can't handle eating breakfast for fear of throwing up, I don't know that I'm ready for whatever these pages contain. A glance at the time, though, shows that I have least fifteen minutes until Emery arrives.

I take a chance. I unfold the first page and start reading.

....

IN ELEMENTARY SCHOOL *we had to write our autobiographies. I had a good time inventing my fictitious history, so much so that I was moved from the bilingual class to the fully English class mid-year. In it, my father was a chef at Niagara Falls, my mother a world-famous diver whom he met one night on a smoke break (really, my teachers ate this up), my imaginary little sister toddling around Dad's restaurant and charming the stingiest tippers into leaving a few more bills. Andreas says he's been to Niagara Falls and the food sucks, so what do I know?*

In reality, I was born in a town in Texas too small to be mapped. Right after I arrived, Dad went back to our apartment because two-year-old Victor had croup. Victor was born in Guadalajara. It was as if he was warning my parents then: there is nothing to rejoice.

There was always music in Texas, and not that twangy acoustic; I mean rumba and merengue and chumba. Dad washed dishes and Mom waitressed at a restaurant where afterwards there was dancing. I remember clinging to Dad's leg and watching the high heels and slick black dress shoes spin and stomp throughout the dining room, strobe lights casting irregular dazzles over the floor. I always wanted to run in and join. "Too dangerous, m'ijo," he said. I took this very seriously, but now I think he meant the stilettos. In the summer, I'd play in the back parking lot with Victor. He'd make up all sorts of stories: "If you climb up that tree, you can see all the way to Russia."

I turned four the summer of the immigration raids. The whispers ran all through our building. Factories. Bars. Farms. They could happen at any moment.

Dad quizzed Victor before we left for the restaurant and when we arrived home at midnight, one in the morning, Dad was carrying both of us because we were half asleep. "You were born at Austin Memorial Hospital. Can you remember that? Say it with me. You can't have an accent. You have to say it naturally. Like you never knew Spanish."

Later: "Where is your birth certificate?"

"Burned," Victor said.

"With what else?"

"The whole house."

"Very good," Dad said.

The night they sat us down, Mom couldn't stop crying quiet tears that turned her already-running makeup into a stream.

"You're going to live with Uncle Patrick," Dad said finally.

"What do you mean?" Victor said.

Dad took Mom's hand. She shook her head. "It's not safe for Mom and me," Dad said. "We have to go home."

"We are home," I said, but already I could see my life in boxes crammed in the back of a car, the room and apartment and restaurant falling away.

I asked questions. I don't remember what they were, but I thought that if I asked enough, maybe there would be one Dad couldn't answer. Maybe he'd realize that they had to stay. Victor said nothing. He already knew these answers. He started to cry, and my mom put her arms around him. Soon the water over my eyes blurred the room into round shapes, and Mom pulled me into an embrace.

I don't know where I got the image of my life in boxes. I owned almost nothing. Some clothes. The obligatory soccer ball. Mom always asked if I wanted toys, but I said no. I had music and the trees behind the restaurant and Victor. What did I need toys for?

Uncle Patrick's real name is Jesus, but he took his middle name, Patricio, and made it English. Most often he's asked if he's Irish, or at most, Spanish. The elite class of Spanish, with faces that burn in the sun.

Like my father, Uncle Patrick embraced public rejection of his heritage. He spoke only English at home. He named his children Michael and Madison.

He was naturalized before I was born, a process that took fifteen years. He treated us generously: new clothes, karate lessons, an English tutor for me in the early elementary school years because both languages jumbled together in my brain. But I wondered what he would do if anyone questioned him about Victor. Would he give up my brother? The older I grew, the more I believed he might.

Victor sensed it, too. At seventeen, he shook hands with Uncle Patrick and moved into the apartment. Last year, I joined him. We're lucky to have this place to ourselves. At any moment, it seems as though someone's house will burst and people will spill out—relatives, friends, strangers.

My first night at Victor's reminded me of the restaurant in Texas—music, all the time. Conversations, TVs, arguments, laughter. Police sirens. "Bastards ruining it for the rest of us," Victor says. Early in the morning, trucks with groups of men drove over the broken asphalt. Kids played in the street despite the garbage that built up until the weekly pick-up. One of them had a plastic lightsaber and the others joined the battle with ladles.

At first all I could do was sit outside and stare. Then Victor said, "Let's go, pendejo. You want to waste your life sitting around like those guys?" Down the road, I could see two men drinking on the curb.

I joined Victor at Pav's Place, busing tables. Most people don't sit down at Pav's. But those who did looked past me, seeing a shadow or nobody at all.

Victor was a big hit—whipping up surprise concoctions, speaking in crisp English to the businessmen and smooth Spanish to the laborers, to the men from our neighborhood. Even in the off-season, he came home with over one hundred dollars in tips a night. He finally quit in August when the packaging company gave him steady hours and better wages.

He could stand the looks at Pav's. I couldn't. "There's nothing wrong with being invisible," he said. "Nobody bothers you when they can't see you."

Except when they can, like the guys from school who came down to ask for a job but we had no openings. They looked at me and I heard them saying the usual things on their way out. Fuck this, fuck them all. And they piled into one kid's Porsche and drove away.

One night this summer, Victor and I left Pav's and a man stumbled across our path, face bloodied. "Ayúdame, hermano."

Victor stared ahead.

"¿Me explico?"

"I don't speak Spanish." Victor pulled me forward. "Sorry."

He was Uncle Patrick at that moment.

I am not as wise as my brother, I guess. Otherwise I wouldn't get so upset on behalf of others so easily.

CHAPTER THIRTY-ONE

I STARE AT the letter until Emery honks outside. It makes my heart ache for tiny Marcos and Victor in Texas, saying goodbye to their parents. For Marcos now, who carries the shadow of fear that's hardened over time.

Cassie, my oldest and best friend, won't let me in. When she does, it's in patches and angles, all of it on her terms, and then she shuts down as quickly as the shutter on her camera.

In those pages, Marcos has finally let me in.

"Ready to rock this, champ?" Emery has the bass thudding and the G-man pumping.

I slide in next to her. "Ready as I'll ever be."

. . . .

THE FLOOR EXERCISE is filled with bodies: tiny girls in sparkly leotards and perky ponytails, older girls with knees and ankles and wrists bound by tape and braces. They stretch in precise lines, holding handstands, leaping, and turning.

I want to run out the door.

"What took you so long in the bathroom?" Emery's glittery eyelids narrow. With her brown hair pulled slick into a tight bun and her ratty shorts replaced by the blue-and-silver long-sleeved leotard, she looks like a different person. She pulls me to the beam landing mats, the only free space in the gym. "I thought you made a break for it."

"And blow that seventy bucks? No, thanks."

"Thank God for your cheapness."

Sitting down to stretch makes me feel almost normal. I bury my face in my knees and close my eyes, relishing the deep pull in my hamstrings.

"We're starting on beam, F.Y.I."

Awesome. One event, followed by three hours of nothing.

Matt crouches next to me. "How's the knee?"

"Okay," I say. "No weird cracking yet."

When it's time for march-in, we stand on the floor with the other teams. We wave when the announcer says, "South Ocean Gymnastics!" A few people politely applaud. The national anthem plays—a slow, dramatic rendition. On the perimeter of the floor, Matt stifles a yawn.

I always used to make a wish at this time, as if "The Star-Spangled Banner" was equivalent to "Happy Birthday." Maybe "prayer" is a better word. Either way, I'd give my last-minute shout-outs to karma or whoever else was listening.

Please let me stay on beam, and also let me qualify, and don't let Vanessa yell at me while you're at it.

Today it's simple: *Please don't let me break.*

. . . .

THE WORST THING about competing beam? The warm-up.

Emery and I are the last to compete out of twenty girls in our squad. The other eighteen are from

Express Gymnastics, so cleverly named for its location near the Long Island Expressway. They wear shiny black leotards with two yellow stripes down each arm. Ridiculous, if they weren't so good.

On the warm-up beam, the first Express girl crams all her skills into two minutes. Then she goes to the competition beam, where in between competitors she gets a generous thirty seconds—the touch warm-up—to practice. Then it's time to compete. Feeling shaky? Beam not to your liking? Too bad—you're up.

Express Girl #1 scores a 9.575.

Express Girl #2 scores a 9.6.

Express Girl #3 scores a 9.4 and her coaches shake their heads.

By the time the fifth Express Girl salutes, my attention's roamed to the girl who just stuck her vault. Then the tall girl whose legs bend wildly on her giants. Then the tiny one on floor who taps her toes in time to "Friend Like Me" from *Aladdin*.

Vanessa used to swat my ponytail if she caught me watching other gymnasts. "Get in the building, Savannah!" she'd hiss.

Back then, I'd get fired up. *I can beat them*, I thought when I watched the Express gymnasts bang out identical perfect routines. No despairing like my teammates did. "That was so good," they'd lament. "I'm not gonna place." Meanwhile, I'd see a girl stumble on floor. *Got her*, I thought.

Today, I only feel dread. What am I doing here?

Wrist guards. Preemptively taped ankle. The Beast. At this rate, I'm more "walking physical therapy ad" than human. The goddamn Beast draws everyone's attention. All of the Express girls—they've seen me compete throughout the years, and they can tell that this is new. Some of them were probably at Regionals when my knee imploded.

"South Ocean," calls the girl holding a stopwatch next to the warm-up beam.

I'm not ready. Not today, not six weeks from now. Cassie was right. Hell, Vanessa was right. Coach Barry had every right not to reply to my last-ditch e-mail. He too knows I'm a sham. Olympians don't trifle with people like me.

My feet slip as soon as I climb up on the beam. I fall on every layout step-out. My leap looks like a large step, but not for mankind. Spectators gasp as I stumble out of my full turn and catch myself an instant before my face hits the beam. Now my wrists hurt, and this isn't even the real competition.

Under normal circumstances, this would be funny. I almost want to laugh now, except I see Emery's face. Her cheeks bulge from the straight, set line of her mouth. She's worried. Sure, judges are "objective," but I'm slated to compete before she does, and if I go up there and perform like that, I'm setting the tone that South Ocean Gymnastics is a joke.

Matt says nothing to me. He doesn't have to. I couldn't possibly have done worse.

Get in the building.

The thirty-second warm-up is much less disastrous, yet I still feel unsteady, like landing will make my knee crumble within the Beast.

Now there's only one gymnast ahead of me. I don't watch her; I learned one thing from Vanessa. Instead, I read the glittery posters that a few boys lift after a girl dismounts bars. I smell the hot dogs from the concession area. Feel the pulse of energy as one section bursts into cheers while another lets out a disappointed "ohh." The crest and fall of the wave.

Normally I'd see my parents in the middle row—not up front with the hardcore parents, but not in the back where they couldn't see. Worksheets to be graded on my father's lap. He never got through much grading.

I could have told them.

Nope.

Matt nudges me toward the beam. "You can do this. Confidence and attack, okay?"

"Yeah." It's a whisper. The ghost of the formerly cocky kid.

I stand next to the beam as the judges scribble their scores from the previous routine. I'm sure they don't have much to deduct. I'm sure they don't need to confer about their scores. I'm sure this doesn't need to take ten minutes.

I could walk away while they're writing. Walk past Matt's hand reaching out to stop me, past Emery's protests—

"Savannah?" The head judge—salt-and-pepper hair, dark-blue glasses that match her navy blazer—raises her hand.

I raise my arms and flash the tense smile of prom photos. No turning back now.

I press up to a handstand. I don't hold it for as long as I can, but a few people applaud. I'm on.

My movements feel crisper than practice, a sharpness born of fear. I lift one hand up and flick the wrist, the same way Vanessa made us practice in the mirror when I was ten.

Pike jump, straddle jump. The beam reverberates beneath me.

Now for the flight series. I raise both arms over my head with my stomach clenched and the Beast squeezed behind my left leg. I pause long enough to think, *Oh, God.*

As soon as I lift in the air for the layout, I'm crooked. Save it save it save it—left foot hits the beam, right foot reaches to the ground, and I'm off.

Dammit!

"Get it back, Savannah!" Emery calls.

Get what back? I'm allowed thirty seconds to remount, but I'm already up on the beam again, ears burning. My full turn wobbles so severely that I look like a surfer on a tsunami. I stay on and hear applause.

Screw their clapping. Pose. Pose. I shouldn't be here. Pivot turn. Jumps. Leap pass. Split jump-back tuck with a wobble so huge, the beam's shaking might register on the Richter scale. Pose. *Get off. Get out of here.*

I run to the end of the beam, punch with two feet, flip and twist once, land on my ass.

A smattering of hands as I salute the judges. Matt walks toward me and I sidestep him. Why did he make me feel like I could do this? Was Vanessa right, that this was his dream and not mine?

His hand reaches for a low-five. "Way to stick it."

I walk to my gym bag and pull on my warm-ups a little too ferociously. The armpit stitches pop out to create a nice hole.

"What are you getting uppity about?" Matt says. I try to focus on someone's *Requiem for a Dream* floor music instead of listening to him. "You've been practicing full beam routines for three weeks. What did you expect?"

Not to fail.

"This was about getting yourself back out there, physically and mentally," he continues. "It'll be easier next meet."

Next meet, seriously? I'm not going through this again.

Matt's attention turns to Emery. "Bring it home, Em," he calls. I give a half-assed clap.

Well, she brings it home big time. She nails every move in her routine, and as she lands her dismount, my inglorious 7.5 lights up the electronic scoreboard.

"Good job, Savannah," she says as the Express girls pass by and offer her their compliments. "You have serious cojones."

"Right."

Emery grins. "Reenacting the Snowflake Invitational hissy fit all over again?"

"That was totally justified! Monica spilled Gatorade on my grips."

"The grips that you said didn't fit you?"

"So?"

"Then you placed third."

True. My last recorded success on bars.

Her gym bag bounces against her hip as she walks. I jog to keep up. "If it weren't for your knee, I bet you'd do a killer floor routine to make up for it," she says.

"What are you trying to say?"

Emery stops. "Nothing." Her green eyes are wide. "You just never back down. It's awesome."

Mean it? Her gaze stays steady. Sincere. Not trying to trick me into anything the way Matt did.

"Thanks," I say.

Her 9.825 is posted and everyone near the beam bursts into applause. Yep, that's how you get a full ride. Matt high-fives her. "Let's keep the ball rolling on floor."

If my father were here, we'd make eye contact from across the gym. He'd lift his head as if to say, *Next event. Get going.* Except today, I don't have a next event. I have at least three more hours of watching everyone else compete.

I sit at the edge of the floor and feel the shake of each tumbling pass. The *thud-thud*-pause-*thud*. This floor is so springy that Emery nearly bounces off when she lands her double back. She looks concerned. Matt signals her to get her ready for the next turn. He knows she'll be fine. Funny how I can believe Matt believing in Emery, but not in me.

The girls cease tumbling and practice their dance: quick spinning turns, sharp straddle jumps, leaps that stretch beyond a full split. The smallest Express girl struggles to keep up. She stumbles out of every jump. Her face reddens. The curls slip from her ponytail. Each attempt progressively worsens until the coach yanks her arm and says, "If you don't cut the crap, I'm scratching you from floor."

Scratching you? This kid who can't be more than ten and surely nervous enough to pee her leotard, just because of a few jumps? What does it matter if she bombs the warm-up? What does it matter if she bombs one floor routine on one afternoon in one gym? What happens when she grows up and breaks an ankle or tears every ligament in her knee and wishes she had one more routine left for one more day?

Suddenly my breathing comes quickly. I shed my warm-ups as Matt walks over. "You're first," he says. "Get that salute ready." The rule is that even if you're scratching an event, you still must officially present yourself to the judges so you can earn that zero.

I feel the carpet under my feet as I step onto the floor. My legs wobble. *Get going.*

"Savannah?" says the judge, a young blonde.

I raise my arms and smile. Now I'm supposed to turn and walk off the floor, letting Emery take my place and earn more near-perfect scores.

What kind of girl are you? That's what my father wanted to know.

My right toe points behind me, my right arm covers my face, and my left arm stretches behind me. My breathing is so loud that surely the judges can hear it.

This kind.

A long, long pause. Then Matt says to the music person, "Put it on Track 3."

Although it's been months since I heard this music, my arms strike the violin chords just as they used to. My jumps snap up and down. I pivot into the corner, stare down the diagonal, and sprint like there's no way in hell I can fail.

Please don't let me break.

I lift into the air—*oh God oh God oh God*—pull in my arms—spin twice—land with such momentum that I bounce over the white line. Out of bounds, an automatic one-tenth deduction.

Emery screams, "Yes!" Applause from all sides of the floor. "Go, Savannah!" voices shout. Who is cheering and why? Who am I to them?

My leaps are high and fast the way they used to be. Everything is right. Everything is the music and motion and hitting every beat. Until I stand in the corner for the final pass as the music hits a crescendo and my vision turns blurry and I feel the leaden cry of every muscle that wants to collapse.

As I start to run—jog—a tremendous wave of noise erupts from the bleachers. The sound of dozens of feet pounding the metal. "Let's go, Savannah!"

I rise on that wave. Close my eyes, bring my knees to my chest, flip and land with a stumble, leap to the ground, pose. Music ends.

When I stand to salute, chest heaving, the wave is even louder. Marcos. Marcos and the entire varsity soccer team stand in the bleachers, pumping fists and high-fiving each other like I've just scored the winning goal. Like I've done something worth celebrating. Around the floor, every Express girl applauds.

Emery jumps on me with a hug so ferocious that I almost fall over. "You are my *hero!*" she shouts in my face.

Matt's hug is just as tight, if more dignified. "Surprised?" I gasp out.

He shakes his head. "Never surprised. Just impressed."

Dimitri and Andreas wave frantically as the meet director walks over to shush them. "Sa-van-nah!" they chant in unison.

My legs cramp so tightly that I can hardly walk. Then again, I shouldn't consider walking when I can't even breathe without gasping. Emery's music starts and I try to watch, but my vision's still rocky and my mind runs faster than my breathing.

Did that just happen? And did I really just survive it?

One more routine on one more day.

....

I VAULT, TOO. A front handspring with a full twist, where I hit the table with my hands, pop off, spin once, and land on my feet. No flips, no frills. It's a vault I haven't played with since I was ten, but it achieves my second-highest score of the day: 8.3. Five of the Express girls faceplant their vaults. So does Emery. But she stands up and laughs.

I attempt a bar routine that merits a shocking 8.425. The soccer team whoops in approval the way they have after all of my routines. The stands have cleared out around them. "You qualified for States!" Matt exclaims, spinning me around.

"What? No."

"Yes." He places me on the floor and the gym wobbles. "32.225."

After he punches the numbers into his phone and shows me, I take it and tally the scores myself.

A year ago, I would have been aghast. A 32 all-around? An 8.0 on floor? I would have been praying that Coach Englehardt didn't search the Internet for my scores.

Today, they feel like a gift.

Matt takes the phone back. "I gotta text Vanessa and let her know to start looking for hotels in Brockport."

I can't stop smiling.

CHAPTER THIRTY-TWO

TOMORROW WILL BE hell on my knees, but the lightness hasn't left. I want to gallivant in the road, spin in the sand, wave the Beast over my head, and let loose a mighty holler.

"Marcos faked a stomach virus this morning, but he has to work the dinner shift," Andreas told me after the meet. "He says you need a cape to complete your superhero look."

"That was freakin' awesome," Dimitri added. "How do Dre and I sign up?"

Out of the whole soccer team, they seemed the most wowed by the experience. (Although I also fielded several, "Your friend Emery—she single?" remarks.

"You promised, Savannah!" Andreas winked at Emery as she joined us. "The sport of gymnastics will never be the same."

Marcos sent me a text before he went into work. *You were amazing out there. I've never seen you so happy.*

We need to talk. I know this.

I also know this: he believes in me. Not once has he suggested that I back down and put the Beast and my dreams out to pasture the way I was ready to.

Cassie texted me, too. *So sorry I couldn't make it today. Let me know how you do!*

Burritos? I replied, because that seems like the easiest icebreaker.

Now I'm crossing the late-afternoon shadows on Main Street, waiting for Cassie. My wet hair swings across my eyes, and I ignore the wind. I like this chill. It keeps the lightness buoyant.

Nothing happens in Ponquogue on a Sunday afternoon. Middle school boys on bicycles loiter outside of Anthony's Pizza. A cheer spills out from Sitting Duck—touchdown for the Jets.

A hand lifts in the window of Tastes by Tabitha. Cassie. Her eyes squint against the sun as she walks out to meet me. Her beaded necklace takes flight and then settles onto her chest.

"You're going to get sick with that wet hair," she greets me.

"Now you're the responsible one?"

She pushes my hair out of my face. "You should let me dye it. I think you'd look great with copper highlights. How'd the meet go?"

"I did the all-around and qualified for States," I say proudly as we approach Pav's. The chili pepper lights wink under the façade, and my stomach grumbles in anticipation of the spicy deliciousness.

"Wow." For the first time in a long while, her voice perks up at something gymnastics-related. "Do you think you'll make it to Regionals?"

"What the fuck!" a voice calls from behind Pav's.

In the middle of putting her arm around me, Cassie freezes. The little boys on bicycles look at us then look at each other, not daring to move.

The voice continues, "Look, I don't know what you want."

I know that voice. I tug Cassie's hand.

"I don't—shit!"

Bones slam against bones, so much louder than the hallway scuffle. There's a scream and a guy in a black sweatshirt and jeans sprints up the alley, his sneakers slapping against the pavement. He passes so close I can hear his urgent breath. Our eyes meet. Crystalline blue eyes. Then he bolts the other way, a limp in his run. Blood on his back.

"What the hell?" says Cassie. I can hardly hear her over the pounding of my heart. It can't be Marcos, it can't–

We round the corner to find a facedown, unmoving boy in a lime-green Pav's Place shirt, and I almost throw up.

Cassie starts crying, fast and sudden as a downpour, a hand on my shoulder to brace herself.

"What?" I say. Annoyed at her. Dizzy. I can't stop looking at the blood and concrete. Can't stop thinking out of control thoughts, like what if somebody walks by and implicates us in this?

She looks at me and that look slices straight through the thoughts. "Savannah, it's Marcos."

A punch to the chest. I knew the voice, but confirmed by Cassie, it's so much worse. That God-awful shirt. *Pav's Place, where the fiesta never ends!* on lime-green, a seductive woman holding a tray with a single beer.

The back door of Pav's swings open. Two guys and Juliana rush out. "We heard screaming–" Juliana halts. "Crap, crap, crap." Her face pales, her hands shake, and she kneels on the concrete. "We gotta roll him over."

"What if he has a neck injury?" I join her, my head woozy.

"What if he can't breathe?" she retorts. So together we gingerly roll him over, probably breaking every rule of basic first aid.

As soon as he's on his back, I swallow back the nausea. The gash in his forehead leaks blood down his cheeks. I hastily yank off the brand-new sweatshirt I bought after the meet and wrap it around his forehead to staunch the flow.

He groans. I feel a flutter of relief—*he's breathing*. Who knows what kind of damage has been done to his head? And the way his arm twists...I've seen enough gymnasts trip off the low bar, fall to the mat, and start screaming to know what a dislocation looks like.

One of the guys swears. He drops his phone twice before calling 911.

We sit in silence, waiting for the ambulance. I can't form words. I can't think. I just grab the moist hand of the boy who's still breathing but not moving. Juliana keeps blinking rapidly. Cassie sits between us, face ashen. "Where's the ambulance?" I say. "Where are the police? What about whoever did this?" My voice reaches a panicked pitch.

"Chill, Savs, we're doing all we can." Cassie's voice wobbles. I wait for *I told you so*, but it doesn't come.

Blood dribbles from under the sweatshirt onto the concrete. I don't care who provoked whom or if his hero complex got the best of him. He doesn't deserve this.

An eternity later, red and blue lights spill over the pavement. Juliana strides over to the police officers. The EMTs check Marcos's heart rate and blood pressure as I strain to hear what she's saying. "All I know is he went to take out the trash and then we heard screaming."

"Do you think he knows who was involved?" one officer asks.

"If someone was waiting for him, I wouldn't be surprised." She glances toward me. "It's not the first time people have stirred up shit here."

"That's for sure," Cassie mutters.

Marcos groans again. I squeeze his hand and for a moment, his grip tightens.

Eventually the police have collected their answers—I keep describing the guy I saw although they ask me only once, and the officer keeps saying, "I understand, miss." Marcos's arm has been braced, and I'm forced to pull away when he's hoisted onto the stretcher, stumbling against Cass as we watch him get lifted into the ambulance. The door shuts. I squeeze my eyes shut against the beating lights, and we stand there as the siren reverberates down Main Street and slowly fades.

"What do we do now?" My throat is dry and my heart aches.

"You have Victor's number?" Juliana says. I shake my head. "I'll tell him to go to the hospital."

"What about you?"

Her lips press together. She nods to her coworkers, who linger by the door. "We gotta go back inside and do damage control."

"And the police are going after that guy," I say.

Juliana's ponytail shakes. "He's probably long gone."

Those words puncture the numbness. *Long gone.* Getting away with this.

I look at Cassie, but she stares at the pavement. "They're letting him go?"

Juliana rolls her eyes. It lacks her usual verve. "I mean, that's not what they said, but obviously the guy got a head start. I didn't get the impression that there was gonna be a manhunt, did you?"

"You're telling me this is it, then." Anger kicks up with each word. That someone won't be held responsible for this—it's unthinkable. Apparently it's all right for blood to seep into the concrete without repercussions, without ensuring that it never happens again.

"Yes, Savs, she is," Cass says. "We'll get my car and go to the hospital, okay?"

I can't sit in a hospital waiting room. I can't linger, floating down, resigning myself to whatever happens next.

I rise to my feet. There's no ache in them from the meet. "Not yet."

Cassie looks at me sharply. I grab her elbow more roughly than I need to. "Let's go."

She yanks it back. She's never failed to read me, and this is no exception. "You think that guy's hanging around waiting for us to say hi?"

"He's getting farther away the longer we sit here."

"Are you serious?" Juliana nearly shouts. "He's dangerous."

"What's going to stop this asshole from hurting us?" Cassie adds.

The fact that she's making sense hardly registers. For once she's the logical one and I'm the one trying to make the bad idea sound feasible—and we're running out of time.

Physically, I can't do anything else for Marcos. But I can make this right, and I'm not going to let them stop me. "You can stay here, or you can come with me."

We stare at each other. As kids, Cass was the staring contest queen, outlasting me when my eyes watered or she made a silly face to make me laugh. My legs are tingling, ready to run, but I can't do this alone. I need fearless Cass at my side.

She blinks first. Long and slow, like she'll open her eyes and I'll have changed my mind. When she sees me still staring at her, the worry in her eyes hardens.

I take that as a yes.

After a moment, her footsteps echo behind mine.

"Where the hell are you going?" Juliana calls after us. "Cassie!"

You're an idiot, I think as we cross Main Street, cars honking.

That guy is going to hurt you, I think as we follow drops of blood leading into the dirt motocross trail in the woods by the high school.

My legs never tire and Cassie doesn't flag beside me. Leaves crunch under our feet, branches fly up, a deer scuttles out of the way. We follow the dirt motocross trail.

Hurry up, hurry up.

"There's no way we're going to find him," Cassie says, panting. "Just let me take you to the hospital."

I'm not stopping. If I do, that means it's okay that this happened. I've done enough sitting back in the last few months.

The trail winds over roots—I trip and Cassie catches me, keeping me from hitting the ground—and the longer we run, the more I start to wonder if she's right. If this is stupid and useless, if I'm better off staring at the ceiling in the waiting room—

At the exact same time, we halt.

There he is. With his back to us, hands on his knees, gasping so loudly he must not have heard the branches snap under our feet.

Cassie's hand clamps my shoulder. "I'm not doing this," she hisses.

"C'mon."

"I'm *not*."

"You can't leave me out here alone." Now that we're here, I have no idea what the hell I'm going to say or do, but I know that I'm not turning back.

"This wasn't my idea."

I search Cassie's face for a breaking point. She's the girl with an opinion about what to do, the girl who's the first to make the dare and the first to take the dangerous leap. I look for sympathy, however reluctant. "I'd do it for you, Cass," I hiss.

I see fear.

Cassie is never afraid.

I can't turn back now. The decision has been made.

I walk forward on shaking legs, my heart sprinting past my feet. Cassie tries to snatch me back. I keep moving. "Excuse me."

Blue eyes. He straightens, confused.

"What the hell happened back there?" I say.

He looks up to the trees and stumbles back a step. The fading afternoon sun through the trees hits a shock of red hair. "I don't know what you're talking about." He's monotone, trying to be uninterested, but his eyes dart almost as quickly as my heart.

"Let's go, Savannah." Cassie's voice quakes.

"What'd he do to you?" I say. "Did he look at you the wrong way? I bet he's cleaned your table at Pav's. Wiped your spit and threw out your crap. Did you leave him a tip?"

"What, is he your boyfriend or something? Sent you to fight for him?" There's a laugh, and then another guy, grass stains across his jeans, steps onto the path. Cassie grabs my wrist. We both know without speaking that this one is no amateur. His arms are thick as tree trunks.

The words keep spilling out. "He's unconscious," I say, and with heart pounding, "and he's not breathing."

That catches both of them.

"Maybe he needs a little mouth-to-mouth," the first guy says, laughing, but the other guy doesn't crack a smile.

"You think it's hilarious that you almost killed someone?"

"Savannah, shut up," Cassie mutters. "He's not dead."

"What's Goldilocks saying?" says the one with the blue eyes.

"Cut the bullshit," the other says. "There are some things you don't understand, little girl."

In the next instant, my toes scrape the dirt and an arm as firm as a deadbolt wraps around my stomach. The second guy's arms, powerful as falling boulders, nearly knock the wind out of me.

I kick his shins. My fists lash out for his face, but he dodges. He laughs. The laugh of older brothers who hold the basketball above your head, higher and higher, the more you swipe at it. They never drop it; they never let go.

"Thing is," his voice says from somewhere behind me, "it'd be better if you didn't see us. Am I right?"

"What are you doing?" says Cassie, thin and quaking.

"CASSIE, GET—" The second guy's thick hand swallows the last word. I thrash my head. His hand tight, untrembling, presses my lips against my teeth.

"Jesus, this girl's out of control," he says.

"You can stay here with your friend and we'll make sure you'll regret it," the one with blue eyes tells Cassie. "Or you can get the hell out of here, and pretend you never saw us. Nice girls from Ponquogue don't call the police if they want to stay out of trouble."

She looks at me. I thrash harder, the way I would to kick out of a riptide. My eyes plead with hers.

Then she turns away and runs.

"Real friend you got there," the Boulder says behind me, his words muffled by my hair.

She's getting help. She has to be. Running for the police station or back to Marcos or to someone, anyone who can get me out of this—

Blue Eyes leans close to me. I see the freckles across his cheeks and nose. When Marcos said there were guys causing problems at Pav's, I pictured older thugs. This kid has to be my age, maybe younger. He could be from Galway Beach or from Ponquogue and I never noticed. He could be Tommy Brown, Always Late Nick, any kid who walks the hallway like he's friends with everyone. His breath is too fast. He's nervous. I scare him. Maybe I can make him more afraid of me than I am of him.

"You're all alone out here with the two of us," he says.

I shake my head.

"She's not coming back."

A more ferocious shake. Of course Cass is coming back, and if she's not, she's sending someone else who will. She'll run to Juliana. Juliana will know what to do.

He nods to the Boulder. "Let's go."

I swing my feet for the back of the Boulder's knees. He dances back. I swing harder and his right leg buckles for a moment. "Help me out with this bitch, will you?" he grunts.

I have to get out of here. I have to get back to Marcos—

Blue Eyes reaches for my legs, but I kick his chest and he stumbles back. He comes back and I kick again. This time he dodges my feet.

I'm fading. I can feel it. Not my will, nor my anger, but there are two of them and one of me and I know they will carry me off, no matter how hard I fight.

So I kick harder. He grabs my shoe and my foot wrestles its way out. I wriggle violently from side to side, hoping the Boulder will lose his grip. I'm slipping, I can feel it, my head down lower on his chest, and if he tries to readjust, I'll break out. Then what? Run like hell, that's what, with one shoe.

"Let's go," Blue Eyes says. "Hurry up, you idiot, we have to get out of here—"

"That's enough, gentlemen," says an unmistakable voice. "Put her down."

He stands next to his bicycle, one hand holding it steady. Helmet and jersey. Skinny legs beneath tight Spandex shorts. Dirt spattering his wheels and legs.

"Who is this clown?" says the Boulder in my ear.

Blue Eyes swaggers a bit. "Yeah? What are you gonna do?"

My father does not move. "I will kill you. Do I need to be more explicit?"

CHAPTER THIRTY-THREE

"**D**ID CASSIE FIND you?" Those are the first words I speak to my father. Not thank him, not reflect on what just happened.

His brows crease. "She was out here, too? Did they scuffle with her?"

I tug out my phone, drop it in the dirt, pick it up again, hit her name on speed dial. The ringing I've come to know too well. My entire body vibrates, yet there's a weird calmness within me, the eye of the hurricane. "Hey, mates..." her voicemail begins.

"Cass, it's me. My dad's here. I'm okay. You must have just missed him," I say more confidently, creating stories that I want to believe. "Um, yeah, call me?"

As we emerge from the woods, I'm met with the first bit of luck all afternoon: a series of texts.

At hospital w/ Victor wtf is life!!

Vic says Marc is conscious and talking. Going in for a CAT scan. Doc says prob a concussion.

Btw this is Dre.

I almost drop my phone with relief. Thank God for Andreas. Thank God that Marcos is *okay.* I pull it together enough to request frequent updates and then to text Marcos. *Call me when you can.*

"You don't think they followed her, do you?" I ask Dad when we reach the police station. He shakes his head but says nothing. There's a special kind of hell for this silence.

I call her again when we're out in the parking lot, after I repeated the story over and over until I started to think that the Boulder's eyes were red instead of blue. The officers gave me hot chocolate and handed me a scuzzy blanket that I gratefully wrapped around my shoulders. I couldn't stop shaking.

No updates on Marcos from Andreas. "Can we go to the hospital?"

Dad looks exhausted. Older. No hint of the Smirk, of *you're not mature enough.* "What did they do to you?"

"I'm okay," I say quickly. "I want to see how Marcos is."

"Let's get you home first," he says, "unless you want to ride on a bike all the way there."

"What about Cassie's house?" My words are still too fast, too high-pitched, and Dad agrees.

Three miles is a long way to ride on bicycle handles. By the time Dad turns right at the stop sign for Cassie's road, I jump off and start running.

Click, click, click. The bicycle pulls up behind me when I stop short in front of Cassie's house, where the grass is a tad too long and the pile of fallen leaves grows.

I can't move.

Because there's Cassie's car in the driveway, parked askance the way it always is, and there's the light in her bedroom. Neither of those things tell me why she won't answer the phone, why she didn't come back or send someone my way.

For the first time in my life, my dad curses. Then his hand is on my shoulder. "Let's get you home, sweetheart."

....

I HOBBLE UP our driveway, afraid to look back. Dad could lecture me on any number of points and for once I'd have no excuse, with "attempting to fight vicious skinheads in the woods by myself" at the top of that list.

He unclicks his helmet and casually tugs off his gloves, as if this was simply another ride. He sets them down on the shelf, spins one pedal and frowns. The bike hums as he rolls it gently into its holder.

Just when I think he's forgotten that I'm standing there, he says, "I'm sorry about your friend."

I don't know which one he means. Marcos, face down and those strong shoulders moving up and down with his breathing, but nothing more.

Cassie, the little-girl quiver of her bottom lip. The most unmotivated person I know with a rare determination in her eyes. *I am not following you.*

Cassie would save her own ass before she saved yours, Marcos told me. *I guarantee it.*

The memory makes me shake all over again. Marcos had sensed it, and I hadn't believed him. Of course I knew Cassie better. Of course she'd never leave me.

When Mom sees me running up the stairs with tears running down my cheeks, she doesn't try to stop me.

....

MY LIMBS HAVE turned to lead. I want to go to the hospital, I want to see Marcos's eyes open and that blood wiped off his face, except I can barely do more than toy with my phone that never rings. The last message was from Andreas: *They got him doped up real good for his arm.*

"You dropped something." My mother slips into the room without knocking. I managed to doze for a few minutes, jerking awake at any sound.

"Thanks," I say without turning my head.

The bed by my feet tilts down, and I look up in surprise. Mom sits with my medals in her hand. The meet. That was this morning.

"What'd you place second on?" she says.

"Bars."

Mom smirks, almost like Dad. "Really?"

"They probably confused me with someone else." It feels strange to be joking when I haven't seen Marcos yet, when I don't know what the hell Cassie did.

"Why didn't you tell us? I would have loved to have seen you back in action."

"If it helps, I qualified for States."

I expect Mom to hug me and say something about how she's glad I had a safe competition, and isn't it nice that I'm doing gymnastics again? Instead she has the look in her eye that she usually reserves for mapping out Richard's current location. "When is States? How about Regionals? I'm taking off from work."

Regionals. Now we're getting ahead of ourselves. I'm smiling, though, just a crack.

"What happened with you and Cassie?" she says.

I turn back onto my elbow, ignoring the stab of pins and needles. "Nothing."

"You came home covered in dirt and I expected Cassie to show up behind you, lying through her teeth about whatever you guys were up to. Trying to fight guys in the woods seems like a Cassie thing to do."

That's what I had thought when I'd asked her to come with me. Apparently I was wrong.

Mom rolls the medal in her hands. Strong hands. She's never been a pusher, like Dad. She doesn't need to know every one of my test grades. She didn't care who my competitors were. As long as she knew I'd landed on two feet, she was happy.

"You were always on Cassie's side, no matter what," she says. "I'd started to think you couldn't make your own decisions."

A Cassie decision. As if there are two kinds of decisions: the ones that Cassie makes, spontaneous and making for a good story, and the ones that I make. The kind that stir no ripples.

Today, I made a Cassie decision, except she didn't back me up the way she's always expected me to follow her. She didn't do anything.

....

I'M DREAMING IN dirt and leaves and voices that sneak up behind me, until they start singing and I realize it's my phone.

Cassie, it has to be, and I pick up without looking.

"Hey, it's me." A female voice, clipped and familiar.

"Who?"

"Juliana."

Wow.

"Thank God you answered," she says. "Freakin' Cassie won't pick up her phone. I thought you guys were still out there doing your vigilante thing."

Cassie wouldn't admit that she backed down. That she walked out of the story at the best part. I take a breath. "Yeah, about that."

"You guys found him?"

"Well, I found him. And his friend." My free hand clenches the blanket. "By myself."

A long silence. In the background, water runs and dishes clank. Then she swears under her breath. "She left you out there?"

I pluck at a thread sticking out from my comforter. "I thought she was going to get help. Except I haven't heard from her since, and her car is in her driveway, so she obviously made it back."

She falls into a silence so deep that I wonder if she put the phone down and walked away. "Shit," she says finally. "That's...terrible, Savannah. I'm sorry."

It feels uncomfortable to accept sympathy from Juliana, the girl of steel. It only solidifies the sinking pit in my stomach.

I assume the next ping of my phone is from Cassie. Making sure that I'm alive, perhaps even, I don't know, apologizing. It could happen. Instead, it's Emery. *What are you up to tonight, champ?*

Before I can stop myself, I write, *My boyfriend's in the hospital and my best friend ditched me, so...crying in my bedroom.*

Emo-gency! she replies. *Be there in fifteen.*

. . . .

FOURTEEN MINUTES LATER, Emery walks in with a plastic container of chocolate chip cookies and says, "Hey, Mr. Gregory, what do you think about our state qualifier here?"

My father turns off the sink. "Who?"

"That floor routine was a revelation." Emery tosses me the container. "Did your boyfriend's friends film it? I bet it'll go viral."

"Who?" Dad says again.

"Savannah," Emery says through a mouthful of cookie. So graceful, she is, the crumbs trickling down her chin. "She made her comeback this morning."

Dad looks at me, measuring Emery's words with my face. Scanning my eyes the way he does the answers to his students' tests. Right or wrong? He believes her. I see it, though his voice is skeptical. "Really," he says.

Emery gleefully gives the play-by-play of the competition, certain not to leave out my pissy post-beam stomping around. She magnifies my split-decision floor routine—"I swear, the judges had tears in their eyes"—and describes the soccer team's ruckus. "32.225," she concludes, licking chocolate from her fingers. Really. No shame. "With two falls and a floor routine with no real tumbling."

"And an improvised bar routine," I add. For the first time since the meet, I almost feel happy.

Dad raises an eyebrow.

"My vault was legit," I say.

"Oh, yeah. A real crowd-pleaser," Emery says.

"Did you know about this?" Dad says to Mom.

Mom wipes a glass with more concentration than usual, a slip of a smile on her face.

. . . .

SHE CALLS ME when I'm asleep. I answer with the cool clearness that arrives when the only light in your room comes from the waxing moon.

"What are you up to?" she says.

"Sleeping. You?"

She sighs. "Nothing, really."

She waits for me to continue the conversation. I wait, too. I watch the white glow on the pink carpet.

"Unbelievable about Marcos, huh?" she says finally.

My fingers tighten around the phone. "I guess so."

"I can't believe you went after those guys like that. What the hell were you thinking? You knew we were overmatched."

Of course, Cass. Make it seem like I'm the wrong one.

"I warned you about Marcos," she continues, and I imagine her eyes staring up at the ceiling, crafting all of her evidence. "These were the consequences. There are some risks that aren't worth taking. You have to know when to bail out."

Yes. All my fault.

This time, I'm not buying it.

"Hello?" she says.

"What would you do if I got hurt?"

A sharp inhalation. "What did they do to you, Savs?"

"Let me get this straight." I am not burning. I am cool as the moon's white glow, and just as clear. "You leave me in the woods. You wait twelve hours to call me. And you don't ask if I'm okay."

She exhales, long and shaky. "I went to get help."

"So that's how my dad appeared in his Spandex glory yet never saw you along the way?"

The silence extends for so long that I almost hang up, because goddammit, I'd rather she come up with an excuse than admit that she left me with no intention of helping.

"I'm sorry." Her voice hitches like she might cry.

Don't budge.

"I couldn't think. I couldn't do anything. The whole thing felt surreal. I'm sorry."

That's the closest she'll give me to the truth, and even if that's the way it went down, it's still not enough.

"After all the times I've been there for you, Cass, I really thought you'd be there for me. Just this once."

She's quiet.

Both of us let the moment stretch until my eyelids droop. Then she says, "I thought you'd be there for me too with everything that's happened."

Eyes wide open. "Every time I try to have a real conversation, you blow me off."

"Because I don't want a goddamn conversation!" I hold the phone away from my ear. Her voice quiets, but not by much. "Don't you understand? I just want to move on. I thought you'd get that, but you don't. It's all about your gymnastics and all about your boyfriend, and you don't want to listen to anything I have to say about either of those."

"You kept telling me to stop!" I no longer care that I'm yelling or that my parents might hear. "You never supported me."

"Of course I did. I didn't want you to get hurt," she says. "I am looking out for you. Even if today wasn't my shining moment."

I don't know what to believe anymore. Cassie's perception of the truth, or my truth? Looking back now, the way she talked to Beth and Marcos under the guise of looking out for me seems extreme. She didn't have to tell off Beth because I couldn't make it to her birthday party. She didn't have to be so cold to Marcos, the person who pulled her from freezing water. She's wanted all of me, and yet at the same time, it's not enough for her.

"You don't need to protect me," I say, "which you demonstrated so well today. I'm capable of making my own mistakes."

"You're the one who wants to freaking talk about our feelings every five seconds," Cassie says. "Why did I do this or that or the other thing? God, Savannah, that's what I have therapy for. I'm still trying to figure it out myself. You were supposed to just..." She falters. "Just know. You always knew me better than anyone."

A pause.

"Well, I guess not anymore," I say, and hang up the phone.

CHAPTER THIRTY-FOUR

I SUFFER THROUGH Monday morning with only Marcos's texts to go by. *Did your knee hurt as much as my head does?* he writes. The verdict: concussed, stitched up, and with his elbow popped back into place. He assures me there's no need to visit him and that he'll be back in action in a few days. It seems too far away.

When I walk into AP Chem to find Cassie's seat empty, my palms sweat and I itch to text her. *Where are you? Are you okay?* She didn't go looking for me, yet that doesn't stop me from wanting to search for her.

I send a message to Juliana instead. *Do you know where Cassie is?*

She responds immediately. *We're on a field trip at the MoMA. She's quiet. Keeping an eye on her.*

I'm not sure how to reconcile the aching in my head and heart, as if our fight on the phone left me emotionally hungover, with the same blaze of disappointment that made me hang up. I don't know if it's right to feel relieved and angry at the same time.

Of course the entirety of Ponquogue High School knows what happened this weekend, although their accounts vary. "I hear you kicked some serious ass this weekend," Jason Kortis says to me approvingly as

I fumble my way through the chem lab. "I always knew there was a bad-ass within you."

"Savannah! Are you okay? Is Marcos okay?" Jacki Guzman pounces at our lockers.

"Alive and kicking." Figures Cassie would have a conveniently timed field trip. I'm regretting not taking up my father on his rare "Are you sure you want to go to school?" offer this morning. I don't want to answer questions. I don't want to talk to anyone. I want to crawl back in bed and sleep until it's time for practice. Sleep until June while I'm at it.

"Savannah?"

I whirl around. There's no way.

Jacki squeals. "You're alive!"

"Guess so." Marcos's voice is gravelly. Forehead covered with a gauze pad, his arm in a cast, two dimples that can't be quelled despite the scratches across his cheeks, he looks at me and grins.

My heart flips. He's patched back together. He's *here*. "You said you weren't back yet."

He shrugs. "They let me out this morning—"

I don't hesitate. I wrap my arms around him and kiss him, ignoring the chorus of catcalls and "Get it, Gregory!" from my classmates.

He stumbles backward, cast knocking into the orange locker. "I should dislocate my elbow more often."

"Please don't," I mumble into his shoulder, "or I will need to break your skull." I inhale deeply. Still fresh as cotton, still strong despite being thrown to the concrete.

He hugs me back just as fiercely as someone can with one arm. "If you were anyone else, I'd think you were kidding."

"How are you feeling?"

"Concussed, generally shitty, and these bones are killing me," he says into my neck.

"Maybe hugging isn't the wisest choice."

His arm tightens around me. "I'll take that chance."

· · · · · · · · · · · · · · · · · ·

WE'RE BOTH EXCUSED from gym—him for his elbow and concussion, me because Dad must have bragged about my meet in the faculty room; when I approached the locker room, Coach Doroski said, "We need to keep you in one piece for States!" Like he has any idea what States are. If it means no mesh jerseys for the day, though, I'll take it.

As our classmates play flag football, Marcos and I walk along the tree line, sidestepping twigs and pinecones. I take a breath of the cool air. "I'm sorry I didn't want to listen to you about Cassie," I say. "I didn't want to believe you. I still don't want to, if I'm being honest. I think that things have been changing between us for a long time now."

If I met Cassie today, would we still be friends? I don't know. I want my friends to be loyal, willing to be honest without making it about their own benefit. She makes me laugh, pushes the messy strands of hair into place, and makes the unbelievable seem plausible. She sat with me for hours on end when all I could do was stare up at the ceiling after my surgery. She'll turn on my favorite song from when we were twelve to cheer me up.

But she calls the shots. She makes the decisions, and God forbid I want to do something else. She'll dig and dig until I relent. It was easier to do what she wanted, because I genuinely thought she wanted what was best for both of us.

She left me.

I failed her, too. I didn't answer the phone when she called me that night. I wasn't under the bridge as the sun broke over the horizon to lock the car door and keep her from walking out.

I didn't fail Marcos. Yes, I made a risky and not-so-smart decision to chase after those guys. I refused to hang back, though. I took the chance anyway.

"I'm sorry for scaring you," he replies, dropping the leaf to lace his fingers through mine. They're chilly but firm. "When I woke up in the ambulance, I realized that all of this had gone too far."

"It wasn't your fault on Sunday," I say. That's what Juliana had said—that he'd gone outside to throw out the trash.

"Yeah, I know. I remember that much. It had been building, though. You know what I mean? One thing led to another and, God, it was the scariest experience of my life." He shakes his head gently. "Not worth the risk. Andreas and I had a good talk at the hospital. We're both going to work harder on controlling our impulses."

"Your heart's in the right place," I say. "I think you just sometimes run up against the wrong people."

He nudges me. "Speaking of risks, if I had any idea you'd gone after that guy—"

"I know. It was stupid." Dangerous. Terrifying. "Even Cassie warned me."

We pause by a majestic pine and both of us breathe in deeply, the shouts of class and screeches of the whistle far behind.

"It's hard for me not to assume the worst about people when I've met so many shitty ones," he admits. "It's easier to stick with the ones I know best so I don't have to worry about others disappointing me."

Unfortunately, the ones you know best can also be the ones who disappoint you the most.

"I loved your letter," I tell him. "It really means a lot to me that you trusted me enough to let me in. I know I can't fully understand everything about your life." Just the way I've never been able to follow Cassie down her dark roads. "I'll do my best, though. Promise."

He nods. "I still owe you a track team tryout, don't I?"

"Don't be scared that I'm faster than you," I tease.

"You sure about that? I've had many years of experience chasing after Dre's ass."

"Wanna find out?" I tip my head back toward the class. The football tumbles in a wobbly spiral, landing on the ground with a distant thump.

He holds out his cast indignantly. "Have you seen my arm?"

"Look who you're talking to. My coach made me run laps with a bum wrist."

"First, there's one more thing," he says, and then he leans in as the branches sway above us and I forget all about running.

. . . .

I THOUGHT CASSIE would make a dramatic gesture to earn back our friendship. Instead, she recedes.

Marcos makes up a test during lunch on Tuesday, so I walk into the cafeteria and sit with Andreas and Dimitri. Although there's an empty chair next to Andreas, Juliana takes the one next to me. She spends most of the period making fun of Andreas's hyperactivity the way everyone does, but there's a fondness I never noticed in her before. She speaks like an older sister to a pesky and loveable younger brother. Before the bell, she balls up her aluminum foil and says to me, "See you later," the same way she says it to Andreas.

I follow her into the hallway, where Cassie lingers by her locker. "Want to go out to the fountain?" I hear Cassie say over the burst of sneakers on linoleum.

"Nah," Juliana says. "I have a project to work on."

Seeing her with her head tilted, her golden curls rolling across her shoulders, I can't forget her face in the woods. Her vanishing footsteps. The resounding silence the rest of the day.

"Remember, you owe me a gymnastics lesson." Andreas bounds up beside me. "Do I need to wear a leotard?"

"Nobody wants to see that, Dre," Dimitri says.

"What? You know I'd look freakin' fly."

"That's one word for it," I say, grateful for the distraction.

"Am I too tall?" Dimitri asks. "Would I hit the ceiling? I might hit the ceiling."

They banter back and forth and I feel her looking at me, but I don't turn my head.

When I crashed from my knee injury, there was nothing waiting for me at the bottom. Just Cassie. She wants all of me, in specific, moldable ways. A girl who will follow her lead, say farewell to gymnastics, tell Marcos goodbye, and understand every emotion that she's not sharing. I can't be that person. I don't think anybody can be.

While I wanted her to help me escape everything I was afraid of, it's been up to me to put my world back together all along. I had to figure out what was right for me, not what Cassie thought was best.

All of these years, I chose her. But she didn't choose me.

. . . .

THERE'S ANOTHER STEP I need to take. After school, I write to Coach Englehardt and Coach Barry to tell them that I qualified for States (leaving out the "barely"). I tell them that my next meet is in January. Dad had said, "We let you off easy last time, but we're coming to this one, like it or not."

Then I shut the laptop and go for a run.

The first snowflakes of the season brush against my eyelashes. As I approach the bay, I ball my fingers inside my sweatshirt sleeves for extra warmth. The wind pushes me back as I make my way up the bridge. I grit my teeth and run harder. Force myself to be faster, the way I would for the final tumbling pass of my floor routine. To run as quickly as I did through the woods, except this time without the urgency.

Despite the wind and the gentle swirl of snowflakes that land on the sand and vanish, the tide is calm. I can almost see why Cassie chose here. There's something soothing in the infinity of the waves flowing endlessly to the horizon.

I take strength from the waves. I will not sink.

When I return home, flushed from the cold air, there are messages. *D and I are coming 2 open gym tonight. GET READY, OLYMPICS!* Andreas writes.

Can your boyfriend hook us up with free food at Pav's after practice? Wrong that I'm already pondering my next meal? asks Emery.

Andreas's high-fives every time we pass in the hallway, Juliana's acknowledgment that I'm a human, Emery and I sweating our asses off in the gym and immediately refueling with burritos—it's not the same without Cassie. None of it replaces her. It's not 2 a.m. Slurpees and driving around for the sake of driving and teasing each other while listening to our favorite songs. It's not the same as knowing each other since we were seven. I'm starting to believe that something different is good for me, though.

I'm about to reply to them when it happens:

Inbox: (1).

CHAPTER THIRTY-FIVE

"PULL AWAY FROM the curb," the DMV employee says coolly.

I signal and obediently check the mirrors. Behind us are other cars with nervous aspiring drivers, their parents in the passenger seat. I've left Dad standing by the tree whose leaves were red and golden in October. Now they bloom verdant green in April. It's taken until spring for my eighth road test. You could say that I've been preoccupied. Luckily, I've had some good instructors along the way.

I wait for the last-minute panic to kick in—the sweating palms, the doubt, the out-of-control thoughts. Instead, my mind is quiet.

The speedometer hovers at 36 in the 35. The man makes no comment. He gazes out the window as though we're out for a nice afternoon drive.

I stop at the stop sign. And the next. And the next.

"Should I turn up here?" I say at the sixth intersection. I mean, this is getting excessive.

"Sure."

Uh. "Which way?"

"Whichever."

Unreal. Abso-freaking-lutely unreal. Who is this man?

He must have asked himself the same question. "Left," he says, straightening up.

My left turn is dead on. Centered beautifully between the double yellow and the curb. I don't know that I've ever turned so perfectly. I don't know that anyone has ever turned so perfectly. I half expect the men standing outside of 7-Eleven to applaud. Can you get bonus points?

"Look, I don't know what your life goals are," the man says suddenly. "But make sure you never work for the state. Three-point turn here."

I'm so startled that I hit the brakes too forcefully. With a hasty look in the side-view mirror, I roll to the left.

"You think that after twenty-two years, they wouldn't screw you over," the man says as I transition into reverse. "You never call in sick. Never take a damn personal day. Not one. And this is how they treat you. Like that plastic bag over there."

I'm trapped in a vehicle with this man, ladies and gentlemen.

"Parallel park," he says as I draw near an old Volvo that has two wheels up on the sidewalk. Where would the rest of the Volvo be, had its driver parked it successfully? In fact, where was the DMV when its driver took his road test? I halt a healthy two feet away.

If you do this, you're home free.

My heartbeat kicks up.

Get this man back to the DMV, and you pass.

I cut the wheel three quarters of the way. Rolling past the Volvo's windows...the tremendous dent on the back door...bumper-to-bumper and I'm only one foot away...

This is your moment, Gregory.

Oh, holy crooked parking job. I'm a mile from the curb. Toast. Dunzo. Outta here. What were Dad's wise words about idiot drivers? Will I never have the chance to join their ranks? Will my parents have to escort me back and forth from college? Please, no.

"Hmm," the man says.

I will the curb to move closer.

He opens the door and examines the distance. "Interesting." Yep. I'll never be able to look at Dad again without him laughing.

"All right, our work here is done," the man says.

I don't cry the whole drive back. I want to. I very nearly do. I manage to stay composed. *Later*, I keep telling myself.

I pull up across the street from where the hopefuls line up for their tests. As a young buck in a cowboy hat hugs his mother goodbye, I realize: Screw it. So what if Dad has to drive me to school for the rest of senior year and back and forth from college? So what if I'll be able to hear Richard laughing when Mom tells him on the phone? So what if Dad, Richard, my mom, or some combination of the three will bring up the goddamn squirrel on my wedding day? At least I've tried. I've admitted all of my failures. I've done my best to improve. That's all they can ask of me.

"Thank you for your time," I say with all the dignity I can muster.

"Congratulations," he replies.

Wait. What?

"Took one point off. That parallel park was a little brutal. But you'll never need to parallel park again unless you're in the city, and who wants anything to do with New York these days, anyway? Have a good one," he says as he opens the passenger seat door. "And remember what we talked about."

So this is how you pass a road test. It has nothing to do with your skills or how much you've practiced or how many times you've failed. It's all about the kind of person you get on that particular day.

Dad appears at the door. "Any furry friends along the way?" he asks. Waiting for me to surrender the keys so he can drive and I can sulk the whole ride back. It's the system. Or, rather, it was the system.

I crank up AC/DC and say, "Oh, did you want a ride?"

....

I HONK OUTSIDE of Emery's apartment. "I don't freaking believe it!" she yells, gym bag bouncing against her back as she runs to the car. "Should I wear a helmet?"

"Earplugs." I turn up "Live and Let Die." And then I almost roll into a garbage can.

Cruising at a blistering thirty-five miles per hour, we arrive at practice fifteen minutes late. By now, all of the recreational class parents have cleared out, so I drift into a spot without fear of sideswiping anyone. There's Matt's SUV, Vanessa's sporty little thing, me, and a blue minivan with tinted windows.

When we walk in, the first thing I notice is how quiet the gym is. Second, there are Nicola and Erica's super wide *you won't believe what's happening* eyes as they turn at the sound of the door. Third, there's the bona-freakin'-fide Olympian standing next to the floor.

She's shorter than I am. I've never met anyone simultaneously older yet shorter than me. I blame this for why I can't say anything.

"Great to see you again!" says Coach Barry with a clap on my back. Oops. Didn't notice he was here. "We were in the area to watch the Manhattan Invitational, and we thought we'd swing by and see how your comeback is going."

Nobody "swings by" here from Manhattan. My palms are sweating profusely. The two coaches are here for me, Savannah Gregory and her Beast.

"Admissions let me know that you were accepted," he continues, reaching out to shake my hand in congratulations, except I'm blatantly staring at the girl next to him. "This is our new assistant coach, Angela Cardena."

"Well, duh," I say. "I only account for half of the thousands of YouTube hits on your gold medal routine from the Olympics. You're the reason that I ate Champion's Choice turkey for an entire year."

Great. They're going to slap me with a restraining order before I set a foot on campus.

Bless her soul, former Olympic champion Angela Cardena laughs like she's genuinely amused and maybe a little flattered. "And you are—"

"Kaitlyn Savannah Gregory," I say, shaking her hand. Too much information. Might as well offer up my firstborn while I'm at it. "It's a pleasure to meet you."

. . . .

"DAD, I'M GOING to Owego," I yell into the phone at our first water break. Due to the Olympian walking among us, Vanessa actually looks at me and smiles when she sees me on the phone.

Does my father break down in relieved tears? Chide me for making this decision without telling him? Tell me how proud he is?

"About damn time," he says. "Now, what were you calling me about?"

. . . .

TODAY, I'M COMMITTING.

Ponquogue Commits Day is dedicated to all of the students who will be joining college teams come the fall. While Division I athletes—the ones receiving athletic scholarships—are the ones who actually sign letters of intent, those of us competing for Division II and III schools are welcome to the event, which primarily involves everyone loitering by the crumb cake table and making awkward conversation. Andreas will be playing soccer for Suffolk, and he shakes everyone's hand like he's singlehandedly won the World Cup. There's a lovely table set up with a maroon cloth and a backdrop of our mighty Dolphin. On the table rests a silver fountain pen.

Grant Klein—the athletic director who called my dad in for a conference when, in ninth grade, my ripped palms started bleeding in paddleball and I told him it was the stigmata—lives for this day. "Let's get signing, folks!" he says when the first local sportswriter walks into the library, a lost-looking man with a camera around his neck.

Each athlete takes a turn posing at the table, pen in hand. Handshakes. Parents with hands on the shoulders of their child. I can't help it: I'm excited to be part of this. Like I've done something worth celebrating and photographing, something that should be remembered.

"Next up, Kathryn Savannah Gregory," Klein says. "Kathryn is a gymnast committing to Owego State College." He emphasizes the "nast" rather than the "gym."

"It's Kaitlyn," I say to the reporter, who nods miserably.

"Stand right there, Mom and Dad," says Klein.

We form a trio in front of the Dolphin, me in the center, and smile at the reporter. I have a practiced smile from years of Picture Days. Always I'd look at the camera and think, "You're posing after just winning the Olympic all-around." This would require, I imagine, a healthy mix of joy and dignity—not too much joy, or otherwise my cheeks would swallow my eyes.

Behind the reporter, the library door swings open. First enters Marcos, backpack on his shoulders. He grins. Is he laughing at me?

Hot on Marcos's heels is a blonde hurricane. Arms and legs pumping toward the table, camera in hand. "Excuse me, Mr. Klein? We're going to have to start over."

"Look who showed up," Dad says over my head.

"We can't start over," says Klein. "We're on the last recruit."

"Well, you have to," Cassie says. "The *Ponquogue Compass* needs a cover photo."

Klein gestures to me. "Get her before she turns into a pumpkin."

When Cassie used to lift the camera and take a photo of me, she held the power to make me look stupid or meaningful, skilled or sloppy.

Today, there's a division. Cassie, who stays behind the camera. Me, who will be leaving. It doesn't matter if I'm squinting from the smile or looking the wrong direction, or that Dad's parabola tie is way too prominent.

She clicks, and I smile wider.

Cassie argues with Klein as my parents and I leave the library. Marcos wanders nearby, pretending to take an interest in the Board of Trustees plaque. As soon as my parents move ahead, he puts his arm around me. He comes over to my house almost every weekend and my parents like him, but there's only so much teasing from them that I'm willing to tolerate.

"You committed," he says, kissing my cheek.

"Don't tell anybody."

"Looks like you'll be the cover story for the *Ponquogue Compass*."

"What more could you want from life?"

"Well, an autographed copy, for starters. I'm not supposed to tell you this, but Rena has big plans to publicly embarrass you very soon. Something about decorating your locker."

"Should I be absent that day?"

"You're a big-shot college athlete now. You can do whatever you want."

What does this commitment mean for the boy with the coconut smell in his hair and me? I lean my head on his shoulder and inhale. That's enough for right now.

"Excuse me, Ms. Gregory, shouldn't you be in class?"

Thanks, Dad, I think immediately. No. Something's off. The voice is too deep, too tall to be his. It's one I haven't heard in person for almost a year—

"Richard!" my mother says.

I beat her to him. "Holy shit!" I yell to the lobby of Ponquogue High School. My head collides with my brother's chest, which vibrates against my temple as he laughs. I expected the smell of smoke and sunburn, but instead I inhale soap, the old skin scrubbed off him.

"Language, Savannah," Mom says, but she's laughing, too. Soon she hugs Richard and then he and Dad exchange a manly hug, the kind with hands slapped against backs. Richard offers a handshake to Marcos, who seems mildly intimidated but smiles regardless.

"How's base? How long are you home for? I got into college and I finally passed my road test," I say without waiting for his answer. It's like I'm six years old again, jumping up and down in front of him so that he'll pick me up for an airplane ride.

There are more than a few confused looks as students pass our reunion. Backpacks hustle away from our enthusiastic embraces. "Is Mr. Gregory actually *hugging* someone?" one scholar whispers. A kid knocks against me with a trumpet case as he asks his friend, "Is it, like, army recruiting day?" because although he's not in uniform, my brother's short dark hair and strict posture give it away. There are too many eyes on us, and somehow, I don't mind.

Richard flicks my ponytail. "Mom told me you were signing your letter of intent today. Y'all and your surprises."

"It's been a little hectic. Since when did you acquire a Southern accent? Do you wear cowboy boots now, too?"

His hazel eyes crinkle. "You've got a month to break it down for me, kid. Maybe I'll even take you to McDonald's, get some breakfast sandwiches."

"If you're buying, I'm driving," I say.

"God help us all," Dad says.

The library door cracks open. I don't need to look, but I do anyway. Two blue eyes watch us.

. . . .

I PRETEND TO not see Cassie approach my locker, looking up at the last possible moment. "That's really cool," she greets me. "About Owego and stuff."

"Thank you." Too formal. We've spent the intervening months sharing classes without speaking. She'll pass me a handout and her lips twitch like she's about to speak, and then I look away and the moment passes. She should have been the first person I told about Owego. She should be trying to convince me to go somewhere brighter and brassier, rolling her eyes when I say something like, "I hear the snow is really scenic."

"I miss hanging out with you." Her eyes dart away from me.

So do I. We can't go back, though. "We've changed."

"What?" She looks at me, startled, like she didn't expect me to counter her.

"Last year, you would have been right up there with me in the woods, even thought it was scary and probably a stupid thing to do."

She's shaking her head—disagreeing with me, chastising herself, I don't know. "I replay that day all of the time. I just...I don't know. I failed. I'm sorry."

I believe her. Yet it's not enough to make me step forward, say, "It's okay," and let her embrace me.

There are the nightmares. I wake up some nights convinced I'm back in the woods with those leering faces so close to mine that I can see Blue Eyes's nose hairs, red as the hair on his head, and the freckles on the Boulder's face. I yell except there's a hand on my mouth that keeps my lips from opening. I kick but everything moves so slowly, as if through water, and I wake up thrashing in my bed.

Where did they plan to take me? What were they going to do with me? To me? In the dreams, I never get out of the Boulder's grip. Reality might have ended up the same way.

Why did I go into the woods that day? Was it adrenaline from the meet, or something more? Did something change within me the moment I decided to do a floor routine, or has this change been building since the moment I failed my road test and drove to South Cross? Was it the right decision? On those nights, I just feel empty.

Cassie interrupts my thoughts. "You've changed too, you know." Her voice is wistful. "You stopped telling me everything."

"I didn't mean to," I say. "Once I stopped, it was harder to start again." Gymnastics, Marcos, all the little moments—I'd started keeping them to myself when Cassie was in the hospital, not wanting to overwhelm her. Somehow, it became habit.

"Yeah," she says with a short, humorless laugh. "I guess I get that, too. I wish I could control what it's like in my head, but I can't. Sometimes, everything's great. Other times, I wish Marcos never found me under the bridge. I know that's terrible, but it's true, and there's nothing I can do about it."

It still hurts me to hear her say that she's struggling. I want to say, "I'll help you through this." I can't, though. I don't know the right words, and even if I did, she might not want to hear them.

The thing between us that had seemed unbreakable is no longer the same. It may not be entirely severed, but it's damaged for sure, and it's too soon to tell if it will ever be repaired. "What are you going to do?" I say.

She shrugs. "My doctors advised me to take a gap year after we graduate to figure out what I really want to do, maybe just work for a while. I've been reading these stupid college forums online and everyone says that I need to stand out in order to get into art school, so I joined the newspaper. I think I'm going to apply for spring admission for next year." Her voice trails off. "I don't know what else to do."

"You have so much talent," I say. "Don't forget that." It sounds like something you'd write in the yearbook of someone you never plan to see again.

The bell rings.

CHAPTER THIRTY-SIX

IN MY ANGRY moments, I hate seeing Cassie's hair bouncing on her shoulders in the hallway. I hate when I hear her laughing from across the cafeteria where she sits with some of the summer crew while I eat with Andreas, Rena, Dimitri, Juliana, and Marcos. If she's laughing, she's not missing our friendship. Sometimes Juliana ventures into her territory. I don't.

Still, it's better than thinking about her under the bridge.

I intentionally let it slip when Rena pauses from rambling to ask, "What about you and Cassie? Are you girls still friends? It seems pretty damn chilly between you."

"I wish none of this happened," I say.

That's all I need. Although she doesn't know the extent of this, Rena will repeat it to Andreas, who will tell Juliana, who may mention it the next time she's across the cafeteria. Message in a bottle. Cassie will receive it eventually.

. . . .

FOR THE FIRST time, I own Ponquogue High School athletic garb. After all, I did make a deal with Marcos. "Planning to flip over the hurdles?" Jason Kortis calls when he passes my locker. Beth, the track team captain, mandated that we all wear our team tank tops to school in honor of our home meet. Maroon background, white winged foot.

Although I only have about an hour of practice available a day before I head to the gym, the coaches don't mind. Compared to the stress of staying on beam, running around in circles is kind of relaxing.

Crammed through the cracks of my locker, just above my precalc textbook, is a blank manila envelope.

I fold back the silver tab. It reminds me of opening the acceptance letter from Owego, with the second letter offering a full academic scholarship. I'd already known I was in, but the scholarship was a nice surprise. Marcos received his full tuition scholarship from Suffolk and continues to give me far too much credit for my contributions to his math grades.

A folded piece of notebook paper flutters to the tiles.

Next, a photograph. I catch it before it falls. Black and white. The subject's legs are crossed, toes pointed. Her arms wrap over her chest and pull to the left side. They're wrapped as tightly as her leotard, and the muscles in her arms clench beneath the glitter. Her eyes are half-closed and her teeth are gritted in concentration. The short ponytail is a sunburst. She is upside down, suspended above the ground. The background blurs. Her knees are braceless, holding themselves together.

I unfold the paper.

Savs,

I was throwing out my crappy old photos when I found this one. It's the day you broke your knee doing the triple-double or whatever your dad called it. I debated giving it to you, since that's kind of messed up of me to remind you of that day. Then I realized that I've done a lot of messed up things recently.

I'm sorry that I wasn't more supportive when you said you were going back to gymnastics. I was always jealous. You had this world that I didn't get, and you were so good at it. Look at you in this photo—you're untouchable. When you started hanging out with Marcos, I felt the same way. Once again, you were joining a new world without me.

That doesn't excuse anything that I've done. But maybe it is a bit of an explanation.

I wouldn't trade any of our memories. Not for Juliana, or art school, or any stupid person from the summer.

I hope you can forgive me someday.

Love,

Cass

"You ready?" says Marcos, leaning against the next locker in his own Ponquogue Varsity Track and Field maroon-and-white jersey.

"Matching? For real? You guys are gonna make me puke," Andreas calls as he bounds past.

"The only people that will be puking will be Southampton when we beat them," I say.

He high-fives me. "Damn straight!"

I see Cassie behind him. She stands still as the crowd bucks around her, looking straight at me. Even from here, I know she's cracking her knuckles.

The girl in the photo does not know what will happen in the next moment. She doesn't know that when she lands, everything changes.

I smile at Cassie. Not a large smile that says, *Everything's great and I forgive you.* Because it's not and I haven't. But a smaller one that acknowledges that I read her letter and that maybe there's hope for both of those things someday.

"I am," I say to Marcos, and looping my arm through his, we make our way into the crowd.

ACKNOWLEDGMENTS

One of my writing mentors, Roger Rosenblatt, started class by writing a W.B. Yeats quote on the board: "A line will take us hours maybe; yet if it does not seem a moment's thought, our stitching and unstitching has been naught."

Thank you to everyone who helped me stitch and unstitch this story. To Danielle Ellison, editor extraordinaire, who plucked this book out of Pitch Wars and who has tirelessly helped me find the heart of it. To the team at Spencer Hill—especially Traci Inzitari, Britta Gigliotti, Harmony Beaufort and everyone else—for their help in making this book shine. To Jenny Perinovic for the gorgeous layout. Publishing's quite the ride, and I'm so grateful for having Tina Wexler and Lyndsay Hemphill guide me on the way. Also, a shout-out to Dahlia Adler, who read an early version and encouraged me to keep going.

To my writing teachers, especially Victoria Boynton, David Franke, and Roger Rosenblatt, for their unflagging support. Everyone should be lucky enough to have teachers like you. To Susan Scarf Merrell, who happily answered my publishing questions. To all of my coaches throughout the years who cheered me on, tossed me into the air, and caught me on the way down.

To my parents, who attended every gymnastics competition and didn't bat an eye when I decided to major in writing. Thank you for always encouraging me to pursue what I love. To my brothers, who keep me from taking anything too seriously.

To Lena, best friend and query queen. I might not have written fiction without you, and I definitely wouldn't have started gymnastics if you didn't make me watch the 1996 Olympic beam finals with you.

To Flo, who has read this story almost as many times as I have, analyzed *Make It or Break It* episodes with me, and reignited my love of YA fiction.

To Tony, who has been there since the first draft with ice cream, chai, and support in spades.

To Alex and Ali for the popcorn, LOTR marathons, adventures in the Qrypt, and general awesomeness. Team 150 all the way!

To Beth, who inspired the opening chapter, and Regina, who filled me in on the details of CPEP. To Katrina, Neely, and Goldy for the humor, emails, and enthusiasm.

To the girls I coach, who make me laugh every day and who may see pieces of themselves in Savannah's story. I know you'll always find a way to land on your feet.

ABOUT THE AUTHOR

Though Diana Gallagher "... be but little, she is fierce!" She's also a gymnastics coach and judge, former collegiate gymnast, and writing professor. Her work has appeared in *The Southampton Review*, *International Gymnast*, *The Couch Gymnast*, *The Gymternet*, and on a candy cigarette box for *SmokeLong Quarterly*. She holds an MFA from Stony Brook University and is represented by Tina Wexler of ICM Partners. To learn more, visit dianagallagher.blogspot.com.